COMING SOON
BOOK**SHOTS**

HUNTED
Someone is luring men from the streets to play a mysterious, high-stakes game. Former Special Forces officer David Shelley goes undercover to shut it down—but will he win?

113 MINUTES
Molly Rourke's son has been murdered. Now she'll do whatever it takes to get justice. No one should underestimate a mother's love....

$10,000,000 MARRIAGE PROPOSAL
A mysterious billboard offering $10 million to get married intrigues three single women in LA. But who is Mr. Right…and is he the perfect match for the lucky winner?

FRENCH KISS
It's hard enough to move to a new city, but now everyone French detective Luc Moncrief cares about is being killed off. Welcome to New York.

KILLER CHEF
Caleb Rooney knows how to do two things: run a food truck and solve a murder. When people suddenly start dying of food-borne illnesses, the stakes are higher than ever....

THE CHRISTMAS MYSTERY
Two stolen paintings disappear from a Park Avenue murder scene—French detective Luc Moncrief is in for a merry Christmas.

BLACK & BLUE
Detective Harry Blue is determined to take down the serial killer who's abducted several women, but her mission leads to a shocking revelation.

THE MATING SEASON

Documentary ornithologist Sophie Castle is convinced that her heart belongs only to the birds—until she meets her gorgeous cameraman, Rigg Greensman.

SACKING THE QUARTERBACK

Attorney Melissa St. James wins every case. Now, when she's taken on football superstar Grayson Knight, her heart is on the line too.

BODYGUARD

Special Agent Abbie Whitmore has only one task: protect Congressman Jonathan Lassiter from a violent cartel's threats. Yet she's never had to do it while falling in love....

DAZZLING: THE DIAMOND TRILOGY, PART I

To support her artistic career, Siobhan works at the elite Stone Room in New York City...never expecting to be swept away by Derick Miller.

RADIANT: THE DIAMOND TRILOGY, PART II

After an explosive breakup with her billionaire boyfriend, Siobhan moves to Detroit to pursue her art. But Derick isn't ready to give her up.

HOT WINTER NIGHTS

Allie Thatcher moved to Montana to start fresh as the head of the trauma center. And even though the days are cold, the nights are steamy...especially when she meets search-and-rescue leader Dex Belmont.

TRIPLE THREAT

THRILLERS

JAMES PATTERSON

BOOK**SHOTS**

GRAND CENTRAL
PUBLISHING
NEW YORK LONDON

Copyright © 2016 by James Patterson
Excerpt from *The Trial* copyright © 2016 by James Patterson

Grand Central Publishing
Hachette Book Group
1290 Avenue of the Americas, New York, NY 10104
grandcentralpublishing.com
twitter.com/grandcentralpub

First Edition: August 2016

Grand Central Publishing is a division of Hachette Book Group, Inc. The Grand Central Publishing name and logo are trademarks of Hachette Book Group, Inc. The BookShots name and logo are trademarks of JBP Business, LLC.

The publisher is not responsible for websites (or their content) that are not owned by the publisher.

The Hachette Speakers Bureau provides a wide range of authors for speaking events. To find out more, go to hachettespeakersbureau.com or call (866) 376-6591.

ISBN 978-0-316-31782-5
Library of Congress Cataloging-in-Publication Data has been applied for.

Printed in the United States of America

RRD-C

10 9 8 7 6 5 4 3 2 1

CONTENTS

CROSS
KILL

JAMES PATTERSON

CHAPTER 1

A LATE WINTER STORM bore down on Washington, DC, that March morning, and more folks than usual were waiting in the cafeteria of St. Anthony of Padua Catholic School on Monroe Avenue in the northeast quadrant.

"If you need a jolt before you eat, coffee's in those urns over there," I called to the cafeteria line.

From behind a serving counter, my partner, John Sampson, said, "You want pancakes or eggs and sausage, you come see me first. Dry cereal, oatmeal, and toast at the end. Fruit, too."

It was early, a quarter to seven, and we'd already seen twenty-five people come through the kitchen, mostly moms and kids from the surrounding neighborhood. By my count, another forty were waiting in the hallway, with more coming in from outside where the first flakes were falling.

It was all my ninety-something grandmother's idea. She'd hit the DC Lottery Powerball the year before and wanted to make sure the unfortunate received some of her good fortune. She'd partnered with the church to see the hot-breakfast program started.

"Are there any doughnuts?" asked a little boy, who put me in mind of my younger son, Ali.

He was holding on to his mother, a devastatingly thin woman with rheumy eyes and a habit of scratching at her neck.

"No doughnuts today," I said.

"What am I gonna eat?" he complained.

"Something that's good for you for once," his mom said. "Eggs, bacon, and toast. Not all that Cocoa Puffs sugar crap."

I nodded. Mom looked like she was high on something, but she did know her nutrition.

"This sucks," her son said. "I want a doughnut. I want two doughnuts!"

"Go on, there," his mom said, and pushed him toward Sampson.

"Kind of overkill for a church cafeteria," said the man who followed her. He was in his late twenties, and dressed in baggy jeans, Timberland boots, and a big gray snorkel jacket.

I realized he was talking to me and looked at him, puzzled.

"Bulletproof vest?" he said.

"Oh," I said, and shrugged at the body armor beneath my shirt.

Sampson and I are major case detectives with the Washington, DC, Metropolitan Police Department. Immediately after our shift in the soup kitchen, we were joining a team taking down a drug gang operating in the streets around St. Anthony's. Members of the gang had been known to take free breakfasts at the school from time to time, so we'd decided to armor up. Just in case.

I wasn't telling him that, though. I couldn't identify him as a known gangster, but he looked the part.

"I'm up for a PT test end of next week," I said. "Got to get used to the weight since I'll be running three miles with it on."

"That vest make you hotter or colder today?"

"Warmer. Always."

"I need one of them," he said, and shivered. "I'm from Miami, you know? I must have been crazy to want to come on up here."

"Why did you come up here?" I asked.

"School. I'm a freshman at Howard."

"You're not on the meal program?"

"Barely making my tuition."

I saw him in a whole new light then, and was about to say so when gunshots rang out and people began to scream.

CHAPTER 2

DRAWING MY SERVICE PISTOL, I pushed against the fleeing crowd, hearing two more shots, and realizing they were coming from inside the kitchen behind Sampson. My partner had figured it out as well.

Sampson spun away from the eggs and bacon, drew his gun as I vaulted over the counter. We split and went to either side of the pair of swinging industrial kitchen doors. There were small portholes in both.

Ignoring the people still bolting from the cafeteria, I leaned forward and took a quick peek. Mixing bowls had spilled off the stainless-steel counters, throwing flour and eggs across the cement floor. Nothing moved, and I could detect no one inside.

Sampson took a longer look from the opposite angle. His face almost immediately screwed up.

"Two wounded," he hissed. "The cook, Theresa, and a nun I've never seen before."

"How bad?"

"There's blood all over Theresa's white apron. Looks like the nun's hit in the leg. She's sitting up against the stove with a big pool below her."

"Femoral?"

Sampson took another look and said, "It's a lot of blood."

"Cover me," I said. "I'm going in low to get them."

Sampson nodded. I squatted down and threw my shoulder into the door, which swung away. Half expecting some unseen gunman to open fire, I rolled inside. I slid through the slurry of two dozen eggs and came to a stop on the floor between two prep counters.

Sampson came in with his weapon high, searching for a target.

But no one shot. No one moved. And there was no sound except the labored breathing of the cook and the nun who were to our left, on the other side of a counter, by a big industrial stove.

The nun's eyes were open and bewildered. The cook's head slumped but she was breathing.

I scrambled under the prep counter to the women and started tugging off my belt. The nun shrank from me when I reached for her.

"I'm a cop, Sister," I said. "My name is Alex Cross. I need to put a tourniquet on your leg or you could die."

She blinked, but then nodded.

"John?" I said, observing a serious gunshot wound to her lower thigh. A needle-thin jet of blood erupted with every heartbeat.

"Right here," Sampson said behind me. "Just seeing what's what."

"Call it in," I said, as I wrapped the belt around her upper thigh, cinching it tight. "We need two ambulances. Fast."

The blood stopped squirting. I could hear my partner making the radio call.

The nun's eyes fluttered and drifted toward shut.

"Sister," I said. "What happened? Who shot you?"

Her eyes blinked open. She gaped at me, disoriented for a moment, before her attention strayed past me. Her eyes widened, and the skin of her cheek went taut with terror.

I snatched up my gun and spun around, raising the pistol. I saw Sampson with his back to me, radio to his ear, gun lowered, and then a door at the back of the kitchen. It had swung open, revealing a large pantry.

A man crouched in a fighting stance in the pantry doorway.

In his crossed arms he held two nickel-plated pistols, one aimed at Sampson and the other at me.

With all the training I've been lucky enough to receive over the years, you'd think I would have done the instinctual thing for a veteran cop facing an armed assailant, that I would have registered *Man with gun!* in my brain, and I would have shot him immediately.

But for a split second I didn't listen to *Man with a gun!* because I was too stunned by the fact that I knew him, and that he was long, long dead.

CHAPTER 3

IN THAT SAME INSTANT, he fired both pistols. Traveling less than thirty feet, the bullet hit me so hard it slammed me backward. My head cracked off the concrete and everything went just this side of midnight, like I was swirling and draining down a black pipe, before I heard a third shot and then a fourth.

Something crashed close to me, and I fought my way toward the sound, toward consciousness, seeing the blackness give way, disjointed and incomplete, like a jigsaw puzzle with missing pieces.

Five, maybe six seconds passed before I found more pieces and I knew who I was and what had happened. Two more seconds passed before I realized I'd taken the bullet square in the Kevlar that covered my chest. It felt like I'd taken a sledgehammer to my ribs and a swift kick to my head.

In the next instant, I grabbed my gun and looked for...

John Sampson sprawled on the floor by the sinks, his massive frame looking crumpled until he started twitching electrically, and I saw the head wound.

"No!" I shouted, becoming fully alert and stumbling over to his side.

Sampson's eyes were rolled up in his head and quivering. I grabbed the radio on the floor beyond him, hit the transmitter, and said, "This is Detective Alex Cross. Ten-Zero-Zero. Repeat. Officer down. Monroe Avenue and 12th, Northeast. St. Anthony's Catholic School kitchen. Multiple shots fired. Ten-Fifty-Twos needed immediately. Repeat. Multiple ambulances needed, and a Life Flight for officer with head wound!"

"We have ambulances and patrols on their way, Detective," the dispatcher came back. "ETA twenty seconds. I'll call Life Flight. Do you have the shooter?"

"No, damn it. Make the Life Flight call."

The line went dead. I lowered the radio. Only then did I look back at the best friend I've ever had, the first kid I met after Nana Mama brought me up from South Carolina, the man I'd grown up with, the partner I'd relied on more times than I could count. The spasms subsided and Sampson's eyes glazed over and he gasped.

"John," I said, kneeling beside him and taking his hand. "Hold on now. Cavalry's coming."

He seemed not to hear, just stared vacantly past me toward the wall.

I started to cry. I couldn't stop. I shook from head to toe, and then I wanted to shoot the man who'd done this. I wanted to shoot him twenty times, completely destroy the creature that had risen from the dead.

Sirens closed in on the school from six directions. I wiped at my tears, and then squeezed Sampson's hand, before forcing myself to my feet and back out into the cafeteria, where the first patrol officers were charging in, followed by a pair of EMTs whose shoulders were flecked with melting snowflakes.

They got Sampson's head immobilized, then put him on a board and then a gurney. He was under blankets and moving in less than six minutes. It was snowing hard outside. They waited inside the front door to the school for the helicopter to come, and put IV lines into his wrists.

Sampson went into another convulsion. The parish priest, Father Fred Close, came and gave my partner the last rites.

But my man was still hanging on when the helicopter came. In a daze I followed them out into a driving snowstorm. We had to shield our eyes to duck under the blinding propeller wash and get Sampson aboard.

"We'll take it from here!" one EMT shouted at me.

"There's not a chance I'm leaving his side," I said, climbed in beside the pilot, and pulled on the extra helmet. "Let's go."

The pilot waited until they had the rear doors shut and the gurney strapped down before throttling up the helicopter. We began to rise, and it was only then that I saw through the swirling snow that crowds were forming beyond the barricades set up in a perimeter around the school and church complex.

We pivoted in the air and flew back up over 12th Street, rising above the crowd. I looked down through the spiraling snow and saw everyone ducking their heads from the helicopter wash. Everyone except for a single male face looking directly up at the Life Flight, not caring about the battering, stinging snow.

"That's him!" I said.

"Detective?" the pilot said, his voice crackling over the radio in my helmet.

I tugged down the microphone, and said, "How do I talk to dispatch?"

The pilot leaned over, and flipped a switch.

"This is Detective Alex Cross," I said. "Who's the supervising detective heading to St. Anthony's?"

"Your wife. Chief Stone."

"Patch me through to her."

Five seconds passed as we built speed and hurtled toward the hospital.

"Alex?" Bree said. "What's happened?"

"John's hit bad, Bree," I said. "I'm with him. Close off that school from four blocks in every direction. Order a door-to-door search. I just saw the shooter on 12th, a block west of the school."

"Description?"

"It's Gary Soneji, Bree," I said. "Get his picture off Google and send it to every cop in the area."

There was silence on the line before Bree said sympathetically, "Alex, are *you* okay? Gary Soneji's been dead for years."

"If he's dead, then I just saw a ghost."

CHAPTER 4

WE WERE BUFFETED BY winds and faced near-whiteout conditions trying to land on the helipad atop George Washington Medical Center. In the end we put down in the parking lot by the ER entrance, where a team of nurses and doctors met us.

They hustled Sampson inside and got him attached to monitors while Dr. Christopher Kalhorn, a neurosurgeon, swabbed aside some of the blood and examined the head wounds.

The bullet had entered Sampson's skull at a shallow angle about two inches above the bridge of his nose. It exited forward of his left temple. That second wound was about the size of a marble, but gaping and ragged, as if the bullet had been a hollow point that broke up and shattered going through bone.

"Let's get him intubated, on Propofol, and into an ice bath and cooling helmet," Kalhorn said. "Take his temp down to ninety-two, get him into a CT scanner, and then the OR. I'll have a team waiting for him."

The ER doctors and nurses sprang into action. In short order, they had a breathing tube down Sampson's throat and were racing him away. Kalhorn turned to leave. I showed my badge and stopped him.

"That's my brother," I said. "What do I tell his wife?"

Dr. Kalhorn turned grim. "You tell her we'll do everything possible to save him. And you tell her to pray. You, too, Detective."

"What are his chances?"

"Pray," he said, took off in a trot, and disappeared.

I was left standing in an empty treatment slot in the ER, looking down at the dark blood that stained the gauze pads they'd used to clean Sampson's head.

"You can't stay in here, Detective," one of the nurses said sympathetically. "We need the space. Traffic accidents all over the city with this storm."

I nodded, turned, and wandered away, wondering where to go, what to do.

I went out in the ER waiting area and saw twenty people in the seats. They stared at my pistol, at the blood on my shirt, and at the black hole where Soneji's bullet had hit me. I didn't care what they thought. I didn't—

I heard the automatic doors *whoosh* open behind me.

A fearful voice cried out, "Alex?"

I swung around. Billie Sampson was standing there in pink hospital scrub pants and a down coat, shaking from head to toe from the cold and the threat of something far more bitter. "How bad is it?"

Billie's a surgical nurse, so there was no point in being vague. I described the wound. Her hand flew to her mouth at first, but then she shook her head. "It's bad. He's lucky to be alive."

I hugged her and said, "He's a strong man. But he's going to need your prayers. He's going to need all our prayers."

Billie's strength gave way. She began to moan and sob into

my chest, and I held her tighter. When I raised my head, the people in the waiting room were looking on in concern.

"Let's get out of here," I muttered, and led Billie out into the hallway and to the chapel.

We went inside, and thankfully it was empty. I got Billie calmed down enough to tell her what had happened at the school and afterward.

"They've put him into a chemical coma and are supercooling his body."

"To reduce swelling and bleeding," she said, nodding.

"And the neurosurgeons here are the best. He's in their hands now."

"And God's," Billie said, staring at the cross on the wall in the chapel before pulling away from me to go down on her knees.

I joined her and we held hands and begged our savior for mercy.

CHAPTER 5

HOURS PASSED LIKE DAYS as we waited outside the surgical unit. Bree showed up before noon.

"Anything?" she asked.

I shook my head.

"Billie," Bree said, hugging her. "We're going to find who did this to John. I promise you that."

"You didn't find Soneji?" I asked in disbelief. "How could he have gotten away if you'd cordoned off the area?"

My wife looked over at me, studied me. "Soneji's dead, Alex. You all but killed him yourself."

My mouth hung open, and I blinked several times. "You mean you didn't send his picture out? You didn't look for him?"

"We looked for someone who looked like Soneji," Bree said defensively.

"No," I said. "He was less than thirty feet from me, light shining down on his face. It was him."

"Then explain how a man who all but disintegrated right before your eyes can surface more than a decade later," Bree said.

"I can't explain it," I said. "I…maybe I need some coffee. Want some?"

They shook their heads, and I got up, heading toward the hospital cafeteria, seeing flashbacks from long ago.

I put Gary Soneji in prison after he went on a kidnapping and murder spree that threatened my family. Soneji escaped several years later, and turned to bomb building. He detonated several, killing multiple people before we spotted him in New York City. We chased Soneji into Grand Central Station, where we feared he'd explode another bomb. Instead he grabbed a baby.

At one point, Soneji held the baby up and screamed at me, "This doesn't end here, Cross. I'm coming for you, even from the grave if I have to."

Then he threw the infant at us. Someone caught her, but Soneji escaped into the vast abandoned tunnel system below Manhattan. We tracked him in there. Soneji attacked me in the darkness, and knocked me down and almost killed me before I was able to shoot him. The bullet shattered his jaw, ripped apart his tongue, and blew out the side of one cheek.

Soneji staggered away from me, was swallowed by the darkness. He must have pitched forward then and sprawled on the rocky tunnel floor. The impact set off a small bomb in his pocket. The tunnel exploded into white-hot flames.

When I got to him, Soneji was engulfed, curled up, and screaming. It lasted several seconds before he stopped. I stood there and watched Soneji burn. I saw him shrivel up and turn coal black.

But as sure as I was of that memory, I was also sure I'd seen Gary Soneji that morning, a split second before he tried to shoot me in the heart and blow Sampson's head off.

I'm coming for you, even from the grave if I have to.

Soneji's taunt echoed back to me after I'd gotten my coffee.

After several sips, I decided I had to assume Soneji was still dead. So I'd seen, what, a double? An impostor?

I supposed it was possible with plastic surgery, but the likeness had been so dead-on, from the thin reddish mustache to the wispy hair to the crazed, amused expression.

It was him, I thought. *But how?*

This doesn't end here, Cross.

I saw Soneji so clearly then that I feared for my sanity.

This doesn't end here, Cross.

I'm coming for you, even from the grave if I have to.

CHAPTER 6

"ALEX?"

I startled, almost dropped my coffee, and saw Bree trotting down the hall toward me with a wary expression.

"He made it through the operation," she said. "He's in intensive care, and the doctor's going to talk to Billie in a few moments."

We both held Billie's hands when Dr. Kalhorn finally emerged. He looked drained.

"How is he?" Billie asked, after introducing herself.

"Your husband's a remarkable fighter," Kalhorn said. "He died once on the table, but rallied. Besides the trauma of the bullet, there were bone and bullet fragments we had to deal with. Three quarters of an inch left and one of those fragments would have caught a major artery, and we'd be having a different conversation."

"So he's going to live?" Billie asked.

"I can't promise you that," Kalhorn said. "The next forty-eight to seventy-two hours will be the most critical time for him. He's sustained a massive head injury, severe trauma to his upper-left temporal lobe. For now, we're keeping him in a medically induced coma, and we will keep him that way until we see a significant drop in brain swelling."

"If he comes out, what's the prognosis, given the extent of the injury you saw?" I asked.

"I can't tell you who he'll be if and when he wakes up," the neurosurgeon said. "That's up to God."

"Can we see him?" Bree asked.

"Give it a half hour," Kalhorn said. "There's a whirlwind around him at the moment. Lots of good people supporting him."

"Thank you, Doctor," Billie said, trying not to cry again. "For saving him."

"It was an honor," Kalhorn said, patted her on the arm, and smiled at Bree and me before returning to the ICU.

"Damage to his upper-left temporal lobe," Billie said.

"He's alive," I said. "Let's keep focused on that. Anything else, we'll deal with down the road."

Bree held her hand and said, "Alex is right. We've prayed him through surgery, and now we'll pray he wakes up."

But Billie still appeared uncertain forty minutes later when we donned surgical masks, gloves, and smocks and entered the room where Sampson lay.

You could barely see the slits of his eyes for the swelling. His head was wrapped in a turban of gauze, and there were so many tubes going into him, and so many monitors and devices beeping and clicking around him, that from the waist up he looked more machine than man.

"Oh, Jesus, John," Billie said when she got to his side. "What have they done to you?"

Bree rubbed Billie's back as tears wracked her again. I stayed only a few minutes, until I couldn't take seeing Sampson like that anymore.

"I'll be back," I told them. "Tonight before I go home to sleep."

"Where are you going?" Bree asked.

"To hunt Soneji," I said. "It's what John would want."

"There's a blizzard outside," Bree said. "And Internal Affairs is going to want to hear your report on the shooting."

"I don't give a damn about IA right now," I said, walking toward the door. "And a blizzard's exactly the kind of chaotic situation that Gary Soneji lives for."

Bree wasn't happy, but sighed and gestured to a shopping bag she'd brought with her. "You'll need your coat, hat, and gloves if you're going Soneji-hunting."

CHAPTER 7

OUTSIDE A BLIZZARD WAILED, a classic nor'easter with driving wet snow that was already eight inches deep. It takes only four inches to snarl Washington, DC, so completely that there's talk of bringing in the National Guard.

Georgetown was a parking lot. I trudged to the Foggy Bottom Metro station, ignoring my freezing-cold feet, and reliving old times with big John Sampson. I met him within days of moving up to DC with my brothers after my mother died and my father, her killer, disappeared, presumed dead.

John lived with his mother and sister. His father had died in Vietnam. We were in the same fifth-grade class. He was ten years old and big, even then. But so was I.

It made for a natural rivalry, and we didn't much care for each other at first. I was faster than him, which he did not like. He was stronger than me, which I did not like. The inevitable fight we had was a draw.

We were suspended for three days for fighting. Nana Mama marched me down to Sampson's house to apologize to him and to his mother for throwing the first punch.

I went unhappily. When Sampson came to the door equally annoyed, I saw the split lip and bruising around his right cheek and smiled. He saw the swelling around both of my eyes and smiled back.

We'd both inflicted damage. We both had won. And that was that. End of the war, and start of the longest friendship of my life.

I took the Metro across town, and walked back to St. Anthony's in the snow, trying to will myself not to remember Sampson in the ICU, more machine than man. But the image kept returning, and every time it did, I felt weaker, as if a part of me were dying.

There were still Metro police cars parked in front of the school, and two television trucks. I pulled the wool hat down and turned up the collar of my jacket. I didn't want to talk to any reporters about this case. Ever.

I showed my badge to the patrolman standing inside the front door, and started back toward the cafeteria and kitchen.

Father Close appeared at his office door. He recognized me.

"Your partner?"

"There's brain damage, but he's alive," I said.

"Another miracle, then," Father Close said. "Sister Mary Elliott and Theresa Ball, the cook, they're still alive as well. You saved them, Dr. Cross. If you hadn't been there, I fear all three of them would be dead."

"I don't think that's true," I said. "But thank you for saying so."

"Any idea when I can have my cafeteria and kitchen back?"

"I'll ask the crime-scene specialists, but figure tomorrow your students bring a bag lunch and eat in their homerooms. When it's a cop-involved shooting, the forensics folks are sticklers for detail."

"As they should be," Father Close said, thanked me again, and returned to his office.

I returned to the cafeteria and stood there a moment in the empty space, hearing voices in the kitchen, but recalling the first shots and how I'd reacted.

I went to the swinging industrial doors and did the same. We'd done it by the book, I decided, and pushed through them again.

I glanced at where the cook and nun had lain wounded, and then over where Sampson had lain dying before turning my attention to the pantry. This was where the book had been thrown out. In retrospect, we should have cleared the rest of the building before tending to the wounded. But it looked like femoral blood and…

Three crime-scene techs were still at work in the kitchen. Barbara Hatfield, an old friend, was in the pantry. She spotted me and came right over.

"How's John, Alex?"

"Hanging on," I said.

"Everyone's shaken up," Hatfield said. "And there's something you should see, something I was going to call you about later."

She led me into the pantry, floor-to-ceiling shelves loaded with foodstuffs and kitchen supplies, and a big shiny commercial freezer at the far end.

The words spray-painted in two lines across the face of the fridge stopped me dead in my tracks.

"Right?" Hatfield said. "I did the same thing."

CHAPTER 8

I WAS UP AT four o'clock the following morning, snuck out of bed without waking Bree, and on three hours of sleep went back to doing what I'd been doing. I got a cup of coffee and went up to the third floor, to my home office, where I had been going through my files on Gary Soneji.

I keep files on all the bad ones, but Soneji had the thickest file, six of them, in fact, all bulging. I'd left off at one in the morning with notes taken midway through the kidnapping of the US secretary of the treasury's son, and the daughter of a famous actress.

I tried to focus, tried to re-master the details. But I yawned after two paragraphs, drank coffee, and thought of John Sampson.

But only briefly. I decided that sitting by his side helped him little. I was better off looking for the man who put a bullet through John's head. So I read and reread, and noted dangling threads, abandoned lines of inquiry that Sampson and I had followed over the years but which had led nowhere.

After an hour, I found an old genealogy chart we and the US marshals put together on Soneji's family after he escaped prison. Scanning it, I realized we'd let the marshals handle the pure fugitive hunt. I saw several names and relations I'd never talked to before, and wrote them down.

I ran their names through Google, and saw that two of them were still living at the addresses noted on the chart. How long had it been? Thirteen, fourteen years?

Then again, Nana Mama and I had lived in our house on 5th for more than thirty years. Americans do put down roots once in a while.

I glanced at my watch, saw it was past five, and wondered when I could try to make a few calls. No, I thought then, this kind of thing is best done in person. But the storm. I went to the window in the dormer of the office, pushed it up, and looked outside.

To my surprise, it was pouring rain and considerably warmer. Most of the snow was gone. That sealed it. I was going for a drive as soon as it was light enough to see.

Returning to my desk, I thought about going back downstairs to take a shower, but feared waking Bree. Her job as Metro's chief of detectives was stressful enough without dealing with the additional pressure of a cop shooting.

I tried to go back to the Soneji files, but instead called up a picture on my computer. I'd taken it the afternoon before. It showed the fridge and the spray-painted words the shooter had left behind.

CROSS KILL
Long Live Soneji!

I had obviously been the target. And why not? Soneji hated me as much as I hated him.

Had Soneji expected Sampson to be with me? The two pistols he'd fired said yes. I closed my eyes and saw him there in the doorway, arms crossed, left gun aimed at me, right gun at Sampson.

Something bothered me. I turned back to the file, rummaged around until I confirmed my memory. Soneji was left-handed, which explained why he'd crossed his arms to shoot. He was aiming at me with his better hand. He'd wanted me dead no matter what happened to John.

It was why Soneji shot for center of mass, I decided, and wondered whether his shot at Sampson was misaimed, if he'd clipped John's head in error.

Left-handed. It had to be Soneji. But it couldn't be Soneji.

In frustration, I shut the computer off, grabbed my notes, and snuck back into the bedroom. I shut the bathroom door without making a peep. After showering and dressing, I tried to get out light-footed, but made a floorboard squeak.

"I'm up, quiet as a mouse," Bree said.

"I'm going to New Jersey," I said.

"What?" she said, sitting up in bed and turning on the light. "Why?"

"To talk to some of Soneji's relatives, see if he's been in touch."

Bree shook her head. "He's dead, Alex."

"But what if the explosion I saw in the tunnel was *caused* by Soneji as he went by some bum living down there?" I said. "What if I didn't see Soneji burn?"

"You never did DNA on the remains?"

"There was no need. I saw him die. I identified him, so no one checked."

"Jesus, Alex," Bree said. "Is that possible? What did the shooter's face look like?"

"Like Soneji's," I said, frustrated.

"Well, did his jaw look like Soneji's? His tongue? Did he say anything?"

"He didn't say a word, but his face?" I frowned and thought about that. "I don't know."

"You said the light was good. You said you saw him clearly."

Was the light that good? Feeling a little wobbly, I nevertheless closed my eyes, trying to bring more of the memory back and into sharper focus.

I saw Soneji standing there in the pantry doorway, arms crossed, chin tucked, and...looking directly at me. He shot at Sampson without even aiming. It *was* me he'd wanted to kill.

What about his jaw? I replayed memory again and again before I saw it.

"There was something there," I said, running my fingers along my left jawline.

"A shadow?" Bree said.

I shook my head. "More like a scar."

CHAPTER 9

THREE HOURS LATER, I'D left I-95 for Route 29, which parallels the Delaware River. Heading upstream, I soon realized that I was not far from East Amwell Township, where the aviator Charles Lindbergh's baby was kidnapped in 1932.

Gary Soneji had been obsessed with the Lindbergh case. He'd studied it in preparing for the kidnappings of the treasury secretary's son, the late Michael Goldberg, and Maggie Rose Dunne, the daughter of a famous actress.

I'd noticed before on a map the proximity of East Amwell to Rosemont, where Soneji grew up. But it wasn't until I pulled through the tiny unincorporated settlement that I realized Soneji had spent his early life less than five miles from the Lindbergh kidnapping site.

Rosemont itself was quaint and leafy, with rock walls giving way to sopping green fields.

I tried to imagine Soneji as a boy in this rural setting, tried to see him discovering the crime of the century. He wouldn't have cared much for the police detectives who'd worked the Lindbergh case. No, Soneji would have obsessed on the information surrounding Bruno Hauptmann, the career criminal convicted and executed for taking the toddler and caving in his skull.

My mind was flooded with memories of going into Soneji's apartment for the first time, seeing what was essentially a shrine to Hauptmann and the Lindbergh case. In writings we found back then, Soneji had fantasized about being Hauptmann in the days just before the killer was caught, when the whole world was fixated and speculating on the mystery he'd set in motion.

"Audacious criminals change history," Soneji wrote. "Audacious criminals are remembered long after they're gone, which is more than can be said of the detectives who chase them."

I found the address on the Rosemont Ringoes Road, and pulled over on the shoulder beyond the drive. The storm had ebbed to sprinkles when I climbed out in front of a gray-and-white clapboard cottage set back in pines.

The yard was sparse and littered with wet pine needles. The front stoop was cracked and listed to one side, so I had to hold on to the iron railing in order to ring the bell.

A few moments later, one of the curtains fluttered. A few moments after that, the door swung open, revealing a bald man in his seventies. He leaned over a walker and had an oxygen line running into his nose.

"Peter Soneji?"

"What do you want?"

"I'm Alex Cross. I'm a—"

"I know who you are," Gary Soneji's father snapped icily. "My son's killer."

"He blew himself up."

"So you've said."

"Can I talk to you, sir?"

"Sir?" Peter Soneji said and laughed caustically. "Now it's 'sir'?"

"Far as I know, you never had anything to do with your son's criminal career," I said.

"Tell that to the reporters who've shown up at my door over the years," Soneji's father said. "The things they've accused me of. Father to a monster."

"I'm not accusing you of anything, *Mr. Soneji*," I said. "I'm simply looking for your take on a few loose ends."

"With everything on the internet about Gary, you'd think there'd be no loose ends."

"These are questions from my personal files," I said.

Soneji's father gave me a long, considered look before saying, "Leave it alone, Detective. Gary's long dead. Far as I'm concerned, good riddance."

He tried to shut the door in my face, but I stopped him.

"I can call the sheriff," Peter Soneji protested.

"Just one question and then I'll leave," I said. "How did Gary become obsessed with the Lindbergh kidnapping?"

CHAPTER 10

TWO HOURS LATER AS I drove through the outskirts of Crumpton, Maryland, I was still wrestling with the answer Soneji's father had given me. It seemed to offer new insight into his son, but I still couldn't explain how or why yet.

I found the second address. The farmhouse had once been a cheery yellow, but the paint was peeling and streaked with dark mold. Every window was encased in the kind of iron barring you see in big cities.

As I walked across the front yard toward the porch, I stirred up several pigeons, flushing them from the dead weeds. I heard a weird voice talking somewhere behind the house.

The porch was dominated by several old machine tools, lathes and such, that I had to step around in order to knock at a steel door with triple dead bolts.

I knocked a second time, and was thinking I should go around the house where I'd heard the odd voice. But then the dead bolts were thrown one by one.

The door opened, revealing a dark-haired woman in her forties, with a sharp nose and dull brown eyes. She wore a grease-stained one-piece Carhartt canvas coverall, and carried at port arms an AR-style rifle with a big banana clip.

"Salesman, you are standing on my property uninvited," she said. "I have ample cause to shoot you where you stand."

I showed her my badge and ID, said, "I'm not a salesman. I'm a cop. I should have called ahead, but I didn't have a number."

Instead of calming her down, that only got her more agitated. "What are the police doing at sweet Ginny Winslow's door? Looking to persecute a gun lover?"

"I just want to ask you a few questions, Mrs. Soneji," I said.

Soneji's widow flinched at the name, and turned spitting mad. "My name's been legally changed to Virginia Winslow going on seven years now, and I still can't get the stench of Gary off my skin. What's your name? Who are you with?"

"Alex Cross," I said. "With DC…"

She hardened, said, "I know you now. I remember you from TV."

"Yes, ma'am."

"You never came to talk with me. Just them US marshals. Like I didn't even exist."

"I'm here to talk now," I said.

"Ten years too late. Get the hell off my property before I embrace my Second Amendment rights and—"

"I saw Gary's father this morning," I said. "He told me how Gary's obsession with the Lindbergh kidnapping began."

She knitted her brows. "How's that?"

"Gary's dad said when Gary was eight they were in a used book store, and while his father was wandering in the stacks, his son found a tattered copy of *True Detective Mysteries,* a crime magazine from the 1930s, and sat down to read it."

Finger still on the trigger of her semiautomatic rifle, Virginia Winslow shrugged. "So what?"

"When Mr. Soneji found Gary, his son was sitting on the

floor in the bookstore, the magazine in his lap, and staring in fascination at a picture from the Lindbergh baby's autopsy that showed the head wound in lurid detail."

She stared at me with her jaw slack, as if remembering something that frightened and appalled her.

"What is it?" I asked.

Soneji's widow hardened again. "Nothing. Doesn't surprise me. I used to catch him looking at autopsy pictures. He was always saying he was going to write a book and needed to look at them for research."

"You didn't believe him?"

"I believed him until my brother Charles noticed that Gary was always volunteering to gut deer they killed," she said. "Charles told me Gary liked to put his hands in the warm innards, said he liked the feeling, and told me how Gary'd get all bright and glowing when he was doing it."

CHAPTER 11

"I DIDN'T KNOW THAT about Gary, either," I said.

"What's this all about?" Virginia Winslow asked, studying me now.

"There was a cop shooting in DC," I said. "A man who fit Gary's description was the shooter."

I expected Soneji's widow to respond with total skepticism. But instead she looked frightened and appalled again.

"Gary's dead," she said. "*You* killed him, didn't you?"

"He killed himself," I said. "Detonated the bomb he was carrying."

Her attention flitted to the boards. "That's not what the internet is saying."

"What's the internet saying?"

"That Gary's alive," she said. "Our son, Dylan, said he's seen it online. Gary's dead, isn't he? Please tell me that."

The way she clenched the rifle told me she needed to hear it, so I said, "As far as I know, Gary Soneji's dead and has been dead for more than ten years. But someone who looked an awful lot like him shot my partner yesterday."

"What?" she said. "No."

"It's not him," I said. "I'm almost certain."

"Almost?" she said before a phone started ringing back in the house.

"I…I have to get that," she said. "Work."

"What kind of work?"

"I'm a machinist and gunsmith," she said. "My father taught me the trade."

She shut the door before I could comment. The bolts were thrown one by one.

I almost left, but then, remembering that voice I'd heard on my way in, I went around the farmhouse, seeing a small, neglected barn around which dozens of pigeons were flying.

I heard someone talking in the barn, and walked over.

Click-a-t-clack. Click-a-t-clack.

Pigeons started and whirled out the barn door.

There was a grimy window. I went to it, and peeked inside, seeing through the dirt sixteen-year-old Dylan Winslow standing there by a large pigeon coop, gazing off into space.

Dylan looked nothing like his father. He had his mother's naturally dark hair, sharp nose, and the same dull brown eyes. He was borderline obese, with hardly a chin, more a draping of his cheeks that joined a wattle above his Adam's apple.

"You need to learn your place," he said to no one. "You need to learn to be quiet. Emotional control. It's the key to a happy life."

Then he turned and walked by the pigeon coop, running a hoop of keys across the metal mesh.

Click-a-t-clack. Click-a-t-clack.

The sound rattled the pigeons and they battered themselves against their cages.

"Be quiet now," Dylan said firmly. "You got to learn some control."

Then he pivoted and started toward me, raking the cages again.

Click-a-t-clack. Click-a-t-clack.

A disturbing little smile showed on the teen's face, and there was even more upsetting delight in his eyes. I have a PhD in criminal psychology and have studied serial killers in depth. Many of them grew up torturing animals for sport.

Had Dylan's father?

I stepped inside the barn. Gary Soneji's son had his back to me again, walking away while raking the front of the cages.

Click-a-t-clack. Click-a-t-clack.

I took another two steps and noticed a large piece of cardboard nailed to one of the barn's support posts.

There was a well-used paper target taped to the cardboard and six darts sticking out of it. The target featured a bull's-eye superimposed over a man's face. It had been used so many times that at first I didn't know who the man was.

Then I did.

"Who the hell are you?" Dylan said, and then gaped when I faced him.

"From the looks of it," I said, "I'm your dartboard."

CHAPTER 12

DYLAN WINSLOW PURSED HIS lips in long-simmering anger, said, "If Mama would let me, I'd use one of her shotguns on it instead of darts."

What do you say to the disturbed son of the disturbed criminal you shot in the face and watched burn?

"I can understand your feelings," I said.

"No, you can't," he said, sneering. "This an official visit, Detective Alex Cross?"

"As a matter of fact," I said. "A man fitting your dead father's description shot my partner in the head last night."

Dylan's sneer disappeared, replaced by widening eyes and that disturbing, delighted grin I'd seen earlier. "It's true, then, what they're saying."

"What are they saying?"

"That you didn't get my dad," Dylan said. "That he escaped the tunnels, badly wounded, but alive, and is still alive. Is that what you're telling me, too?"

There seemed so much hope in his face that, whether he was in need of psychological help or not, I didn't want to destroy it.

"If it wasn't your father who shot my partner, it was his twin."

Dylan started to laugh. He laughed so hard there were tears in his eyes.

Thumping his chest, he said, "I knew it! I felt it right here."

When he stopped, I said, "What do you think is going to happen? That he's going to suddenly appear to rescue you?"

Dylan acted as if I'd read his thoughts, but then shot back, "He will. You watch. And there's nothing you can do about it. It's like they say—Dad was always smarter than you. More patient and cunning than you."

Rather than defend myself, I said, "You're right. Your father was smarter than me, and more patient, and more cunning."

"He still is. They say so on the internet."

"What site?" I asked.

Dylan gave me that disturbing smile again before saying, "One you can't get at in a million years, Cross." He laughed. "Never in a million years."

"Really?" I said. "How about I march back up to your mother and tell her I'm coming back with a search warrant for every computer in your house?"

Dylan's grin stretched wider. "Go ahead. We don't have one."

"How about every computer in your school, in the local library, in every place your mother says you get online?"

I thought that would rock him, but it didn't.

"Knock yourself out," he said. "But unless I have a lawyer present, I am done answering your questions, and I have pigeons to feed."

Or torture, I almost said.

But I bit back the urge, and turned to leave, calling over my shoulder, "Nice to meet you, Dylan. Wonderful getting to know the son of an old enemy."

CHAPTER 13

IT WAS PAST SIX when I finally reached the ICU at GW Medical Center. The nurse at the station said Sampson's vitals had been irregular most of the day, and there'd been little if any reduction in brain swelling.

"You sick in any way?" the nurse asked.

"Not that I'm aware of. Why?"

"Protocol. The shunt draining the wound is an open track straight to the inside of your friend's healing skull. Any kind of infection could be catastrophic."

"I feel fine," I said, and put on the gown, mask, and gloves.

When I pushed open the door, Billie stirred awake in her reclining chair.

"Alex? That you?"

"The man behind the mask."

"Tell me about it," she said, getting up to hug me. "I've been wearing one the past forty hours and I'm getting rubbed raw."

"His vitals?"

Billie scanned the monitors attached to her husband and said, "Not bad at the moment, but his blood pressure took a short, scary dive about four hours ago. I was thinking stroke until he just kind of came up out of it."

"They say talking to people in comas helps," I said.

"Stimulates the brain," she said, nodding. "But that's usually with a non-induced coma, when there aren't drugs involved."

"All the same," I said, and went to Sampson's side.

"I'll be a few minutes," Billie said.

"Be right here until you get back," I said.

When she'd gone out, I held Sampson's giant hand and gave him an account of the day's investigation, sparing him no detail. It felt good and familiar, and right, to talk it out with him, as if Sampson were not drugged down to the reptilian part of his brain, but acute and thoughtful and funny as hell.

"That's it," I said. "And, yes, I want another crack at Soneji's widow and kid before long."

The door opened. Billie stepped back inside, and then several of the monitors around Sampson began to squawk in alarm.

A team burst in. I was pushed to the corner with Billie.

"It's his blood pressure again," Billie said in a wavering voice. "Jesus, I don't know if his heart can take this much longer."

Ninety seconds later, the crisis passed and his vitals improved.

"I don't know what happened," I said, bewildered. "I was telling him about the investigation and…"

"What?" Billie said. "Why did you do that?"

"Because he'd want to know."

"No," she said, shaking her head. "That's done. That's over, Alex."

"What's over?"

"His career as a cop," Billie said. "No matter how he recovers, that part of John's life is over if he wants to continue to be my husband."

"John loves being a cop," I said.

"I know he does…did…but that's over," Billie said sharply. "I will care for him, and defend John until the day one of us dies, but between now and then, his days carrying a gun and a badge are behind him."

CHAPTER 14

"SHE'S GOT THE RIGHT to demand that," Bree said later in the hospital cafeteria. "John took a bullet to the head, Alex."

"I know," I said, frustrated and heartsick.

It felt like part of John had died and was never coming back. And it would never be the same between us, as partners anyway. That was dead, too.

I explained this to Bree, and she put her hands on mine and said, "You'll never have a better friend than John Sampson. That friendship, that fierce bond you two have, will never be broken, even if he's no longer a cop, even if he's no longer your partner. Okay?"

"No," I said, pushing my plate away. "But I'll have to learn to live with it."

"You haven't eaten three bites," Bree said, gesturing at the plate.

"No appetite," I said.

"Then force yourself," Bree said. "Especially the protein. Your brain has to be tip-top if you're going to find Soneji."

I laughed softly. "You're always looking out for me."

"Every moment I can, baby."

I ate quite a bit more, and washed it down with three full glasses of water.

"Not quite Nana Mama's cooking," I said.

"I'm sure there'll be leftovers," Bree said.

"You trying to get me fat?" I said.

"I like a little cushion."

I didn't know what to say to that, and we both burst out laughing. Then I looked over and saw Billie standing in the doorway, watching us with bitterness and longing in her expression. She turned and left.

"Should I go after her?" I asked.

"No," Bree said. "I'll talk to her tomorrow."

"Home?"

"Home."

We left the hospital and were crossing a triangular plaza to the Foggy Bottom Metro station when the first shot rang out.

I heard the flat crack of the muzzle blast. I felt the bullet rip past my left ear, grabbed Bree, and yanked her to the ground by two newspaper boxes. People were screaming and scattering.

"Where is he?" Bree said.

"I don't know," I said, before the second and third shots shattered the glass of one newspaper rack and *ping*ed off another.

Then I heard squealing tires, and jumped up in time to see a white panel van roar north on 23rd Street, Northwest, heading toward Washington Circle, and a dozen different escape routes. As the van flashed past us, I caught a glimpse of the driver.

Gary Soneji was looking my way as if posing for a mental picture, grinning like a lunatic and holding his right-hand thumb up, index finger extended, like a gun he was aiming right at me.

I was so shocked that another instant passed before I started running across the plaza to 23rd, trying to get a look at his license plates. But his plate lights were dark, and the van soon disappeared into evening traffic, headed in the direction of whatever hellhole Gary Soneji was calling home these days.

"Did you see him?" I asked Bree, who was shaken, but calling in the shots to dispatch.

She shook her head after she'd finished. "You did?"

"It was him, Bree. Gary Soneji in the flesh. As if he hadn't been blown up and burned, as if he hadn't spent the past decade in a box under six feet of dirt."

CHAPTER 15

THE NEXT MORNING, I called GW to check on Sampson. His vitals had destabilized again.

Part of me said, *Go to the hospital,* but instead I drove out to Quantico, Virginia, and the FBI Lab.

For almost seven years, I worked for the Bureau in the behavioral science department as a full-time consultant and left on good terms. I have many friends who still work at Quantico, including my old partner, Ned Mahoney.

I called ahead, and he met me at the gate, made sure I got the VIP treatment clearing security.

"What are friends in high places for?" Mahoney asked when I thanked him. "How's John?"

I gave him a brief update on Sampson and my investigation.

"How could Soneji be alive?" Mahoney said. "I was there, remember? I saw him burning, too. It was him. "

"Then who was the guy who shot Sampson and tried to shoot me last night?" I said. "Because both times I've seen him, my brain has screamed *Soneji!* Both times."

"Hey, hey, Alex," Mahoney said, patting me on the shoulder out of concern. "Take a big breath. If it's him, we'll help you find him."

I took several deep, long breaths, trying to keep my

thoughts from whirling, and said, "Let's start with the cyber-crime unit."

Ten minutes later, we went through an unmarked door into a large space filled with low-walled cubicles that were in a soft blue light Mahoney said was supposed to increase productivity. There were three, sometimes four computer screens at every workstation.

"The only thing that separates the IT brainpower in this room from a company like Google is the dress code," Mahoney said.

"No Ping-Pong, either," I said.

"There's agitation in that direction," Mahoney said, weaving through the cubicles.

"Any chance it happens?"

"When the Bureau starts admitting J. Edgar preferred panties," he said, and then stopped in front of a workstation in the middle of the room.

"Agent Batra?" Mahoney said. "I want to introduce you to Alex Cross."

A petite Indian woman in her late twenties in a conservative blue suit and black pumps spun around from one of four screens at her station. She stood quickly and put out her hand, so small it felt like a doll's.

"Special Agent Henna Batra," she said. "An honor to meet you, Dr. Cross."

"And you as well."

"Agent Batra is said to be at one with the internet," Mahoney said. "If anyone can help you, she can. Stop by the office on your way out, Alex."

"Will do," I said.

"So," Agent Batra said, sitting again. "What are you looking for?"

"A website where there are active conversations going on concerning Gary Soneji."

"I know that case," Batra said. "We studied it at the academy. He's dead."

"Evidently his admirers don't think so, and I'd like to see what they're saying about Soneji. I was warned we'd never find the site in a million years."

With Special Agent Batra navigating the web via a link to a supercomputer, the search took all of fourteen minutes.

"Quite a few that mention Soneji," Batra said, gesturing at the screen, and then scrolling down before tapping on a link. "But I'm betting this is the one you're looking for."

I squinted to read the link. "ZRXQT?"

"Anonymous, or at least attempting anonymity," Batra said. "And it's locked and encrypted. But I ran a filter that picked up traces of commands going into and out of that website. The density of Soneji mentions in those traces is through the roof compared to every other site that talks about him."

"You can't get in?"

"I didn't say that," Batra said, as if I'd insulted her. "You drink tea?"

"Coffee," I said.

She gestured across the room. "There's a break room over there. If you'd be so kind as to bring me some hot tea, Dr. Cross. I should be able to get inside by the time you come back."

I thought it was kind of funny that Batra had started the conversation as my subordinate and was now ordering me around. Then again, I hadn't a clue about how she was doing what she was doing. Then again, she was at one with the internet.

"Oolong?" I asked.

"Fine," Batra said, already engrossed in her work.

I found the coffee and the tea, but when I returned, she was still typing.

"Got it?"

"Not yet," she said, irritated. "It's sophisticated, multilevel, and…"

Lines of code began to fill the page. Batra seemed to speed-read the code as it rolled by, because, after twenty seconds of this, she said, "Oh, of course."

She gave the computer another command, and a homepage appeared, featuring a cement wall in some abandoned building. Across the wall in dripping black graffiti letters, it read *Long Live The Soneji!*

CHAPTER 16

I WON'T BORE YOU with a page-by-page description of the www
.thesoneji.net website. There may be archives of it still up on
the internet for those interested.

For those of you less inclined to explore the dark side of
the web, it's enough to know that Gary Soneji had developed a
cult of personality in the decade since I'd seen him burn, hundreds of digital devotees who worshipped him with the kind
of fervor I'd previously assigned to Appalachian snake han-
dlers and the Hare Krishnas.

They called themselves The Soneji, and they seemed to
know almost every nuance of the life of the kidnapper and
mass murderer. In addition to an extensive biography, there
were hundreds of lurid photos, links to articles, and an online
chat forum where members hotly debated all things Soneji.

The hottest topics?

Number one that day was *the John Sampson shooting.*

The Soneji were generally ecstatic that my partner had been
shot and barely clung to life, but a few posts stood out.

Napper2 wrote, Gary fuckin' got Sampson!

Gary's so back, The Waste Man agreed.

Only thing better would be Cross on a Cross, wrote Black
Hole.

That day's coming sooner than later, said Gary's Girl. Gary's missed Cross twice. He won't miss a third time.

Aside from being the subject of homicidal speculation, something bothered me about that last post, the one from Gary's Girl. I studied it and the others, trying to figure out what was different.

"They think he's alive," Agent Batra offered.

"Yeah, that's hot thread number two," I said. "Let's take a look there, and come back."

She clicked on the "Resurrection Man" thread.

Cross saw him, came face to face with Gary, wrote Sapper9. Shit his pants, is what I heard.

Cross was hit in first attack, wrote Chosen One. Soneji's aim is true. Cross is just lucky.

Beemer answered, My respect for Gary is profound, but he is not alive. That is impossible.

The believers among The Soneji went berserk on Beemer for having the gall to challenge the consensus. Beemer was attacked from all sides. To his credit, Beemer fought back.

Call me Doubting Thomas, but show me the evidence. Can I put my finger through Soneji's hand? Can I see where the lance pierced his side?

You could if he trusted you the way he trusts me, wrote Gary's Girl.

Beemer wrote, So you've seen him, GG?

After a long pause, Gary's Girl wrote, I have. With my own two eyes.

Pic? Beemer said.

A minute passed, and then two. Five minutes after his demand, Beemer wrote, Funny how illusions can seem so real.

A second later the screen blinked and a picture appeared.

Taken at night, it was a selfie of a big, muscular woman gone goth, heavy on the black on black right down to the lipstick. She was grinning raunchily and sitting in the lap of a man with wispy red hair. His hands held her across her deep, leather-clad cleavage, and he had buried three quarters of his face into the side of her neck.

The other quarter, however, including his right eye, was clearly visible.

He was staring right into the camera with an amused and lecherous expression that seemed designed to taunt the lens and me. He knew I'd see the picture someday and be infuriated.

I was sure of that. It was the kind of thing Soneji would do.

"That him?" Batra asked. "Gary Soneji?"

"Close enough. Can you track down Gary's Girl?"

The FBI cyber agent thought about that, and then said, "Give me twenty minutes, maybe less."

CHAPTER 17

AT FIVE O'CLOCK THAT afternoon, Bree and I drove through the tiny rural community of Flintstone, Maryland, past the Flintstone Post Office, the Stone Age Café, and Carl's Gas and Grub.

We found a side street off Route 144, and drove down a wooded lane to a freshly painted green ranch house set off all by itself in a meticulously tended yard. A shiny new Audi Q5 sat in the driveway.

"I thought you said she's on welfare," Bree said.

"Food stamps, too," I said.

We parked behind the Audi and got out. AC/DC was blasting from inside the house. We went to the front door and found it ajar.

I tried the bell. It was broken.

Bree knocked and called out, "Delilah Pinder?"

We heard nothing in response but the howling of an electric guitar against a thundering baseline.

"Door's open," I said. "We're checking on her well-being."

"Be my guest," Bree said.

I pushed open the door and found myself in a room decorated with brand-new leather furniture and a big curved HD television. The music throbbed on from somewhere deeper inside the house.

We checked the kitchen, saw boxes of appliances that hadn't even been opened, and then headed down the hallway toward the source of the music. The first door on the left was a home gym with Olympic weight-lifting equipment. The music came from the room at the end of the hall.

There was a lull in the song, just enough that I heard a woman's voice cry, "That's it!" before the throbbing, wailing song drowned her out.

The door to that room at the end of the hall was cracked open two inches. A brilliant light shone through.

"Delilah Pinder?" I called out.

No answer.

I stepped forward and pushed the door open enough to get a comprehensive view of a very muscular and artificially busty woman up on all fours on a four-poster bed. Gyrating her hips in time with the beat, she was naked, and looking over her shoulder at a GoPro camera mounted on a tripod.

I just stood there, stunned for a moment, long enough for Bree to nudge me, and long enough for Delilah Pinder to look around and spot me.

"Christ!" she screamed and flung herself forward on the bed.

I thought she was diving for modesty, but she hit some kind of panic button and the door slammed shut in my face and locked.

"What the hell just happened?" Bree demanded.

"I think she was doing a live sex show on the internet," I said.

"No."

"I swear," I said.

The music shut off and a woman shouted, "Goddamnit, whoever you are, I'm calling the sheriff. They are going to hunt you down!"

"We are the police, Miss Pinder," Bree yelled back.

"What the hell are you doing in my house, then?" she screamed. "I've got rights, and you had no right to come into my house or place of business!"

"You're correct," I said. "But we knocked and called out, and we felt we were doing a safety check on you."

"What I do here is perfectly legal," she said. "So please leave."

"We aren't here about your, uh, business," Bree said.

"Who are you, then? What do you want?"

"My name is Alex Cross. I'm a detective with the DC Metro Police, and I'm here concerning Gary's Girl."

There was a long silence, and then the music cranked up. But over it I heard the sound of a door slamming loudly.

"She's running," Bree said, spun around, and took off.

CHAPTER 18

I CAN HOLD MY own in the weight room, but I am no match for Bree in a footrace. She exploded back through the house and barreled out the front door.

Delilah Pinder, who was now dressed in a blue warm-up suit and running shoes, had already sprinted around the end of the house and was charging across the front lawn, heading for the road. I came out the front door in time to see Bree try to tackle the big woman.

Delilah saw her coming and stuck out her hand like a seasoned running back, hitting Bree in the chest. Bree stumbled. The internet sex star raced out onto the road and headed toward the highway.

I cut diagonally through the yard, trying to close in on her from the side. But when I broke through the trees and jumped the stone wall onto the road, Bree was right back behind Pinder.

She jumped on the much bigger woman's back, threw an arm bar around her neck, and choked her. Delilah tried to buck her off, and to pry her hold apart. But Bree held on tight.

Finally, the big woman stopped running. Her massive thighs wobbled, and she sat down hard at Bree's feet.

"Oh, my God," Bree gasped when I ran up. "That was like 'Meet the Amazon.'"

"More like 'Ride the Amazon,'" I said, as she put zip ties on Delilah's wrists.

The woman was regaining her strength. She struggled against the restraints.

"No," she said. "Let me go."

"Not for a while yet," I said, picking her up.

Delilah twisted her head around in a rage, and spit in my face.

"Knock that off!" Bree shouted, and wrenched up hard on Delilah's bound wrists. "That kind of bullshit gets you in trouble, and you're already in a world of trouble. Got it?"

Delilah was obviously in pain, and finally nodded.

Bree eased up on the pressure while I used a tissue to wipe my face.

"I don't know what this is about," Delilah said. "I told you, I have a legitimate business, registered with the state and everything. Delilah Entertainment. Check it out."

"You know exactly what this is about," I said, grabbing one of her formidable biceps and marching her back toward her house. "You're a member of The Soneji. You're Gary's Girl. You like to take selfies of you and Gary together. Isn't that true?"

Delilah looked at me smugly and said, "Every single word of it, Cross. Every single word."

"Where is Gary Soneji?" Bree asked.

"I have no idea," Delilah said. "Gary comes and goes as he pleases. Our relationship is strong enough for that."

"Yeah, I'm sure it is," I said, rolling my eyes. "But you understand you've abetted a man who shot a police officer in cold blood?"

"How's that?"

"You housed him," Bree said. "You fed him. You dressed up goth and had sex with him, maybe even did one of your kinky shows for him."

"Every night, darling," Delilah said. "He loved it. So did I. And that's where yours truly will shut up. I have the right to remain silent. And I have a right to an attorney. I'm taking both those rights, right here and right now."

CHAPTER 19

PALE MORNING FOG SHROUDED much of the cemetery from my view. The fog swirled on the wet grass, the melting snow that remained, and the gravestones. It left droplets on the pile of wilted flower bouquets and empty liquor bottles and remembrances that had to be moved before the backhoe could begin its work.

The last item was a baby doll, naked, with lipstick smeared on the lips.

Shivering against the dank March air, I zipped my police slicker higher and pulled on the hood. I stood off to one side of the grave with Bill Worden, the cemetery superintendent, alternately looking at the baby doll and watching the backhoe claw deeper into the soil. A baby doll, I thought, recalling a real baby tossed through the air with total indifference, if not cruelty.

Someone brought that doll here, I thought. In celebration. In reverence.

That's just sick. How could you worship that?

I glanced at the headstone Worden dug from the ground after I'd brought him an order from a federal judge in Trenton. The grave marker was simple. Rectangular black polished granite.

"*G. Soneji*" was etched in the face, along with the date of his birth. The date of his death, however, had been chiseled away. That was it. No mention of his brutal crimes or his disturbing life.

The man six feet under the headstone was all but anonymous.

And yet they'd come. The Soneji. They'd chipped away at the gravestone. Spray-painted the grass to read *"Soneji Lives."* I took pictures before the backhoe destroyed it.

"How many visit?" I asked over the sound of the digging machine.

Worden, the cemetery superintendent, tugged his hood over his head and said, "Hard to say. It's not like we keep it under surveillance. But a fair number every month."

"Enough to leave that pile of flowers," I said, eyeing the baby doll again.

Worden nodded. "For some it seems almost like a pilgrimage."

"Yeah, except Mr. Soneji was no saint," I said.

Drizzle began to fall, forcing me deeper into the collar of my jacket. A few moments later, the backhoe turned off.

"There's the straps, Bill," the equipment operator said. "I'll hand-dig the last of it."

"No need," Worden said. "Just hook up and lift, brush the dirt off later."

The backhoe operator shrugged and got out cables, which he attached to the bucket. Then he got down into the grave and clipped the cables to the rings of stout straps that had been left after the casket was lowered.

"They're not weakened by being in the dirt ten years?" I asked.

Worden shook his head. "Not unless something chewed through them."

The superintendent was right. When the backhoe arm rose, the straps easily lifted the casket of a man I helped kill.

Wet dirt slid and cascaded off the top of the casket as it came free of the grave and dangled four feet above the hole. The wind picked up. The casket swayed.

"Put it down there," Worden said, gesturing to one side.

I was fixated on the casket, wondering what was inside, beyond the charred remains I'd seen placed in a body bag beneath Grand Central Station a decade before. He was in there, wasn't he?

Every instinct said yes. But…

As the casket swung and lowered, I happened to look beyond it and between two far monuments. The wind had blown a narrow vent in the fog. I could see a slice of the graveyard between those monuments that ran all the way to the pine barrens that surrounded the cemetery.

Standing at the edge of the woods, perhaps eighty yards from me, was a man in a green rain slicker. He was turning away. When his back was to me, he pulled off his hood, revealing a head of thinning red hair. Then he raised his right hand, and pointed his middle finger at the sky.

And me.

CHAPTER 20

I STOOD THERE, TOO stunned to move for the moment it took for the wind to ebb and the fog to creep back, obscuring the figure, who stepped into the pine barrens and disappeared.

Then my shock evaporated, and I took off, drawing my pistol as I sprinted between the gravestones. Peering through the fog gathering again in the cemetery, I tried to figure out exactly where I'd seen him go into the pines.

There it was, those two monuments. He'd been framed between them. I ran to the spot and looked back toward the fog-obscured backhoe and the exhumed casket. When I thought I had the correct bearings, I turned and headed in a straight line toward the edge of the forest.

"Dr. Cross?" the superintendent called after me. "Where are you going?"

I ignored him and charged to the edge of the dripping pines, scanning the ground and seeing a scuff mark that looked fresh, not yet beaten down by the rain. I pushed my way into the trees.

The forest was thick there, crowded with young saplings with wet branches that bent away and wet needles that slid past my clothes. I stopped, unsure where to go, but then noticed a broken branch on the ground.

The inner wood looked bright and new. So did the broken branch to my left at ten o'clock. I went that way for fifty, maybe seventy-five yards, and then broke into an expanse of older trees, more than ten feet high, and growing in long straight rows, a pine plantation.

Despite the fog, I soon spotted dark, discolored spots on the mat of dead needles that covered the forest floor. I went to them, and saw where he'd kicked up the duff as he'd run down one of those lanes through the trees.

I ran after him, wondering if I could catch up, and numerous times whether I'd lost the way. But then I'd find some disturbance in the pine needles and push on one hundred, two hundred, three hundred yards deeper into the barrens.

What direction was I going? I had no idea, and it didn't matter. As long as Soneji was leaving signs, I was staying with him. I thought I'd cross a logging road or trail at some point, but didn't. There was just the monotony of the plantation pines and the swirling fog.

Then the way began to climb up a hill. I could clearly see where he'd had to dig in the edges of his shoes to keep his footing, and more broken branches.

When I hit the top of the knoll, there was a clearing of sorts with a jumble of tree trunks to one side, as if a windstorm had blown them over. I skirted the jumble, crossed the hilltop, and found myself looking down into a long, broad valley of mature pines.

The forest had been thinned there, as if some of the trees had already been harvested. Despite the fog, I could see down a dozen lanes and deeper into the woods than at any other time since I'd entered it. Nothing moved below me.

Nothing at—

A rifle cracked. The bark of a tree next to me exploded and I dove for the ground behind one of those downed tree trunks.

Where was he?

The shot came from the valley. I was sure of it. But where down there?

"Cross?" he called. "I'm coming for you, even from the grave if I have to."

If it wasn't him, he'd studied Soneji's voice, right down to the inflection.

When I didn't answer, he shouted, "Hear me, Cross?"

He sounded to my right and below me, no more than seventy yards. Raising my head as high as I dared, I scanned the valley there. The fog was in and out, but I thought I'd see him move or adjust his angle if he wanted another shot at me.

But I couldn't make him out.

"I know I didn't hit you," he called, his voice cracking weirdly. "I did, you would have gone down like the shit bag you are."

I decided not to engage, to let him think he'd gotten lucky, taken me out with one bullet. And it was odd the way his voice had cracked, wasn't it? Gone to a higher pitch?"

Tense moments passed, a minute and then two, while my eyes darted back and forth, trying to spot him, hoping he'd come in to make sure of the kill.

"How's your partner?" he called, and I heard him chuckle hoarsely. "He took a hit, didn't he? What I hear, best-case scenario, he'll be a veg."

It took every fiber of my being, but I did not engage with him, even then. I just lay there and waited, scanning and scanning and scanning.

I never saw him go, or heard anything like a distant twig breaking to suggest he was on the move again. He never said another word, and nothing told me he'd left but the time that kept ticking away.

I lowered my head after ten minutes and dug out my phone. No service.

The rain started in earnest then, drumming, beating down the fog and revealing the plantation. Nothing moved but a doe a hundred yards out.

I wanted to get up and go down there, look for him. But if he was waiting, I'd be exposed again. After fifteen more minutes of watching, I crawled back in the direction I'd come until I was well down the backside of the hill.

There was a bitter taste in my mouth when I got to my feet and started back toward the cemetery.

I hadn't gotten halfway there when my cell phone buzzed in my pocket.

A text from Billie.

"Alex, wherever you are, come. John's taken a bad turn. We're on deathwatch here."

CHAPTER 21

BY THE TIME I reached the cemetery, the superintendent had already loaded the casket into the FBI van that would take it to Quantico for examination. I explained the urgency of my situation, and left.

I called ahead to New Jersey, Delaware, and Maryland state police dispatchers, asking for help. When I reached I-95, there were two Jersey state trooper cruisers waiting. One in front, the other behind, they escorted me to the border, where two Delaware cruisers met me. Two more waited when I reached the Maryland line. At times we were going more than a hundred.

Less than two hours after I'd read the text, I got off the elevator to the ICU at GW Medical Center, still in damp clothes and chilled as I ran down the all-too-familiar halls to the waiting area. Billie sat at the back, her feet drawn up under her. Her elbows rested across her knees and she had a skeptical, faraway look in her eye, as if she couldn't believe that God was doing this to her.

Bree sat at her left, Nana Mama on her right.

"What happened?" I asked.

"They decided to bring him up out of the chemical coma," Billie said, tears streaming down her cheeks.

"He flatlined. They had to paddle him," Bree said. "He came back, but his vitals are turning against him."

"Billie's called in the priest," Nana Mama said. "He's giving John the last rites."

Whatever control I'd maintained until that point evaporated and I began to grieve in gasps of disbelief and an explosion of sorrow and tears. It was real. My best friend, the indestructible one, Big John Sampson, was going to die.

I sank into a chair and sobbed. Bree came over and hugged me. I leaned into her and cried some more.

The priest came in. "He's in God's hands now," he said, consoling us. "The doctor says there's nothing more they can do for him."

"Can we go in?" Billie asked.

"Of course," he said.

Nana Mama, Billie, and Bree got up. I looked at them, feeling numb.

"I can't do it," I said, feeling helpless. "I just can't watch this. Can you forgive me?"

"I don't want to either, Alex," Billie said. "But I want him to hear my voice one last time before he goes."

Nana Mama patted me on the shoulders as she followed Billie into the ICU. Bree asked if I wanted her to stay, and I shook my head.

"Going in there scares me more than anything has in my entire life," I said. "I need to take a walk, get my courage up."

"And pray," she said, kissed me on the head, and went inside.

I got up and felt like a coward walking toward the men's room. I went inside and washed my face, trying to think of anything but John and all the good times we'd had over the years, playing football and basketball, attending the police academy, and finding our way through the ranks to detective and partners against crime.

That would never happen again. John and me would never happen again.

I left the restroom and wandered off through the medical complex, sure that any minute now I'd get a text that he was gone. Guilt built up in me at the thought that after all we'd been through, I wouldn't be there at Sampson's side when he passed.

I stopped and almost turned around. Then noticed I was standing outside the plastic surgery offices. A beautiful Ethiopian-looking woman in a white jacket came out the door.

She smiled at me. Her teeth gleamed and her facial skin was so taut and smooth she could have been thirty. Then again, she could have been sixty and often under the knife.

"Dr. Coleman?" I said, reading her badge.

She stopped and said, "Yes?"

I showed her my badge, said, "I could use your help."

"Yes?" she said, looking worried. "How so?"

"I'm investigating the shooting of a police officer," I said. "We want to know, how difficult would it be to make one person look almost exactly like another?"

She squinted. "You mean, good enough to be an imposter?"

"Yes," I said. "Is it possible?"

"That depends," Dr. Coleman said, glancing at her watch. "Can you walk with me? I have to give a lecture about twenty minutes from here."

"Yes," I said, glad for the diversion.

We walked through the medical center and out the other side, ending up on the George Washington University campus. Along the way, the plastic surgeon said that similar facial structure would be key to surgically altering a person to look like someone else.

"The closer the subject was to looking like the original to begin with, the better the results," she said. "After that it would all be in the skill of the surgeon."

"So, even the similar bone structure wouldn't guarantee success for your everyday surgeon?"

Dr. Coleman smiled. "If the end product is as close to the original as you say it is, then there is no way an average boob-job surgeon did it. You're looking for a scalpel artist, Detective."

"What kind of money are we talking?"

"Depends on the extent of surgical alteration required," she said. "But I'm thinking this is a hundred-thousand-dollar job, maybe less in Brazil."

A hundred thousand dollars? Who would spend that much to look like Gary Soneji? Or go to Brazil to get it done?

I felt my phone buzz in my pocket, and sickened.

"Here I am," Dr. Coleman said, stopping outside one of the university's many buildings. "Any more questions, Detective?"

"No," I said, handing her a card. "But if I do, can I call?"

"Absolutely," she said, and hurried inside.

I swallowed hard and then got out my phone.

The text was from Bree: "Come now or you'll regret it the rest of your life."

I started to run.

Ten minutes later, I went through the door of the ICU, trying to keep my emotions from ruining me all over again.

When I reached the doorway to John's room, Billie, Bree, and Nana Mama were all sobbing.

I thought I'd come too late, that I'd done my best friend and brother the ultimate disservice, and not been there when he took his last breath.

Then I realized they were all sobbing for joy.

"It's a miracle, Alex," Bree said, tears streaming down her cheeks. "Look."

I stepped inside the crowded room. A nurse and a doctor were working feverishly on John. He was still on his back in bed, still on the ventilator, still hitched up to a dozen different monitors.

But his eyes were open and roving lazily.

CHAPTER 22

WE SAT WITH JOHN for hours as more of the drugs wore off. They removed his breathing tube, and he came more and more to consciousness.

John did not acknowledge his name when Billie called it softly, trying to get him to turn his head to her. At first Sampson seemed not even to know where he was, as if he were lost in some dream.

But then, after the first nap, he did hear his wife, and his face lolled toward her. Then he moved his fingers and toes on command, and lifted both arms.

When I sat beside him and held his hand, his lips kept opening as if he wanted to talk. No sound came out, and he appeared frustrated.

"It's okay, buddy," I said, holding tight. "We know you love us."

Sampson relaxed and slept again. When he awoke, Elizabeth Navilus, a top speech-language pathologist, was waiting. She was part of a team of specialists rotating through the room, performing the various exams on the JFK Coma Recovery Scale, a method of diagnosing the extent of brain damage.

Navilus ran Sampson through a brief battery of tests. She found that John's cognitive awareness as expressed through his language comprehension was growing by the moment. But he was having trouble speaking. The best he could do was chew at the air and hum.

It crushed me.

Out in the waiting area, Navilus told us to take hope from the fact that head trauma patients often exhibit understanding before being able to respond.

Later, when Nana Mama had left for home to cook dinner, and Bree to the office, and Billie to the cafeteria, I sat by John's side.

"I was there when you were shot," I told him. "It was Soneji. Or someone who looked just like him."

Sampson blinked, and then nodded.

"I came close to catching him this morning," I said. "He was watching when we dug up Soneji's body."

He looked away and closed his eyes.

"I'm going to get him, John," I said. "I promise you."

He barely nodded before sagging off to sleep.

Sitting there, watching him, I felt better, stronger, and more humbled and in debt to my Lord and savior than ever before. The idea of Sampson dying must have been as much of an abomination to God as I thought it was.

If that wasn't a miracle, I don't know what is.

CHAPTER 23

I STAYED AT THE hospital until nine, promised Billie I'd be back in the morning, and headed home. Given what had happened the last time I'd exited GW Medical Center and looked for a cab, my head was turning three-sixty.

I saw no threat, however, and stepped to the curb. As I did, Soneji's voice from earlier in the day echoed back to me.

I'm coming for you, even from the grave if I have to.

It sounded so much like Gary, it was scary. I'd had multiple conversations with him over the years, and Soneji's tone and delivery were unmistakable.

After I'd gotten into the cab and given the driver my home address, I almost pushed these thoughts aside. But then I blinked, remembering how his voice had cracked weirdly and turned hoarse when he said, "I know I didn't hit you. I did, you would have gone down like the shit bag you are."

It sounded like he had something wrong in his throat. Cancer? Polyps? Or were his vocal cords just straining under the tensions wound up inside him?

I tried to remember every nuance of our encounter in the pine barrens, the way he'd swaggered into the trees, finger held high. Where was the gun then? Had he been trying to lure me in for a shot?

In retrospect, it felt like he had, and I'd fallen for it. Where was all the training I'd done? The protocol? I'd reacted on emotion, charging into the pines after him. Just the way Soneji had wanted me to.

That bothered me because it made me realize that Soneji understood me, could predict my impulses the way I could predict his a dozen years before. I mean, how else would he have known to be at the cemetery when I was there to exhume his body? What or who had tipped him?

I had no answers for that other than the possibility Soneji or The Soneji had us bugged. Or had it just seemed the rational thing to do at some point, given the fact that I'd seen someone who looked just like him at least three times now?

These unanswerable questions weighed on me the entire ride home. I felt depressed climbing from the taxi and waiting for the receipt. Soneji, or whoever, was thinking ahead of me, plotting, hatching, and acting before I could respond.

Climbing the porch stairs, I was beginning to feel like I was a fish on a hook with some angler toying with me, messing with my lip.

But the second I stepped inside the house, smelled something savory coming from Nana Mama's kitchen, and heard my son, Ali, laughing, I let it go. I let everything about the sonofabitch go.

"Dad?" Jannie said, coming down the stairs. "How's John?"

"He's got a fight and a half ahead of him, but he's alive."

"Nana Mama said it's, like, a miracle."

"I'd have to agree," I said, and hugged her tight.

"Dad, look at this," Ali called. "You can't believe how good this looks."

"The new TV," Jannie said. "It's pretty amazing."

"What new TV?"

"Nana Mama and Ali ordered it off the internet. They just installed it."

I stepped into our once cozy television room to see it had been transformed into a home theater, with new leather chairs, and a huge, curved 4K resolution HD screen on the far wall. Ali had on a repeat of *The Walking Dead,* one of his favorites, and the zombies looked like they were right there in the room with us.

"You should see when we switch it to 3D, Dad!" Ali said. "It's crazy!"

"I can see that," I said. "Does it do basketball?"

Ali took his eyes off the screen. "They're right in the room with you."

I smiled. "You'll have to show me after dinner."

"I can do that," Ali said. "Show you how to run it from your laptop."

I gave him the thumbs up, and then wandered through the dining room to the kitchen upgrade and great room addition we'd put on two years before.

Nana Mama was bustling at her command-center stove.

"Roast chicken, sweet potato fries, broccoli with almonds, and a nice salad," she said. "How's John?"

"Sleeping when I left," I said. "And dinner sounds great. Nice TV."

She made a deep inhaling sound, and said, "Isn't it? I can't wait to see *Masterpiece Theatre* on there. That *Downton Abbey* show."

"I was thinking the same thing," I said.

Nana Mama looked over her shoulder, gave me a sour, threatening look, and said, "Don't you be mocking me, now."

"I wouldn't dream of it, Nana," I said, trying to hide the smile that wanted to creep onto my face. "Oh, I thought you said you weren't going to let the lottery money change our lives."

"I said I didn't want some big mansion to get lost in," she snapped. "Or tooling around in some ridiculous car. But that doesn't mean we can't have some nice things in this house, and still do some good for people. Which reminds me, when is my hot-breakfast program going to be able to start up again?"

I held up my hands. "I'll find out tonight."

"I'm not getting any younger, and I want to see that ongoing," she said. "Endowed. And that reading program for kids."

"Yes, ma'am, and you're sure you're not getting younger? Isn't there a painting of you in some attic that shows your real age?"

She tried to fight it, but that brought on a smile. "Aren't you just the smoothest talker in—?"

"Dad?" Ali cried, running into the kitchen.

He looked petrified, on the verge of crying.

"What's the matter?"

"Someone's taken over my computer," he said.

"What?" Nana Mama said.

"There's this crazy man on the screen now, not *The Walking Dead,* and he won't turn off. He's holding a baby and saying, like, over and over that he's going to come for you, Dad, even from the grave."

CHAPTER 24

IN THE VIDEO CLIP, Gary Soneji was just as I remembered him: out on one of Grand Central Station's train platforms, holding the infant, and taunting me.

I'd never seen the video. Never knew it existed, but it was definitely legitimate. After viewing the clip six or seven times, I could see my own shadow stretched in the space between me and Gary Soneji. The camera operator all those years ago had to have been right off my left shoulder.

Was the cameraman a fluke? A random passerby? Or someone working with Soneji?

The clip started again. It appeared on endless loop.

"Dad, this is giving me the creeps," Jannie said. "Turn it off."

"Gimme the remote and the computer, Ali," I said.

"I've got homework on this computer," he said.

"I'll transfer your homework to the one in the kitchen," I said, and gave him a gimme motion.

He groaned and handed it to me.

Bree came in the front door. I hit the Power button on the remote, but the screen did not turn off. Instead, it broke from that endless loop to Kelly green.

I tried to turn the screen off again, but it jumped to black, slashed diagonally with a golden beam of light. The camera zoomed closer to that light and you could see a silhouette of a person there.

Closer, it was a man.

Closer still, and it was Soneji.

He was giving the lens the same quarter profile we'd seen in the still image that Gary's Girl posted on the website forum, the one where his eye and the corner of his mouth conspired to leer right at me.

But this time Soneji spoke.

In that cracking, hoarse voice I'd heard earlier that day in the pine barrens, Soneji said, "You're not safe in the trees, Cross. You're not safe in your own home. The Soneji are everywhere!"

Then he threw his head back, and barked and brayed his laughter before the screen froze. A title appeared below: www.thesoneji.net.

"What's that, Dad?" Ali asked, upset.

I stormed to the screen, followed the cord to its power source, and tore it violently out of the wall.

"Alex?" Bree said. "What's going on?"

I looked at Ali. "Was that *Walking Dead* episode streaming from Netflix?"

"Yes."

Yanking out my cell phone, I looked to Bree and said, "Soneji hacked into our internet feed."

"I'll shut the router down," Bree said.

"No, don't," I said. I scrolled through my recent calls and hit Call. "I have a feeling it will be better if the link's still active."

The phone picked up. "Yes?"

"This is Alex Cross," I said. "How fast can you get to my house?"

Forty minutes later, as we were finishing up Nana Mama's roast chicken masterpiece, and fighting over who was going to get the last wing and who the last sweet potato fries, there was a sharp knock at our side door.

"I'll get it," I said, put my napkin down, and went out into the great room and unlocked the door that led to the side yard and the alley behind our place.

I did not turn on the light, just opened it quickly and let our visitors inside. The first was Ned Mahoney, my former partner at the FBI. The second was Special Agent Henna Batra of the Bureau's cybercrime unit.

"Who's making sure you're safe in your own home?" Mahoney asked once I'd closed the door.

"Metro in unmarked cars, both ends of the block," I said.

"Soneji's still the type to try."

"I know," I said. "But I think we're good."

"I'm still unclear why you wanted me here, Dr. Cross," Agent Batra said.

"I think Soneji or The Soneji may have made a mistake," I said. "If I'm right, they left a digital trail inside my house, or on our network, anyway."

CHAPTER 25

I GOT TO GW Medical Center early the following morning with my children's howls ringing in my head. Special Agent Batra had taken every computer and phone in the house to Quantico. She'd promised to work as fast as she could, but it was like they'd lost their right hands when the phones were taken away.

I kind of felt the same way walking to Sampson's room, and decided to buy a cheap phone afterward. I was happy to find John sitting up and drinking through a straw.

Billie hadn't arrived yet, so I'd gotten to sit with him awhile, and brought him up to date on all that had occurred the prior day. Though his eyes tended to drift off me, he seemed to understand much of what I was saying.

"If anyone can find this guy, it's Batra," I said. "I've never seen anyone like her before."

John's eyes softened and he smiled. He tried to say something and couldn't. You could see how frustrating it was.

I put my hand on his shoulder and said, "You're in for a long haul, buddy, recovering from this. But if there's any man alive who can do it, you can."

Sampson's lazy, sad gaze came and dwelled around me for several seconds. Then he started struggling, as he got more and more upset.

"Hey," I said. "It's okay. We'll—"

Garbled sounds came out of his mouth.

He tried again. And again.

The sixth time, I thought he said, "Evan-widda."

"Evan-widda?" I said.

"Evan-widda…b…bag," he said, and then smiled and lifted his right hand to point to the surgical bandage. "Ho-ho… n…ed."

I frowned, but got it then, and smiled. "Even with a big hole in your head?"

Sampson smiled, dropped his hand, and winked at me before nodding off to sleep again, as if that had taken every bit of his strength.

But he'd spoken! Sort of. Definitely communicated. And the doctors had said his sense of humor could be gone with a wound to that part of his brain, but here he was making a joke about his situation.

If that wasn't a miracle, I don't know what is.

Billie arrived shortly before eight and beamed when I told her what had happened.

She kissed John, and said, "You spoke?"

He shook his head. "Alack vent…r…wrist…crist."

"What?"

"He said, 'Alex is a ventriloquist.' I think."

John grinned again and said, "Whips do no move."

Billie had tears in her eyes. "Lips don't move."

Sampson made a wheezing sound of delight that stayed with me on the way to work and buying a burner phone.

I went to Bree's office, and I knocked on her doorjamb.

"Long time no see," I said.

Bree glanced at the clock, said, "Are you getting obsessive about me?"

"I've always been obsessive about you, from the very first," I said.

"Liar," Bree said, but she was pleased.

"The truth," I said. "You had me the first time you glanced my way."

That pleased her even more. "Why are you buttering me up?"

"I'm not buttering you up," I said. "I was just flirting with my wife before I told her that Sampson spoke this morning."

"No?" she gasped. "He did?"

"It took a little interpretation, but he was telling jokes."

Bree got tears in her eyes, stood up, came around the desk, and hugged me. I got tears, too.

"Thanks," she said. "What a perfect thing to hear."

"I know," I said, before the cheap phone I'd bought on the way to work buzzed. Who knew the number? I'd just gotten the damn thing. Just activated it.

"Hello?" I said.

"It's Special Agent Batra."

"How'd you get this number?"

"By being good at my job," Agent Batra said, sounding annoyed. "I thought you'd be happy to hear from me so soon."

"I'm sorry," I said, though I was beginning to think there wasn't a box in the virtual universe that Henna Batra couldn't find and unlock if she set her mind to it. "You found something?"

"You were compromised in a troubling fashion."

I wanted to say that I could have told her that, but asked, "How so?"

"They got a bug into your son's computer operating system, piggybacked to a game app he downloaded at school."

"At his school?" I said, feeling queasy.

Soneji or The Soneji were not only threatening me in my house, they were targeting my youngest child.

"What else?" I demanded.

"Your daughter, Jannie, had the same bug in her system," Batra said. "It was uploaded to her computer without her knowledge when she was using her phone as a mobile hotspot at a coffee shop not far from your house."

This was worse. Both my children were being targeted.

"What about my phone? My wife's?" I asked, and turned on the speaker on the burner phone so Bree could hear.

"Clean," Batra said. "I'll have them messengered over in the next hour."

"Thank you," I said. "Is that it?"

"No, as a matter of fact," the FBI cyber expert said. "There was a similarity in the signature of the bug coder and the coder who created www.thesoneji.net."

I looked at Bree, who shrugged in confusion.

"You want to run that by us again?" I said.

The cybercrimes expert sounded irritated when she said, "Coders are artists in their own way, Detective. Just as classical painters had recognizable brushstrokes, great computer coders have a recognizable way of writing. Their signature, if you will."

"Makes sense," I said. "So who coded the website?"

Batra said, "It took me much, much longer than I expected to break through the firewalls that surrounded the identity of the creator and curator, but I did just a few minutes ago."

"Have you been up all night?" I asked.

"You said it was important."

Bree leaned forward, said, "Thank you, Agent Batra. It's Chief Stone here. Do you know who he is? The website creator?"

"She, and I've learned quite a bit about her in the past hour or so, thanks to a friend of mine at the NSA," Agent Batra said. "Especially the boyfriend she's fronting for. In fact, I know about him going right back to what his first-grade teacher said about him the day she recommended he be expelled from school."

I felt fear in the pit of my stomach. "And what was that?"

"She said she thought he was kind of a monster, Dr. Cross. Even then."

CHAPTER 26

AN HOUR LATER, I set in to wait on a bench in a hallway by the door to a loft space on the fourth floor of an older building off Dupont Circle.

I'd gotten into the building by showing my badge to a woman entering with groceries. I told her who I was looking for.

"Out running, that one," she'd replied. "Every lunch hour. Quite a sight."

I'd knocked on the door just in case, but there was no answer. I had a search warrant. I could have called for patrol to break the door down, but I hoped I could get more information by going patient and gentle.

Twenty minutes later, a fit Asian American woman in her late twenties came huffing up the staircase. Her black hair was cut short and her exposed arms were buff and sleeved in brilliantly colored tattoos.

Sweat poured down her face when she reached the landing and saw me getting off the bench. She didn't startle or try to escape as I'd expected.

Instead she hardened, said, "Took you a while, Dr. Cross. The intrusion was almost six hours ago. But here you are. At last. In the flesh."

"Kimiko Binx?" I said, holding up my badge and ID.

"Correct," Binx replied, walking toward me, palms held open at her sides, and studying me with great interest.

The closer she got, I noticed a device of some sort, orange, and strapped to her upper right arm. When I saw it blink, I thought *bomb,* and went for my gun.

"What's that on your arm?" I demanded, the pistol out, pointed her way.

Binx threw her hands up, said, "Whoa, whoa, Detective. It's a SPOT."

"What?"

"A GPS transmitter. It sends my position every thirty seconds to a satellite and to a website," she said. "I use it to track my running routes."

She turned sideways and held up her arm so I could examine the device. It was smaller than a smartphone, commercially made, heavy-duty plastic, with the SPOT logo emblazoned across the front of it and buttons with various icons. One said SOS and another was a shoe tread. The light blinked beside the shoe.

"So it tracks you?" I said.

"Correct," Binx said. "What do you want, Dr. Cross?"

I held the search warrant up and said, "If you could open the door."

Binx read the warrant without comment, fished out a key, and opened the loft. It was an airy work-and-living space with a view of an alley, a hodgepodge of used furniture, and a computer workstation that featured four large screens.

She moved toward the station.

"Do not go near your computer, Ms. Binx. Do not go near anything."

Binx got aggravated and took off the SPOT device. "You want this, too?"

"Please. Turn it off. Put it on the table there, and your phone if you've got it. I'd like to ask you some questions before I call for my evidence team."

"What do you want to know?" she asked, using her thumbs to play at the buttons on the transmitter.

"Why do you worship Gary Soneji?"

Binx didn't answer, hit one last button, and looked up at me before setting the SPOT on the table with the light no longer blinking.

"I don't worship Gary Soneji," she said finally. "I find Gary Soneji interesting. I find you interesting, for that matter."

"That why you built a high-security website about Soneji and me?"

"Yes," she said, sitting down calmly. "Other people find you two interesting also. Lots of them. It was a safe way to handle our common passion."

"Your members cheered when they found out my partner, John Sampson, was shot," I said.

"It's a private forum of free expression. I didn't approve of that."

"Didn't you?" I said angrily. "You provided space for sickos to plot terror in the name of a man who committed utterly heinous acts and died ten years ago."

"He's not dead," Binx said flatly. "Gary Soneji will never die."

I remembered the coffin coming up out of the ground in New Jersey, wondered how much longer the FBI's DNA testing would take, but said nothing of the exhumation of her idol.

Instead I said, "I don't get this, smart woman like you. Virginia Tech graduate. Write code for a living. Paid handsomely. Yet you get involved in something like this."

"Different strokes," she replied. "And it's my personal business."

"Not when it involves the shooting of a police officer. Nothing's personal."

"I had nothing to do with that, either," Binx said evenly. "Nothing. I'll take a lie detector."

"Who did, then?" I asked.

"Gary Soneji."

"Maybe," I said. "Or maybe Claude Watkins?"

Binx shifted her eyes ever so slightly to look just over my right shoulder before shaking her head.

I said, "Watkins's name is on your company's incorporation documents."

"Claude's a limited partner. He lent me some start-up money."

"Uh-huh," I said. "You know his background?"

"He had problems when he was younger," she said.

"He is a sadist, Ms. Binx. He was convicted of carving the skin off a little girl's fingers."

"He was chemically imbalanced back then," she said defiantly. "That was the diagnosis of both the state and his personal psychiatrists. He took the drugs they recommended, paid his dues, and moved on. Claude's a painter and performance artist now. He's brilliant."

"I'm sure he is," I said.

"No," Binx insisted. "He really is. I can take you to his studio. Show you. We've got nothing to hide. It's not far. He rents space in an old factory down by the Anacostia River, west bank."

"Address?"

She shrugged. "I just know how to get there."

I thought for a moment, said, "After my team gets here, you'll take me?"

She nodded. "Be glad to. Can I take a shower in the meantime? You can search the bathroom if you need to. I assure you it's nothing but the usual."

I stared at her for several beats, and then said, "Make it quick."

CHAPTER 27

THE CRIMINALISTS ARRIVED TEN minutes later. I was giving them instructions to call if they turned up anything when Kimiko Binx emerged from her bedroom in jeans, Nike running shoes, and a short-sleeved green blouse.

"Ready, Dr. Cross?" she said, coming toward me and then stumbling over a loose cord and losing her balance.

I reached out before she could fall. Binx grabbed onto my left hand and right forearm and got her balance.

She turned from me, looking back, puzzled. "What was that?"

"You should put your cords under rugs," I said. "Let's go."

We went downstairs to my car.

Binx got in the front seat, said, "Where's the siren?"

"It's not like that," I said. "Where am I going?"

"Toward the Anacostia Bridge. It's an old tool and die factory by the river."

I drove in silence until I realized she was studying me again.

"What are you looking at?"

"The object of Gary's obsession," she said.

"Soneji's sole obsession?" I asked.

"Well," Binx said, and turned to look out the windshield. "One of them."

She was so blithe and relaxed in her manner that I wondered if she was on some kind of medication. And yet, she made me feel strange, scrutinized by a cultist.

"How did you meet Claude Watkins?" I asked.

"At a party in Baltimore," she said. "Have you met him?"

"Haven't had the pleasure."

Binx smiled. "It is, you know. A pleasure to see his paintings and his performances."

"A real Picasso, then."

She caught the sarcasm, turned cooler, and said, "You'll see, Dr. Cross."

Binx navigated me toward a derelict light industrial area north of the bridge, and an abandoned brick-faced factory with a FOR SALE sign on the gate, which was unlocked.

"This is where the great painter and performance artist works?" I said.

"Correct," Binx said. "Claude moves around, takes month-to-month leases on abandoned buildings, where he's free to do his art without worrying about making a mess. When the building and the art's sold, he moves on. It's a win-win for everyone involved. He learned the tactic in Detroit."

It made sense, actually. I parked the car outside the gate, and felt odd, a little woozy, the way you do if you haven't eaten enough or stayed well hydrated. And my tongue felt thick, and my throat dry.

I heard Binx release her seat belt. It sounded louder than it should have. So did the key in the ignition beeping when I opened the door. I took the key out, stood up, felt the warm spring breeze, and felt almost immediately better.

I called up Google Maps on my phone, pinned my location,

and texted the pin to Bree along with a message that said, "Send patrol for backup when you get the chance."

Then I drew my service weapon.

"Sorry to do this, Ms. Binx," I said. "But I need you in handcuffs."

"What? Why?"

"You're technically under arrest. I've just been a nice guy until now."

The computer coder didn't look happy as she came over. I got out my cuffs and buckled down her wrists, arms forward. She'd been cooperative for the most part and didn't seem much of a threat.

"What am I under arrest for?" Binx demanded. "Free speech?"

"How about fomenting and abetting attempted murder of a cop?"

"I did not!"

"You did," I said, pushing her in front of me.

We passed through the gate, crossed fifteen yards of scrub ground where purple crocuses poked out of weeds by a metal double door. Binx seemed on the verge of tears, opening one of the doors and saying, "I would never hurt a cop. My dad was a cop in Philly."

That surprised me. "Was?"

"He's retired," she said. "With a gold shield."

I looked at her differently now, the daughter of a good cop. Why would she get involved in something like this?

"You said you wanted to meet Claude," Binx said, trying to wipe her tears with her sleeves. "Let's go."

At first a voice in my head said not to enter the abandoned

factory, to wait for backup, but then the voice was gone, re-placed by a surge of clarity and confidence.

Keeping Binx squarely in front of me, I went inside.

Whenever you leave a sunny day for a darker quarter, there's always a fleeting moment when you're all but blind before your eyes adjust. It's also a time when you tend to be silhouetted in the doorway and are therefore an easy target.

But I heard no shot, and my vision refocused on a large, airy space, ten, maybe fifteen thousand square feet, with a ceiling that was warehouse-high and crisscrossed with rusted over-head tracks for heavy industrial lifts and booms.

Ten-foot-tall partitions carved the space up like a broad maze. The cement floor right in front of us was cracked, bro-ken in places, and bare but for stacks of pipe and sheet metal, as if a reclaiming operation was under way. Thick dust hung in the air. Waves of it danced and swirled in the weak sunlight streaming through a bank of filthy windows high on the walls.

"I'm not seeing any paintings or studio," I said. "Where's Watkins?"

"He and the studio are in the back," Binx said, gesturing into the gloom. "I'll show you the way."

For the second time that day, that internal voice of mine, born of years of training and experience, raised doubts about following her until I had someone watching my back. And for the second time that day, I felt my heart beat faster, sensed more sharply my surroundings, and surged with another rush of complete confidence in my abilities.

"Lead on," I said, smiling at her, and feeling good, real good, like I was perfectly fine-tuned and ready for anything that might come my way.

Binx took me down one dim hallway, and then another, passing empty workroom after empty workroom before I smelled marijuana, fresh paint, and turpentine. The smells got stronger as we walked a short third hallway that dog-legged left and opened into a large, largely empty assembly-line room with dark alcoves off it on all four sides.

The only lights in the room were strong portable spots trained on one of several large paintings hanging on the far wall about fifty feet away. The painting showed a crane lifting a coffin from the ground. The headstone above the grave read "G. SONEJI." Two men stood by the grave. A Caucasian in a dark suit. And an African American in a blue police slicker. Me.

I almost smiled. Someone who'd been at the exhumation, probably Soneji or one of his followers, Watkins, had painted this, and yet I had to fight to keep from grinning at all the goodwill I felt inside.

The furthest of the three spotlights went dark then, revealing a man I couldn't see before because of the glare. He wore paint-speckled jeans, work boots, and a long-sleeved shirt, but his face was lost in shadows.

Then he took a step forward into a weak, dusty beam of sunlight coming through the grimy windows, revealing the wispy red hair and distinctive facial features of Gary Soneji.

"Dr. Cross," he said in a cracking, hoarse voice. "I thought you'd never catch up."

CHAPTER 28

SONEJI MOVED HIS ARM then, and I saw the gun he held at his side, a nickel-plated pistol, just like the ones he used to shoot Sampson and me.

Take him!

The voice screamed in my head, ending all of those strange good feelings that had been inexplicably surging through me.

I raised my service pistol fast, pushed Binx out of the way, aimed at Soneji, and shouted, "Drop your weapon now or I'll shoot!"

To my surprise, Soneji let go the gun. It fell to the floor with a clatter. He raised his hands, studying me calmly and with great interest.

"Facedown on the floor!" I shouted. "Hands behind your back!"

Soneji started to follow my orders before Binx hit my gun hand with both her fists. The blow knocked me off balance, and my gun discharged just as a spotlight went on from above the paintings, blinding me.

There was a shot.

Then all the lights died, leaving me disoriented, and blinking at dazzling blue spots that danced before my eyes. Knowing I was vulnerable, I threw myself to the floor, expecting another shot at any moment.

It was a trap. The whole thing was a trap, and I'd just walked into...

The spots cleared.

Soneji was gone. So was Binx. And Soneji's nickel-plated pistol.

I held my position, and peered around, noticing for the first time a metal table covered in cans of paint and paintbrushes. And then those alcoves all around the room. They were low-roofed and dark with shadows.

Soneji and Binx could easily have slid into one of them. And what? Escaped? Or were they just waiting for me to make a move?

I had no answers, and stayed where I was, listening, looking. Nothing moved. And there was zero sound.

But I could feel him there. Soneji. Listening for me. Looking for me.

I felt severely agitated at those ideas, almost wired before an irrational, all-consuming rage erupted inside me. Standard protocol was gone, burned up. All my training was gone, too, consumed by the flames of wanting to take Gary Soneji down. Now and for good.

I lurched to my feet and ran hard at the nearest alcove on the opposite wall. Every nerve expected a shot, but there was none. I got to the protection of the alcove, gasping, gun up, seeing the remnants of machine tools.

But no Soneji.

"I've got backup, Gary," I shouted. "They're surrounding the place!"

No response. Were they gone?

I dodged out of the alcove and moved fast along the wall

to the next anteroom, the one directly beneath the painting of the exhumation. At first I saw only large rolls of canvas laid on sawhorses and tables made of plywood.

Then, in the deepest shadows of the alcove, and in my peripheral vision, I caught a flash of movement. I spun left to see Soneji stooping forward on the balls of his feet as he took two halting steps, and straightened up.

His mouth opened as if in anticipation of some long-awaited pleasure. His gun hand started to rise.

I shot him twice, the deafening reports making my ears buzz and ring like they'd been boxed hard. Gary Soneji jerked twice, and screamed like a woman before staggering and falling from sight.

CHAPTER 29

MY HEART BOOMED IN my chest, but my brain sighed with relief.

Soneji was hit hard. He was crying, dying there on the canvas-room floor where I couldn't see him.

My pistol still up, I took an uncertain step toward Soneji, and another. A third and fourth step and I saw him lying there, no gun in his hand or around him, looking at me with a piteous expression.

In a high, whimpering voice, he said, "Why did you shoot me? Why me?"

Before I could answer, Soneji went into a coughing fit that turned wet and choking. Then blood streamed from his lips, his eyes started to dull, and the life went out of him with a last hard breath.

"Oh, my God!" Binx screamed behind me. "What have you done?"

"Soneji's gone," I said, feeling intense, irrational pleasure course through me. "He's finally gone."

Binx was crying. I started to turn toward her. She saw the gun in my hand, turned terrified, and leaped out of sight.

Binx had led me into a trap, I thought. Binx had led me here to die.

I ran after her into the main room, saw her running crazily

back the way we'd come in, and heard her making these petrified whining sounds.

"Stop, Ms. Binx!" I yelled after her.

As I did, I caught a shift in the shadows of an alcove at the
far end of the room. I looked toward it, shocked to see that beyond two fifty-five-gallon drums, Gary Soneji stood there in
the mouth of the alcove, same clothes, same hair, same face,
same nickel-plated pistol in hand.

How was that…?

Before I could shake off the shock of there being two Sonejis, he fired at me. His bullet pinged off the post of one of those
spotlights trained on the paintings. On instinct, I threw myself toward him, gun up and firing.

My first shot was wide, but my next one spun the second
Soneji around just before I landed hard on the cement floor.
Doubled over, he went down too, gasping, groaning, and try-
ing to crawl back into the alcove.

I scrambled to my feet, and charged his position. A
spotlight went on above the alcove, trying to strike me in
the eyes again. But I got my free hand up before it could
blind me.

From high and to my right, a gun went off. The bullet blew
a chunk of cement out of the floor at my feet.

I dove behind the fifty-five-gallon drums, glanced at the
second Soneji, who was still crawling, and leaving a trail of
dark blood behind him.

The voice in my head screamed at me to use my phone and
call it in. I needed sirens coming now.

Then I heard the sirens, distant but distinct, before another
gunshot sounded from up high and to my right again. It

smacked the near barrel, the slug making a clanging noise as it ricocheted inside.

I winced, rolled over, and peered up through the narrow gap between the barrels, seeing a third Gary Soneji standing on the roof of the alcove above the exhumation painting. He was trying to aim at me with a nickel-plated pistol.

Before he could fire, I did.

The third Soneji screamed, dropped his gun, and grabbed at his thigh before toppling off the roof. He fell a solid ten feet, hit the cement floor hard enough to make cracking sounds. He screamed feebly, then lay there moaning.

I stood up then, shaking with adrenaline, and feeling that beautiful rage explode through me all over again, searing-hot and vengeful.

"Who's next?" I roared, feeling almost giddy. "C'mon, you bastards! I'll kill every single Soneji before I'm done!"

I swung all around, my pistol aiming high and low, finger twitching on the trigger, anticipating another Soneji to appear on the roof of the alcove or from the darkness of the three remaining anterooms.

But nothing moved, and there was no sound except for the moans of the wounded and of Kimiko Binx, who sat in the far corner of the main room, curled up in a fetal position, and sobbing.

CHAPTER 30

KIMIKO BINX WAS STILL crying and refusing to talk to me or to the patrol officers who arrived first on the scene, or to the detectives who came soon after.

Not even Bree could get Binx to make any kind of statement, other than to say sullenly, "Cross didn't have to shoot. He didn't have to kill them all."

The fact was, I had not killed them all. Two of the Sonejis were alive, and there were EMTs working feverishly on them.

"Three Sonejis?" Bree said. "Makes it easy for them to cover ground."

I nodded, seeing how one of them could have shot Sampson, while another staked out Soneji's grave, and the third could have driven by Bree and me outside GW Medical Center.

"You okay, Alex?" Bree asked.

"No," I said, feeling incredibly tired all of a sudden. "Not really."

"Tell me what happened," Bree said.

I did to the best of my abilities, finishing with "But all you really need to know is they set up an ambush, lured me, and I walked right into it."

Bree thought about that, and then said, "There'll be an

investigation, but from what you said, it's cut-and-dry. Self-defense, and justified."

I didn't say anything because somehow it didn't seem quite right to me. Justified, yes, but cut-and-dry? They'd tried to kill Sampson, and me, twice. But some of the threads of what had happened just didn't—

"By the way," Bree said, interrupting my thoughts. "The labs came back on the exhumation."

I looked at her, revealing nothing. "And?"

"It was him in the coffin," she said. "Soneji. They compared DNA to samples taken when he was in federal custody the first time. He's dead, Alex. He's been dead more than ten years."

One of the EMTs called out to us before I could express my relief. We went to the Soneji in the far alcove, then the one who'd been crawling away, leaving blood like a snail's track. They'd shot him up with morphine and he was out of it. They'd also cut off his shirt and found the raised latex edge of a mask that could have been crafted by one of Hollywood's finest.

After photographing the mask, we sliced and peeled it off, revealing the ashen face of Claude Watkins, painter, performance artist, and wounded idolizer of Gary Soneji.

The second Soneji was up on a gurney and headed for an ambulance when we caught up to him.

We tore open his shirt, found the latex edge of an identical mask, photographed it, and then had the EMTs slice it off him. The man behind the mask was in his late twenties and unfamiliar to us. But as they wheeled him out, I had no doubt that, whoever he was, he'd been worshipping Gary Soneji for a long, long time.

We waited for the medical examiner to arrive and take custody of the dead Soneji before we cut off the third mask.

"It's a woman," Bree said, her hands going to her mouth.

"Not just any woman," I said, stunned and confused. "That's Virginia Winslow."

"Who?"

"Gary Soneji's widow."

"Wait. What?" Bree said, staring at the dead woman closely. "I thought you said she hated Soneji."

"That's what she told me."

Bree shook her head. "What in God's name possessed her to impersonate her dead husband and then try to kill you? Did she shoot John? Or did Watkins? Or that other guy?"

"One of them did," I said. "I'll put money one of the pistols matches."

"But why?" she said, still confused.

"Binx and Watkins and, evidently, Virginia Winslow made Soneji into a cult, with me being the enemy of the cult," I said, and thought about Winslow's son, Dylan, and the picture of me on his dartboard.

Where was the kid in all of this? Seeing Binx being led out, I thought that if we leaned on her hard enough, she'd eventually want to cut a deal and tell all.

"You look like hell, you know," Bree said, breaking my thoughts again.

"Appreciate the compliment."

"I'm serious. Let's go, let the crime-scene guys do their work."

"No formal statement?"

"You've made enough of a statement to satisfy me for the time being."

"Chief of detectives and wife," I said. "That's a conflict of interest any way you look at it."

"I don't care, Alex," Bree said. "I'm taking you home. You can make a formal statement after you've had a good night's sleep."

I almost agreed, but then said, "Okay, I'll leave. But can we stop by Sampson's room before we go home? He deserves to know."

"Of course," she said, softening. "Of course we can."

I stayed quiet during the ride away from the ambush and shooting scene. Bree seemed to understand I needed space, and didn't ask any more questions on the way to GW Medical Center.

But my mind kept jumping to different aspects of the case. Where had Watkins and Soneji's widow met? Through Kimiko Binx? And who was the other wounded guy? How had he come to be part of a conspiracy to kill me and Sampson?

Riding the elevator to the ICU, I promised myself I'd answer the questions, clean up the case, even though it was all but over.

As the door opened, I felt something sharp on my right arm and jerked back to look at it.

"Sorry," Bree said. "You had a little piece of Scotch tape there."

She showed me the tape, no more than a half inch long, before rolling it between her thumb and index finger and flicking it into a trash can.

I twisted my forearm, to see a little reddish patch, and wondered where I'd picked that up. Probably off Nana Mama's counter earlier in the morning, left over from one of Ali's latest school projects.

It didn't matter because when we reached the ICU, the nurse gave us good news. Sampson was gone, transferred to the rehab floor.

When we finally tracked him down, he was paying his first visit to the physical therapist's room. We went in and found Billie with her palms pressed to her beaming cheeks, and her eyes welling over with tears.

I had to fight back tears, too.

Sampson was not only out of bed, he was out of a wheelchair, up on his feet, with his back to us, using a set of parallel gymnastics bars for balance. His massive arm and neck muscles were straining so hard they were trembling, and sweat gushed off him as he moved one foot and then the other, a drag more than a step with his right leg. But it was incredible.

"Can you believe it?" Billie cried, jumped to her feet, and hugged Bree.

I wiped at my tears, kissed Billie, and broke into a huge grin before clapping and coming around in front of Sampson.

Big John had a hundred-watt smile going.

He saw me, stopped, and said, "'Ow bout that?"

"Amazing," I said, fighting back more emotion. "Just amazing, brother."

He smiled broader, and then cocked his head at me, as if he felt something.

"Wha?" Sampson said.

"I got him," I said. "The one who shot you."

Sampson sobered, and paused to take that in. The therapist

offered him the wheelchair, but he shook his head slowly, still staring at me intently, as if seeing all sorts of things in my face.

"F-get him f-now, Alex," John said finally, with barely a slur and his face twisting into a triumphant smile. "Can't yah see I got dance less. . .sons ta do?"

I stood there in shock for a moment. Bree and Billie started laughing. So did Sampson and the therapist.

I did, too, then, from deep in my gut, a belly laughter that soon mixed with deep and profound gratitude, and a great deal of awe.

Our prayers had been answered. A true miracle had occurred.

My partner and best friend had been shot in the head, but Big John Sampson was not defeated and definitely on his way back.

EPILOGUE

TWO DAYS LATER, I awoke feeling strangely out of it, as if I were nursing the last dregs of the worst hangover of my life.

Department protocol dictated I sit on the sidelines on paid administrative leave while the shootings were investigated. After what I'd been through, and because I was feeling so run-down, I should have taken the time to stay home and recover with my family for at least a week.

But I forced myself out of bed and headed downtown to talk with my union representative, a sharp attorney named Carrie Nan. I walked her through the events in the factory. Like Bree, she felt comfortable with me talking to Internal Affairs, which I did.

The two detectives, Alice Walker and Gary Pan, were polite, thorough, and, I thought, fair. They took me through the scenario six or seven times in an interrogation room I'd used often on the job.

I stuck with the facts, and not the swinging emotions of elation and rage that I'd felt during the entire event. I kept it clean and to the point.

The scene was an ambush. In all three shootings, I'd seen a pistol. I'd made a warning. When the pistol was turned on me, I shot to save my life.

Detective Pan scratched his head. "You sound kind of detached when you describe what happened."

"Do I?" I said. "I'm just trying to talk about it objectively."

"Always said you were the sharpest tack around, Dr. Cross," Detective Walker said, and then paused. "After you shot the third Soneji, did you scream something like 'I'll kill every single Soneji before I'm through?'"

I remembered, and it sounded bad, and I knew it.

"They had me surrounded," I said at last. "I was caught in an ambush, and had already engaged with three of them. Did I lose my cool at that point? I might have. But it was over by then. If there were others, they were long gone."

Pan said, "Kimiko Binx was there."

"Yes. What's she saying?"

Walker said, "We're not at liberty to say, Dr. Cross, you know that."

"Sure," I said. "Just being nosy."

Pan said, "There *were* others there, by the way. In the factory."

Before I could say anything, Pan's cell buzzed. Then Walker's.

"What others?" I asked. "I didn't see anyone else."

The detectives read their texts, and didn't answer me.

"Sit tight," Pan said, getting up.

"You need anything?" Walker asked. "Coffee? Coke?"

"Just water," I said, and watched them leave.

There were others there, by the way. In the factory.

I hadn't seen a soul. But was that true? Different spotlights had been aimed at me from different places and angles. There had to have been a fifth person at the least. There had to—

Two men in suits entered the room along with Chief Michaels and Bree. The first three were stone-faced. Bree looked like she was on the edge of a breakdown.

"I'm sorry, Alex, but…," she said, barely getting the words out before she looked to Chief Michaels. "I can't."

"Can't what?" I asked, feeling as if I were suddenly standing with my back to the rim of a deep canyon I hadn't even realized was there.

"Alex," Michaels said. "The third Soneji, the one you shot off the roof of the alcove, died two hours ago. And some very damning information has come forward that directly contradicts your account of the shooting."

"What evidence?" I said. "Who are these guys?"

One of the suits said, "Mr. Cross, I am Special Agent Carlos Ramon with the US Justice Department."

Coming around the table, the other suit said, "Special Agent Jon Christopher, Justice. You are under arrest for the premeditated murder of Virginia Winslow and John Doe. You have the right to remain silent. Anything you say can and—"

I didn't hear the rest. I didn't need to. I'd recited the Miranda warnings a thousand times. As they handcuffed me, I kept looking at Bree, who was crushed, and wouldn't return my gaze.

"You don't believe them, do you?" I said, as Pan started to urge me toward the door and booking. "Bree?"

Bree looked my way finally with devastated, teary eyes. "Don't say another word, Alex. Everything can and will be used against you now."

ZOO II

JAMES PATTERSON

with MAX DILALLO

CHAPTER 1

I'M RUNNING FOR MY LIFE.

At least I'm trying to.

My clunky rubber boots keep getting stuck in the fresh snowfall. Fifty-mile-per-hour Arctic winds lash my body like a palm tree in a hurricane. The subzero-weather hooded jumpsuit I'm wearing is more cumbersome than a suit of armor.

Mini-icicles crust my goggles. Not that I could see much through them, anyway. All around me is a wall of white, a vortex of icy gusts and swirling snow. I can't even make out my triple-gloved right hand in front of my face.

But that's because it's tucked into my front pocket, clutching a Glock 17 9mm pistol. My one and only hope of survival.

I keep moving—"stumbling" would be more accurate—as fast as I can. I don't know where the hell I'm going. I just know I have to get there fast. I know I can't stop.

If I do, the seven-hundred-pound female polar bear on my tail will catch me and devour me alive.

But, hey, that's life above the Arctic Circle for you. Never a dull moment. One second you're tossing a net into an icy stream, trying to catch a few fish to feed your family. The next, one of Earth's deadliest predators is trying to kill you.

I glance backward to try to see just how close the bear has

gotten. I can't spot her at all, which is even more terrifying. With all the snow swirling around, her milky-white coat makes the perfect camouflage.

But I know the animal is near. I can just feel it.

Sure enough, seconds later, from behind me comes a mighty roar that echoes out across the tundra.

She's closer than I thought!

I push myself to move faster and tighten my grip around the freezing-cold Glock, wishing I had a larger gun. Do I empty my clip at the bear blindly and hope I get lucky? Stop, crouch, wait for her to get nearer, and aim for maximum effect?

Neither sounds promising. So I decide to do both.

Without slowing, I turn sideways and fire four times in her general direction.

Did I hit her? No clue. I'm sure I didn't scare her. Unlike most animals, typical polar bears never get spooked by loud noises. They live in the Arctic, after all. They hear thunderous sounds all the time: rumbling avalanches, shattering glaciers.

But there's nothing typical about this polar bear whatsoever. I didn't provoke her. I didn't wander into her territory. I didn't threaten her young.

None of that matters. She wants me dead.

The reason? HAC. Human-animal conflict. My theory that has helped explain why, for the past half-dozen years, animals everywhere have been waging an all-out war against humanity—and winning. It's why this abominable snow-bear picked up my scent from over a mile away and immediately started charging. I'm a human being and, like every other animal on the planet right now, she has an insatiable craving for human blood.

Another roar booms behind me, revealing the bear's position—even closer now.

I twist to fire off four more rounds. I pray I've hit her, but I don't count on it. With only nine bullets in my clip remaining, I start psyching myself up to turn around, kneel, and take aim.

Okay, Oz, I think. *You can do this. You can—*

I suddenly lose my footing and go tumbling face-first onto the icy ground. It's hard as concrete and jagged as a bed of nails. My gun—*shit!*—goes flying out of my hand and into a snowdrift.

I scramble on all fours and hunt for it desperately, feeling the permafrost beneath me start to tremble from the polar bear's galloping gait.

I could really use that gun right about now.

By the grace of God, I find it just in time. I spin around—right as the bear emerges from the white haze like a speeding train bursting out of a tunnel.

She rears up onto her hind legs, preparing to pounce. I fire four more shots. The first hits the side of her thick skull—but ricochets clean off. The next two miss her completely. The fourth lodges in her shoulder, which only makes her madder.

I shoot twice more, wildly, as I try to roll away, but the bear leaps and lands right on top of me. She chomps down on my snowsuit hood with her mighty jaws, missing my skull by millimeters. She jerks me around like a rag doll. With her razor-sharp claws, she slashes my left arm to shreds.

Pain surges through my limb as I twist and struggle, trying to break free with every ounce of strength I have. Images of Chloe and Eli, my wife and young son, flash through my mind. I can't leave them. I can't die. Not now. Not like this.

I'm still getting tossed around like crazy, but with all the strength I can muster, I shove the tip of my Glock against the bottom of the polar bear's chin, just inches from my own.

I fire my last three shots point-blank.

A mist of hot blood sprays my face as the bullets tear through the behemoth's brain. She stops moving instantly, as if she were a toy and I'd just flipped her off switch. Then all seven hundred pounds of her slump down next to me.

Seconds pass and I begin to catch my breath, relieved beyond belief. Slowly, with all my effort, I reach up and manage to pry my hood from the bear's locked jaw.

I stagger to my feet, instantly light-headed from the adrenaline crash. Or maybe it's the blood loss. My left arm is gushing from easily a dozen lacerations.

Removing the polar-bear-blood-soaked goggles from my face, I survey the massive animal that nearly took my life. Even dead she's a terrifying sight. *Unbelievable.*

I thought my family and I would be safe up here. That's the whole reason we're living in Greenland in the first place, to avoid the sheer hell of constant deadly animal attacks. So much for *that*.

I just have to remind myself: the rest of the world is even worse.

CHAPTER 2

"YOU COULD HAVE DIED out there, Oz! What the hell were you thinking?"

My wife, Chloe Tousignant, paces the cramped quarters of our tiny galley kitchen, anxiously twisting the cuffs of her thick wool sweater, biting her bottom lip.

Chloe's furious with me, and I don't blame her. But I have to admit, I've forgotten how awfully sexy she looks when she's mad. Even scared or angry, my French-born wife is both the most beautiful and most brilliant woman I've ever met.

"Come on, how many times are you going to ask me that?"

This would be number six, for those of you keeping track at home.

The first was when I came stumbling back inside covered in blood—the polar bear's and my own. The second: when Chloe was helping me clean and dress my wounds. The third was when I went back outside again, the fourth when I returned dragging as much of the carcass as I could. The fifth was while she watched me butcher it. (I *think,* but I was focusing pretty intently on the YouTube video I was watching, via our spotty satellite internet connection: *How to Skin a Bear ~ A Guide for First-Time Hunters.*)

"I just don't understand!" she exclaims. "How could you—"

"Shh, keep your voice down," I say gently, gesturing to the tiny room right next to us, where our four-year-old son, Eli, is taking a nap.

Chloe frowns and switches to a harsh whisper. "How could you take such a risk? It was completely unnecessary! You know it's prime mating season all across the tundra. The animals are even crazier than normal. And we still have plenty of food left."

I take a moment to weigh my response.

The reality is, we *don't* have plenty of food left. We've been living in this abandoned Arctic weather station for nearly four months now. Originally settled at Thule Air Base, twenty-five miles away, with President Hardinson and a group of government officials, we had been on our own since they returned to the United States to manage the animal crisis more closely.

Chloe and I had decided to stay. We thought it would be safer. We hoped that living in such a harsh climate, home to fewer wild animals, would mean fewer wild animal *attacks*. And for the most part, it did. It also meant we were left to our own devices.

Yes, Chloe is right that it's prime mating season—because it's late "summer" and, relatively speaking, fairly temperate. But even colder, more brutal weather is just around the corner. Every day I don't go out there and trap a wild caribou or haul in some fresh fish to tide us over through winter threatens our survival.

As I stand over our little propane stove, stirring a gigantic pot of simmering polar bear stew, I decide to keep all of that to myself. Instead, I extend an olive branch.

"You're right, honey. It was pretty dumb of me. I'm sorry."

Chloe probably knows I'm just trying to play nice. A highly educated scientist, she's well aware of the Arctic's weather patterns. And I can guarantee that, as a deeply devoted mother, she's been keeping a worried eye on our rations. Still, she clearly appreciates my words.

"I'm just glad you brought that gun along," she says.

"Are you kidding? That thing's like American Express. I never leave my three-room Arctic hut without it."

Chloe laughs, grateful for a little comic relief. Which makes me feel happy, too. There's no better feeling in the world than being able to make her smile.

She comes up behind me and nuzzles my neck. I wince as she brushes against my bad arm, the bloody slash wounds throbbing beneath the bandages.

"Sorry," she says, backing off. "The pain must be awful."

It is. But Chloe's got enough on her mind. I don't want her worrying about me.

I turn around to face her. Her concern, her love, her beauty are all too much.

"Not too bad," I reply. "But maybe you can help me…forget about it for a while?"

She coyly arches an eyebrow. We start to kiss. Before long, things are heating up faster than the polar bear meat cooking behind me.

Until Chloe suddenly stops. She pulls away. "Wait. Oz, we can't."

I sigh, disappointed. But she's right. Stranded deep inside the Arctic Circle, there's not exactly a corner drugstore we can run to for some condoms or the Pill.

I simply nod and hug her. Tightly.

This isn't a world that either of us would risk bringing new life into.

CHAPTER 3

"YUCK! DADDY, THIS IS GROSS!"

Eli has just taken his first bite of my latest culinary creation: oatmeal mixed with chunks of braised polar bear. He spits it back out into his bowl.

Chloe folds her arms. "Eli, where are your manners?"

How adorably French of her, I think. The world is falling apart and my wife is still concerned about etiquette.

"Oh, go easy on him," I say. "I know it's not exactly the breakfast of champions. But you do have to eat it, buddy. Sorry. We all do. Need the protein."

"No way," Eli says, shaking his head. He proceeds to shovel only the mushy oatmeal into his mouth, avoiding the meat. He uses his fingers, not his spoon.

I don't have the energy to put up a fight, and neither does Chloe. We consume the rest of our meal in silence. All we can hear is the eerie, howling wind outside, whipping against our weather station's aluminum walls. It sounds like something right out of a horror movie.

At least it's not an animal, trying to claw its way inside. It might be soon.

Chloe and I had come to the same chilling conclusion the night before. Because I lost so much blood out there on the ice, leaving a trail leading right to our front door, it's only a matter of time before *other* creatures pick up the scent and come after us. Like a charging herd of enraged musk oxen. Or a throng of feral foxes. Another polar bear, or an entire pack of them.

"All right, who's ready for story time?" Chloe asks, starting to clear our plates.

"Me, me!" Eli shouts, his face lighting up bright.

"Okay, then. Go wash your hands and get ready. I'll be in in a minute."

With a grin practically half the size of his face, Eli disappears into the other room.

When we first moved into the weather station, it was all so rushed and chaotic. Our main focus was making sure we had enough canned food and warm clothing. Toys, games, and books for Eli were the last things on our mind. Thankfully, we discovered the previous inhabitants were voracious readers. They'd left behind a giant library—everything from Charles Dickens to Philip K. Dick, though not exactly young children's literature. Still, Chloe and I have been reading selections to Eli every single day since. Most of the stuff is way over his head, but he loves it.

"Anything new in the world we left behind?" Chloe asks me, rinsing our plates.

She sees I've started skimming the *New York Times* homepage on my laptop. More than half the lead headlines are about the ongoing animal crisis, which shows no signs of slowing down. In fact, it's only getting worse.

I summarize some stories.

"Let's see. Researchers in Cameroon were testing a promising animal pheromone repellent spray when they were mauled by a horde of rhinos. President Hardinson just signed a controversial executive order to set controlled fires in federal parks to destroy thousands of acres of breeding grounds. And the Kremlin's denying it, but apparently a school of blue whales just sunk a Russian nuclear submarine in—"

"Enough!" Chloe snaps. She sighs deeply. She runs her hands through her auburn hair. I feel bad for adding to her stress, but she asked.

My laptop *pings* with a notification—a new email. But not just any message—this has been sent via a classified U.S. government server.

Its subject line reads: "Urgent Request."

I immediately slam my laptop shut.

"Now don't be ridiculous," Chloe says. She'd read the screen over my shoulder. "Open it, Oz. It must be important!"

"As far as I'm concerned," I say, "there are only two things in this crazy world that are important—and they're both inside this weather station with me. I'm done helping the feds, thank you very much. Remember what happened last time? How royally they screwed everything up with their so-called solutions? The idiotic bombing raids? The bungled electricity ban?"

Chloe puts her hands on her hips. Of course she remembers. We lived through every minute of that nightmare together.

But then she snatches my computer away.

"Fine. If you're not going to read it, I will."

She opens the laptop and clicks on the message. She begins to skim it, and I can see her eyes grow wide. Whatever she's reading is big. Very big.

"Let me guess. The Pentagon wants me to come back and try to help solve this thing again. But what's the point? They're not going to listen to me."

Chloe spins the screen around and shows me the email. I read it myself.

It was sent by a Dr. Evan Freitas, undersecretary for science and energy at the DOE. He explains that the powers that be in Washington have finally acknowledged that the animal crisis must be dealt with scientifically, *not* militarily. The Department of Energy is now overseeing America's response, not the Department of Defense. Dr. Freitas is spearheading the new response team personally, and he desperately wants me, Jackson Oz, renowned human-animal conflict expert, to return to the United States and join it.

"This is our chance," Chloe says, grabbing my shoulders, "to get out of this icy hell. To actually stop this thing this time. It's what we've been waiting for!"

I can see tears forming in the corners of my wife's big brown eyes. It's obvious how much this means to her. I'm still skeptical, but I know I can't refuse.

"You're right," I finally reply. "It is what we've been waiting for. It's hope."

CHAPTER 4

THE METAL WALLS OF our little weather station are rattling like a tin can. Outside, something's rumbling, something big. And it's getting louder. Closer.

"Daddy, look!" Eli exclaims. He's standing in front of a triple-paned glass window that looks out across the icy tundra, jabbing his finger at the sky. "It's here!"

The rumbling grows to a crescendo as a gunmetal military transport plane roars overhead, flying dangerously low to the ground.

Which is a very beautiful sight. It means it's about to land. Right on time.

As it touches down—on the snow-covered airstrip about a quarter-mile from our hut—Chloe and I quickly gather up the few small duffel bags we'll be bringing with us. Mostly clothes, toiletries, and a dog-eared copy of *A Tale of Two Cities* we're halfway through reading to Eli.

Other than the hooded jumpsuits we're already wearing, we're leaving the rest of our extreme cold-weather gear behind. I'd started packing our thermal underwear last night, until Chloe saw me and practically slapped the long johns out of my hand.

"I hope you're joking," she said, crossing her arms. "We're

done living in this damned Arctic wasteland. Forever. We're returning to civilization, remember? And we're *saving* it. For real this time."

"Right," I said. "Of course." Then, under my breath: "No pressure or anything."

But my wife had a point. We'd decided to leave our safe little hideout at the edge of the world. We both knew there would be no coming back.

"Okay, bud, time to go," I call to Eli, who eagerly jumps into Chloe's arms.

We assemble by the front door, which we haven't opened in nearly a week—not since I tangled with that polar bear and left a trail of her blood and mine right to our doorstep. Chloe and I were afraid more wild animals would pick up the scent and come calling.

By the evening of the next day, they had.

First was a herd of rabid reindeer. They rammed their hoofs and antlers against the metal siding for hours until finally giving up from exhaustion. Next came a pack of wolverines. Not the scary Hugh Jackman mutant kind but weasel-like critters the size of small dogs. Still, their teeth and claws are as sharp as razors. If they'd found a way in, they'd have had no trouble turning three helpless humans into mincemeat.

I peer through the door's porthole. The coast looks clear—but anything could be out there. Lurking. Waiting. The quarter-mile hike to the airstrip might as well be a marathon.

Which is why I'm holding that trusty Glock—the one that saved my life once before—just in case. I check the clip: seventeen shiny gold bullets. Locked and loaded.

I push open the door and the three of us step outside. With

my very first breath, the frigid air stabs the back of my throat like a knife.

"Come on," I manage to croak. "Let's hurry."

We traipse as fast as we can across the fresh snow; it's up to our knees. Over the crunching of our footsteps and the whistling of the wind, I hear Chloe speaking some comforting words to our son to help keep him calm.

Meanwhile, I'm scanning the icy vista all around us like a hawk. Which is harder than you might think. The endless snow and ice reflect the midday sun brighter than a million mirrors. If a feral animal or two—or ten—came charging toward us, sure, I'd probably spot them in time. But would I be able to see well enough in the glare to aim and fire?

I pray I don't have to find out.

Before long I do spot something looming. It's bluish-gray. And enormous.

It's the C-12 Huron transport plane—its dual propellers still spinning—sent by the Air Force to take us home.

We finally reach it as its rear stairs are hydraulically lowered. I gesture for Chloe and Eli to board first. I take one final glance around, say a silent good-bye to this icy hell, then climb in after them.

"IDs and boarding passes, please?"

One of the two pilots, a surprisingly youngish woman with a megawatt grin, is turned around in her seat to face us. Chloe and I smile back, filled with relief and glad to discover our saviors have a sense of humor.

"Shoot," I say, patting my pockets. "I think I left my wallet in my other subzero bodysuit."

"I'm Major Schiff," the captain says, grinning. "This is First

Lieutenant Kimmel. Sit down, strap in, and let's get you guys out of here."

There are only about a dozen plush leather seats in the plane, which we have all to ourselves. Eli picks one by the window. Chloe sits next to him, and I beside her.

Within seconds, the plane's engines come alive and we're speeding down the bumpy, potholed runway. As we lift off into the sky, I close my eyes for just a moment…

When I hear Eli shriek at the top of his lungs.

"Look, look!" He's pointing out the window. A flock of birds—looks like a mix of gulls and ducks and even owls—has suddenly appeared on the horizon, flying right at us. They can't touch a speeding jet, and we leave the squawking mass of feathers in our atmospheric dust.

I reach over and take Chloe's hand. It's clammy. And trembling.

I realize mine is, too.

CHAPTER 5

THE PLANE'S CABIN IS pitch-black. We've been flying for hours. Eli and Chloe are snoring softly, both sleeping like babies.

Me? Not even close.

I'm exhausted but haven't caught a wink. My first stop, before returning to the United States, is London. There I'll attend an international summit to discuss new global responses to the animal attacks with representatives from around the world.

My mind's been on overdrive pretty much since wheels-up. That world we're returning to after all this time—what does it look like? The government's promise to treat HAC as a scientific crisis, not a military one—how will that actually play out? And what is my role in it all?

The lights inside the cabin come on. Major Schiff turns to face me.

"Time to stow those tray tables. We're about to land."

Now my heart rate really starts to rise. Not because of the summit in London.

No, I'm getting nervous because we're *not* landing in London right now.

And my wife has no idea yet.

Chloe rubs her eyes and sits up in her seat. She gives me a

groggy smile and glances out the window—when her expression instantly turns to shock. Then anger.

"Oz...? Where are we?"

She asks rhetorically, of course. We've just flown past the Eiffel Tower.

"Chloe, look, I'm sorry. If I'd told you the truth—"

"I never would have agreed to it, you're absolutely right!"

"Listen, I can explain—"

"No, let *me,*" she fires back. "While you jet off to London for the conference, then to God-knows-where-else around the world, Eli and I will be staying here. In Paris. With my parents. Because in your head you've convinced yourself that's safer!"

Chloe knows me too well. That was my plan to a T. I'd arranged it secretly with Dr. Freitas of the Department of Energy. And it did sound good in my head. But hearing my wife repeat it back to me, I can't help but wonder if I've done the right thing.

"If there was any way we could stay together," I say, "any way at all, you know I'd choose that in a heartbeat. But be real, Chloe. Let's say they send me to the Amazon. Or Mount Kilimanjaro. Or the *Ant*arctic. Are those any places to take a four-year-old?"

Chloe just rolls her beautiful eyes.

I want to tell her we'll talk every day, no matter where in the world I am. I want her to know that every second I'm not working on solving the animal crisis, I'll be thinking about her and Eli. I want her to believe me when I promise I'll be coming back to get them as soon as I possibly can.

But I don't get a chance to say any of that. Our plane touches down on a private runway at Le Bourget, and before

I know it, Chloe and I are walking down the retractable steps, Eli in my arms. A shiny black Citroën sedan and a handful of people are already waiting for us on the tarmac.

"Chloe, *ma petite chérie!*"

Marielle Tousignant, my wife's bubbly seventy-year-old stepmother, wraps her in an emotional hug. Marielle married her widowed father when Chloe was still fairly young. She never adopted Chloe officially, but it didn't matter. Marielle couldn't have children of her own, and before long, the two became extremely close, as if biological relatives.

I stand in silence as they speak to each other in rapid-fire French. I can't understand a word, but the gist of their conversation is pretty obvious.

"*Salut,* Oz," Marielle says to me, kissing both my cheeks and blotting her eyes. "Thank you for returning to me my daughter."

"Of course, Marielle," I say. "Thanks for taking care of her while I'm gone."

"And who is this handsome *garçon?*" she asks, gently stroking sleeping Eli's hair.

Chloe furrows her brow. Is her stepmother making a joke? Or is it something else?

"Very funny, *Maman,*" she says. "That's your grandson."

After the slightest pause, an embarrassed smile blooms across Marielle's face. "*Oui, bien sûr!* My, how big Eli is getting!"

A suited man standing by the car interrupts us: "Ma'am?"

He has an American accent, and I presume he's one of the U.S. Embassy security escorts Dr. Freitas promised would pick Chloe and Eli up from the airport. "We should get going."

Everyone agrees. Eli is still sleeping, and as Chloe takes him gently from me, I can tell from her expression she's still upset. Is it because I didn't tell her the plan? Because we're going to be apart again? Or because the world has come to this?

Probably all three.

"Where's Papa?" I hear her ask Marielle as we approach the sedan.

"Right here, my dear," comes a scratchy old voice from inside the vehicle.

Jean-Luc Tousignant, my wife's seventy-six-year-old father, is sitting in the backseat. A wooden cane is draped across his knees. As he reaches up to embrace his daughter, his hands tremble terribly.

"Forgive me for not getting out. I do not have the strength."

Chloe can barely hide her shock. Neither can I. The last time we saw him, just a year ago, when he and Marielle visited us in New York, Jean-Luc, a former French Foreign Legion officer, was hale and hearty for his age. Tonight he looks frail and sick.

Wonderful, I think. I figured my wife and son would be safe in Paris with my in-laws. I had no idea that one of them had developed early-stage dementia and the other, Parkinson's.

But at least this is safer than bringing Chloe and Eli with me to dangerous, far-flung lands…right?

I suddenly feel my wife pressing up against me, her arms around my neck, her lips on mine.

"I hate you so much, Oz," she whispers between kisses. "But I love you more."

I tell her I love her, too. I tell her to be safe. To watch over Eli. That I'll be back for them.

"Just as soon as I save the world. *I promise.*"

With that, Chloe gets into the sedan and it speeds away into the night.

As I climb back up the steps of the plane, I swallow the growing lump in my throat. I knew saying good-bye to my family wasn't going to be easy.

Now comes the even harder part.

CHAPTER 6

DAWN IS BREAKING OVER London. It's 2016, but squint, and you'd swear it was back during the Blitz.

Our three-SUV convoy is speeding east along Marylebone Road, one of the city's central thoroughfares. My eyes are glued to the streetscape outside the window, and my jaw is stuck to the floor. I'm getting my first glimpse of just how much the world has changed since I've been gone.

By "changed," I mean "gone to absolute shit."

The sidewalks are splattered with dried blood and strewn with debris and broken glass. Gutters are filled with soggy garbage. Shops are boarded up. Most traffic lights are out. A few other cars and trucks are on the road—police and military vehicles, generally—but I don't see a single pedestrian.

Instead, central London is overrun by animals—in particular, roving packs of rangy, rabid wolves.

Their fur is patchy, but their fangs glisten like icicles. They seem to be stalking down virtually every sidewalk and alley we pass, sniffing the ground, searching for human prey.

Clearly they're the primary animal threat in this part of the city. But I also spot plenty of feral dogs and house cats in the mix. I see squirrels skittering across rooftops, too. A flock of falcons circling and cawing overhead.

When we pass a burnt-out black London cab, abandoned on the corner of Baker Street—near the address of the fictional Sherlock Holmes—I notice that inside, about fifty greasy rats have built a giant, filthy nest. They're gnawing the flesh off a severed human leg, and it doesn't take a crack detective to figure out how they got it.

"Welcome back to the jungle, Oz."

Seated beside me, Dr. Evan Freitas pats me on the shoulder and lets out a grim chuckle. He can't be more than fifty, but the stress of spearheading Washington's scientific HAC response has clearly aged him prematurely. His bushy black beard is streaked with gray. Every time he speaks, his entire face fills with wrinkles like a prune.

"It's…it's just…," I stutter, "unbelievable."

"Worse than you imagined?"

"Worse than—my worst *nightmare!* We had satellite internet back in the Arctic. I'd read that the animals were gaining ground. That huge swaths of major cities had basically been overrun. And abandoned. But this…this is just beyond—"

"London Town ain't been abandoned, mate," says Jack Riley, our driver, a cranky, baldheaded Brit with the Metropolitan Police. "See?"

He gestures to an apartment above what was once a high-end shoe store, now looted and dark. A woman has opened her second-story window a crack. She quickly reels in a line of laundry and slams the window shut.

"The whole bloody lot of us just stay indoors now. Least the smart ones do."

Yep, I'd read about that as well.

In many places, just setting foot onto the street is a death wish. So most people, especially in big cities, remain inside their homes pretty much 24/7, with their doors and windows locked tight. Some have gone even further, converting their buildings into anti-animal mini-fortresses, as Chloe's parents and a few neighbors had done to their Paris apartment complex. It was one of the many reasons I thought my wife and son would be safer there.

Folks communicate with friends and family almost exclusively by phone and internet—even more so than they did before. School and work are done online as much as possible. In terms of food and other necessities, people have come to rely on sporadic deliveries of rations by armed government soldiers. Doctors have gone back to making house calls, at great personal risk…and are almost always packing heat.

"It's like this in Atlanta, too. And the suburbs and surrounding counties? Even worse. People are getting desperate. Civilization is breaking down."

Those ominous words come from the woman sitting in the row of seats behind us, nervously biting her cuticles: Dr. Sarah Lipchitz.

While I'd waited with Freitas at Heathrow for about half an hour for Sarah's plane to arrive from the United States, he explained that she was a brilliant young biologist and pathogen expert currently employed by the Centers for Disease Control and Prevention, who had been handpicked to join our team. (What he *didn't* mention was that the bespectacled Sarah was very pretty, in a geeky, girl-next-door kind of way.)

"Precisely, Doctor," Freitas responds. "And preventing global chaos from becoming total anarchy is why we're all here."

He means me, Sarah, himself, and the rest of the scientists and experts in our three-vehicle convoy. Barely a dozen people, responsible for the lives of millions.

I have about a thousand follow-up questions for Freitas, but they'll have to wait. We pass Hampstead Road and turn down a one-way side street. Our convoy comes to a stop in front of the main gates of University College London. The international symposium we've come to England to attend is a gathering of some of the finest scientific minds in the world, all trying to save humanity.

As armed British soldiers open our doors and escort us inside, I hear a pack of wolves in the distance, howling.

I hope they're not signaling that another innocent person has been mauled.

CHAPTER 7

MY GOD, THESE SCIENTIFIC conferences are dull.

I'd forgotten how absolutely painful they can be. Even when the topic is literally the fate of the planet, the only thing these bland professors and rumpled "experts" seem to know how to do is drone on and on. And on.

It makes me want to pull my hair out. Worst of all, we've been at this for almost five hours now, and I haven't heard one single presenter offer any useful new information or viable solutions.

If this really is a confab of the finest minds in their fields...we're screwed.

A team from Senegal, for example, discussed the inconclusive results of some recent biopsies of the brain tissue of rabid elephants. A Brazilian electrical engineer spoke of her lab's failed attempt to use gamma radiation waves to block the effects of cellphone signals on animal pheromone reception.

A group of officers from Moscow's Valerian Kuybyshev Military Engineering Academy outlined a Kremlin-backed plan to carpet-bomb any and all major underground animal breeding areas. When I angrily interrupted to explain that the American government had tried an almost identical bombing campaign just a few months ago and that it had failed spectacularly, the committee chairman cut the feed to my microphone.

Thank goodness it was time for a fifteen-minute break.

Right now I'm standing in the hallway outside the main meeting room, mainlining some desperately needed caffeine and sugar: a muddy cup of coffee and a rich, gooey Cadbury chocolate-caramel bar.

Sarah is reviewing her notes for a presentation she's giving later about what she's dubbed HMC—Human *Microbial* Conflict—which she believes, based on her research, will be the next, even more terrifying stage in all this madness.

Freitas, meanwhile, is sitting on the floor, talking animatedly on his smartphone and tapping wildly on his iPad. I don't have the foggiest idea to whom or what about—but by the look of it, it's important.

"Feeling nervous?" I ask Sarah when I see she's reached the end of her pages.

"Of course," she replies. "*Exceedingly* nervous."

"Don't worry about it, you'll do great. Just try to imagine that every chubby, balding, pasty scientist in the audience is wearing nothing but his underwear. Actually…no, don't do that. That's a pretty disturbing picture."

Sarah smiles and shakes her head.

"Thanks, Oz. But I'm not nervous about giving the presentation. I'm terrified…about what my *data* show. If you think wild *animals* attacking humans is bad, just wait another few months or so, when I predict wild *bacteria* will join in. There's no way to bomb something microscopic."

"Good God," I mumble, rubbing my temples. The prospect of that sounds beyond horrific. "One crisis at a time, please."

Suddenly Freitas leaps up from the ground and hurries over to us, waving his iPad in the air. Given the glint in his eye, I can tell he's overjoyed about something.

"They're in! The latest worldwide AAPC numbers!"

"Isn't that just a bunch of old fogeys?" I ask.

Freitas doesn't like my joke. The acronym, he says, stands for animal attacks per capita. It's a metric he invented to measure the rate of animal-related incidents and deaths in different countries around the world.

"Over the past few weeks," he explains, "rumors have been flying that all nations are *not* created equal. At least not when it comes to HAC. Allegedly, some have begun seeing a marked decline in attacks, while others have experienced a skyrocketing."

"So," he continues, "I ordered a team of DOE statisticians to crunch all the millions of data points we had and turn them into an easy-to-digest format."

He hands me his iPad. On it is a map of the world shaded every color of the rainbow.

"Uh, okay," I reply skeptically, skimming it. "So it looks like...Finland, Japan, South Korea, and Egypt are seeing fewer attacks. But Brazil, Indonesia, and Canada are seeing more. Big deal. Where does this get us? It doesn't tell us why—or what any of these countries have in common."

"No, it sure doesn't," Freitas responds. "Which is exactly what I want us to find out. Now come on!"

He turns and starts jogging down the hallway—away from the conference room.

"Dr. Freitas!" Sarah calls out, confused. "Where are you going? Our break's almost over. I have a paper to present!"

But Freitas doesn't slow. Instead he glances back and calls out, "Forget your stupid presentation, this is way bigger! We've got a plane waiting to take us to Bali!"

Bali? Is he serious? According to his own data, Indonesia has seen a massive spike in animal attacks recently—and *that's* where he wants to take us?

But when I glance down back at the map on the iPad still in my hands, I see that in the past month, the island of Bali has actually had almost *zero* reported attacks.

That has to be some kind of mistake. Doesn't it?

Or could the key to solving HAC really be right under our nose?

I grab Sarah's arm and practically drag her down the hallway after Freitas.

The day just got a hell of a lot more interesting.

CHAPTER 8

CHLOE IS IN HER old childhood bedroom, lying in her old childhood bed. Eli is curled up in the crook of her arm. The little boy is dozing soundly. Obliviously.

But for Chloe, try as she might, sleep just won't come.

She's been living in her parents' fortified apartment complex for only a few days now, but already she's started losing her mind.

Maybe it's because the air inside is so oppressive and stale: to prevent wild animals from entering, each and every window, chimney, and vent has been double-locked, triple-sealed, and completely boarded up.

Maybe it's because her elderly parents' health has started to deteriorate so rapidly and unexpectedly. Since the last time she saw them, her mother has grown increasingly forgetful, and her father's mobility has become severely limited.

Maybe it's because the apartment's food and supplies are stretched so thin. The government's biweekly rations delivery is inexplicably two days late, so the family is down to their last can of beans, a few shriveled tomatoes from their indoor hydroponic garden, and half of a stale, moldy baguette.

Or, maybe it's because the sounds echoing across the city

each night are so utterly terrifying. Screeching cats. Growling dogs. Yowling foxes. Shrieking vultures.

Screaming humans.

As Chloe snuggles Eli a bit closer, her mind drifts to Oz. She's still mad at him for tricking her into staying with her parents in Paris. But of course she understands. He did it out of love. Frankly, had she been in his shoes, their roles reversed, she'd probably have done the same.

Now she just prays that he's safe. They spoke briefly earlier today; he'd called from a plane, somewhere over the Pacific. Something about going to Mali. Africa? No, that wouldn't make sense. But the connection was lost before she could ask more.

Chloe feels her eyelids finally getting heavy. She's just about to doze off when a pounding on the front door practically shakes the apartment's walls.

Eli jolts awake and begins to cry with fright. As Chloe comforts him, she looks over at the clock on her nightstand: 3:18 a.m. Who could it possibly be at this hour?

No one good, Chloe thinks to herself.

She reassures her son she'll be right back and slips out of bed to investigate.

The pounding continues as she passes through the kitchen—and grabs a glistening chef's knife, just in case. Marielle has been woken up, too, but Chloe gestures for her stepmother to stay back and let her handle this.

"*Monsieur Tousignant!* It is the gendarmerie, with rations. Open the door!"

Chloe looks through the peephole. She sees two soldiers standing outside in the eerily dim hallway. One is carrying an assault rifle, the other a cardboard box. Both wear black fatigues and body armor.

Chloe exhales with relief. She sets down the knife, unlocks the deadbolt, and opens the door.

"*Bonsoir,*" she says. "Thank you very much for finally coming. I can take them."

She reaches for the box of food, but the soldier pulls it away.

"I am sorry, *mademoiselle.* This is to be delivered to Jean-Luc Tousignant only."

"It's fine. I'm Chloe Tousignant, his daughter." She glances up and down the hallway, making sure the coast is clear. "Now please give me the rations and shut the door, before an animal manages to—"

"You could be Marie Antoinette, for all I care," the other soldier snarls. "It does not matter." He holds up his smartphone, which is connected to a tiny digital fingerprint scanner. "The thumbprint of each recipient is required for delivery verification."

Chloe can't believe this. "He's in bed. He's sick. The man can barely walk! And I have a four-year-old son who's very hungry. Please."

The first soldier gives her a sympathetic look, but he won't back down.

"The rules are the rules. I am sorry. If you want the rations, your father must accept them personally. If not, we have many more deliveries to make tonight."

Chloe groans in annoyance. French citizens are dying in the streets, they're starving in their homes, and the army is worried about sticking to protocol?

"*Merde!* Fine! Wait here while I—"

Chloe suddenly sees two beady little eyes appear on the hallway ceiling.

In an instant, a furry four-legged animal squeals and leaps down at her.

She bats it away—a giant raccoon just inches from her face. *"Non!"* she yells as it lands on its back on the floor, then quickly rights itself and comes at her again.

Chloe screams and struggles to fight it off as it scrambles up her legs and torso toward her head, its claws digging into her flesh every inch of the way.

The soldier holding the box of rations drops it and frantically comes to Chloe's aid. He rips the rabid animal off her and flings it into the apartment. His partner swiftly aims his rifle and sprays a flurry of gunshots, killing the creature instantly.

Chloe is out of breath. In total shock. Her legs and chest are crisscrossed with bloody scratches. She's otherwise unharmed, but scared. And furious.

"Merci," she snaps at the soldiers—as she scoops up the box of rations they dropped and slams the door in their face, before either has a chance to protest.

Chloe locks the door and grips the box tightly. Marielle, who witnessed the entire episode, is too stunned to say a word. All she and her stepdaughter can do is stare at the raccoon's bloody carcass, and the trail of bullet holes along the floor and wall.

And be thankful that Chloe is still alive.

CHAPTER 9

THIS MUST BE WHAT heaven looks like.

A pristine coastline, dotted with swaying palm trees, stretching as far as the eye can see. White sand, finer than baby powder. Blue water, clear as glass. The sun warm, the breeze cool.

But best of all?

We've been standing out in the open for nearly fifteen minutes now, less than half a mile from thousands of acres of lush tropical forest, brimming with wildlife…

And there hasn't been a single animal attack yet.

I have to admit, it's more than a little eerie. But it's also an incredible relief, a feeling I can barely describe. A definite cause for hope.

"Careful with that," Freitas says to one of the porters. They're unloading our crates of scientific gear off the hotel shuttle from Ngurah Rai International Airport. Along with Freitas, Sarah, and I, sorting the equipment to be brought to our rooms, are Dr. Ti-Hua Chang, an epidemiologist from the Chinese Ministry of Health; Dr. Woodruff, an immunologist from the University of Illinois; and a few other scientists I've exchanged only a handshake with.

Actually, "rooms" is an understatement. They're more like personal luxury villas, designed in the style of traditional Balinese wooden huts. Built on stilts, they're perched directly above the sparkling water. Absolutely gorgeous.

Which could describe the entire hotel. Definitely not the kind of lodging that stingy old Uncle Sam would normally spring for. But thanks to the worldwide economic slump and the island's drastic drop in tourism, Freitas was able to score these stunning accommodations for his team for pennies on the dollar.

They're also in a prime location, on the beach and also near the jungles where we'll be doing the bulk of our testing. Our goal is simple: figure out why animals are running amok around the rest of the world but here in Bali are living with humans in harmony.

I take a quick break and shake out the front of my t-shirt. It's already damp with sweat and clinging to my chest. Not that I'm complaining or anything, but after all those months in the frigid Arctic, I can't remember the last time I was this hot and sticky.

Feeling thirsty, I look around for something to drink. There's a tiki bar on the other end of the open-air hotel lobby, but it looks empty and closed. Maybe there's a water fountain nearby. Or, heck—the sea looks so clear, maybe I'll just drink that.

"Indonesian iced tea, sir?"

A trim young Balinese man in a crisp white uniform is suddenly by my side. He's holding a silver platter on which sits a tall glass of amber liquid with a twist of lemon.

I don't think I've ever seen a more tempting beverage in all my life.

"Wow, yes, thank you. You guys are mind readers!"

I gulp down the sweet, refreshing tea so fast, rivulets of it trickle down my chin.

"Not mind readers, sir. We are simply very good at treating our guests well. And so is our wildlife, as you can see."

I wipe my mouth with the back of my hand, my top lip cold against my warm skin.

"I sure can," I say, intrigued by the hotel attendant's words. Perhaps he knows something that will point us in the right direction. "Any idea why that might be?"

The man thinks for a moment, furrowing his brow.

"Well, most Balinese are Hindu. And most Hindus are vegetarian. We believe in practicing nonviolence against all life forms. Perhaps our animals feel the same way."

I stifle a laugh—at least I try to—which I hope doesn't offend this friendly hotel employee bearing the divine iced tea. He can't be serious, can he? I'm no world religion scholar, but I'm pretty sure there are plenty of Hindus and vegetarians alike in places like India, Pakistan, Nepal, Malaysia. And those countries are reeling from some of the worst animal attacks on the planet.

"Interesting theory" is all I say, placing the empty glass back on the tray and extending my other hand to shake. "I'm Oz, by the way. Thanks again."

"My name is Putu. Welcome to Bali. I hope you find what you are looking for."

That makes two of us.

The porters are wheeling the last of our gear to our villas. I know Freitas will want us to head out as soon as possible to begin running tests. So first, I take out my new international satellite phone, issued to all team members so we can stay in constant touch no matter where in the world we go. Thrilled to see I have a few bars of reception, I scroll down my very short list of contacts until I find the one I so desperately want to call: "Chloe ~ Paris."

"Did he tell you what time the bar opens?"

I look up. Sarah has walked over to me. She's carrying an industrial metal laptop case and wheeling a crate of empty test tubes and plastic specimen bags.

She's also stripped down to cargo shorts and a tight gray tank top. Like me, her skin is glistening with sweat. But unlike me, on her it actually looks pretty sexy.

"Sorry. I didn't ask. And with so few guests, I bet they don't even open it at all."

"Too bad," Sarah replies. "I was thinking, after we spend the day trekking around the island, we could...have a drink. Compare notes."

Huh? I don't believe it. Is star CDC biologist Dr. Sarah Lipchitz...hitting on me?

I can't tell if that glint in her eye is professional curiosity or something more. Sure, it's a scary time to be single and alone in the world. But Sarah knows I'm happily married. This is a path I definitely don't want to go down—especially with a woman as smart and dangerously cute as she is. Maybe I'm reading too much into it.

"Maybe, uh...another time." Then I hold up my satellite phone. "Excuse me."

I step into a quiet corner of the lobby and dial. It rings. And rings.

Finally, I hear a click. The sound of rustling. Then a familiar voice.

"Allô?"

"Chloe? It's Oz! Can you hear me? How are you and Eli doing?"

The connection is awful, full of crackling static. I can barely make out what my wife replies.

"We're fine but…and food is low…and animals keep trying to…please hurry…"

"Chloe, honey," I interrupt, "I can't understand what you're saying. I'm going to hang up. Give Eli a hug for me. I love you both. And…I will hurry. I promise."

I wait for her to answer, but all I hear is more white noise. Then the line goes dead. Which gives me a sudden sinking feeling deep in the pit of my stomach.

My wife and child are under siege in Paris and I'm here in paradise.

I'd better get to work.

CHAPTER 10

MOST MORNINGS, I LIKE to start the day with a shower. Today I feel like taking a dip in the sea, right outside my front door.

I'm standing by the entrance of my wooden villa, gazing out at the crystal water all around me. The sun is just starting to rise, casting vibrant streaks of pink and orange along the horizon.

It's a precious moment of peace before what I know will be another grueling day.

After arriving in Bali yesterday afternoon, our team wasted no time getting down to business. Freitas, Sarah, the other scientists, and I spread out to cover as much ground as we could. We took samples of the water, soil, pollen, and air. We tested the island for unusual patterns of radiation and electromagnetic activity. We dug through mud as thick as tar to collect insects and worms. We waded into a rushing river to net fish and plankton. We even trekked through the punishing jungle in Padangtegal to trap a feisty twenty-two-inch-long macaque. Before we left, Sarah told me to bag a stinking pile of the monkey's dung. I thought she was kidding—or maybe stung by my rejection earlier—but Freitas insisted I obey.

By the time we all made it back to the hotel, well after midnight, I could barely keep my eyes open. I knew the next day would be even more exhausting: the plan was to head further inland into the mountains to capture additional animals to study, including a Komodo dragon and a six-foot Burmese python. I flopped onto the bed the moment I walked in, still wearing my filthy clothes, and fell fast asleep.

But now, thanks to a mix of jet lag and nerves, I'm wide awake at dawn. It's almost 11:00 p.m. in Paris, too late to call Chloe. To clear my head, I decide to take a dip.

I strip down to my boxers and cannonball into the calm sea, as if I were a little kid again at the local pool. I'm surprised by how warm the water feels, like a soothing bath.

I flick my wet hair from my eyes and float on my back at first, letting the gentle current carry me. Then I flip over and use a slow breaststroke to swim farther out.

I glance over my shoulder at the coastline. The swaying palm trees, the quaint villas, the stunning beach—it's like something you'd see on a postcard. I make a mental note to bring Chloe and Eli back here someday, when all this HAC craziness is finally over, for a family vacation. Lord knows they deserve it.

I know I should probably start heading back to my hut, but something beckons me to swim a little farther out.

Big mistake.

Just up ahead, maybe twenty yards in front of me, I spot a rippling, pinkish-purple mass of something underwater heading my way—fast. Thanks to the way the light is being refracted, I can't quite make out what it is. But I have a very bad feeling.

My first instinct says it's a school of angry jellyfish. Toxic ones.

As the giant blob keeps coming toward me, I realize yes, it *is* a school of jellyfish…with some venomous sea snakes mixed in and a few tiger sharks behind it.

Oh, shit!

"Help, help!" I shout as I twist around and start swimming frantically back toward the shore. "Sarah! Dr. Freitas!"

I'm flapping my arms and kicking my legs wildly, as fast as I can move them. I think I might be getting away, but when I steal a glance behind me, the jellyfish, sea snakes, and tiger sharks are even closer.

I thought Bali was supposed to be safe! What the hell is going on?

I keep swimming and screaming, but it's no use. I can feel the water churning behind me as the mad sea creatures close in. And I can see out of the corner of my eye that they've even started to spread out in a semicircle, flanking me on both sides.

My heart is pounding. My mind is racing.

Is this really how I'm going to die?

Then, in the distance, I hear a glorious sound: the low rumble of a ship engine speeding in my direction. As it gets closer, I hear voices, too, calling to me in Balinese.

Thank God, I think—I hope they're not too late.

I feel a stinger pierce my right ankle and a set of fangs chomp down on my left calf. I howl in pain and try desperately to shake the creatures off…as another jellyfish latches onto my shoulder and a second sea snake latches onto my hip.

I writhe and splash, pain coursing through my body, praying the boat gets here fast. The tiger sharks must be mere yards away, circling, preparing to finish me off.

Finally I spot the noisy vessel. It's a local fishing trawler manned by a group of shirtless Balinese men. Three of them dive into the water and paddle over to me…

And as if by magic, the jellyfish, sea snakes, and tiger sharks all swim away.

I'm too stunned and light-headed to make sense of this. But, Jesus, am I thankful.

The fishermen pull me over to their boat and gently lift me aboard. I'm shocked by all the blood I see. Not mine—the *gallons* of it staining the deck.

While I start to triage my throbbing wounds, I can't help but notice the awful conditions of the sea life on board. Filthy tanks full of bloody fish, crammed together like sardines. Blue crabs stuffed into rusty cages, their shells crushed and mutilated. Even an adorable baby dolphin, tangled in a net, struggling to take its last breaths.

I'm beyond grateful to be alive, but appalled by the horror I'm seeing.

And confused by it, too.

Putu, the hotel attendant I met yesterday—he said most Balinese were Hindu vegetarians who revered all animal life. Clearly that isn't exactly true. Judging by the scene on this boat, fish have plenty to fear from Bali's fishermen. That army of sea creatures fled when the fishermen showed up, but they sure as hell had no problem trying to kill *me*. Why?

My head spins. Maybe animals can distinguish among the human race by scent—whether Hindu vegetarians or dangerous predators—and react accordingly.

For now, as I try to catch my breath and tend to my painful snakebites and jellyfish stings, there's only one thing I know for sure.

Bali isn't the HAC-free paradise we thought it was.

CHAPTER 11

*"**IT WAS NOT ANOTHER** of the dreams in which he had often come back; he was really here. And yet his wife trembled, and a vague but heavy fear was upon her."*

Chloe stops reading aloud from *A Tale of Two Cities* and places the well-worn paperback down on her lap, suddenly overcome by emotion.

Charles Dickens wrote those words—about one of the novel's main characters, worried about her husband's safety—in 1859. Yet tonight, for Chloe, they hit painfully close to home. Her mind drifts to Oz, halfway around the world. A "vague but heavy fear" is definitely what she's feeling.

"Mommy, keep reading," says Eli. He's nestled in bed beside her under the covers. It's one of the novels that she and Oz have been reading to Eli, a few pages a night, ever since they were in the Arctic. "Why did you stop?"

"Just lie there, honey. Something tells me you'll fall asleep pretty soon."

Chloe sets down the book, walks to the door, and is about to turn off the light…

When she hears a loud scratching noise coming from outside.

She's used to the occasional sounds of wild animals trying to find their way in, but tonight it's alarmingly loud.

She nervously peels back the bedroom window curtains—and gasps.

Through a crack in the boards between the glass and wrought iron grate she glimpses at least five or six furry, reddish-brown creatures scurrying up the side of the building, tongues dangling out of their mouths, fangs glistening in the moonlight.

She tries to stay calm. She reminds herself how safe she and her family are—relatively speaking—inside this modest Paris apartment, the one in which she grew up. Every door and window has been heavily reinforced and is kept locked practically around the clock. Beyond the fact that all possible entry points had been sealed up, just a few nights ago, after stomping to death a dazed rabid mouse that had managed to crawl in through the shower drain, Chloe even plugged up much of the apartment's plumbing, too.

Still, the sight of this pack of feral animals—dogs? wolves?—scrabbling up the side of her building fills her with quiet dread.

For good measure, Chloe checks the screws securing the iron grate over the window, making sure they're nice and tight. Satisfied, she smooths out the curtain.

"*Bonne nuit,* Eli," she says to her son. "Good night, my love."

He responds with a gentle snore. The boy is fast asleep.

Chloe tiptoes back to the bedroom door, which is suddenly pushed open from the other side. Marielle, her stepmother, is standing at the threshold.

"*Maman?* What is it?"

At first Marielle doesn't speak. She simply blinks, clearly confused.

"I...I'm sorry. I was looking for the bathroom."

Chloe sighs. Looking for the bathroom? She's lived in this apartment for forty years. Clearly her forgetfulness is getting worse. Chloe has suggested they see a doctor, but Marielle has refused. Not that they could get an appointment even if they wanted to. Practically every hospital in the city is strained to capacity treating victims of animal attacks. An old lady with early-stage dementia isn't exactly a top priority.

"It's all right," Chloe says soothingly. "This is Eli's room. My old room, when I was a little girl. Remember? The bathroom is that way. Second door on the left."

"Of course it is," Marielle says, waving her stepdaughter off with a mixture of frustration and embarrassment. But then she adds, with a bashful smile, "And I only had to open every *other* door to find it."

Marielle pads back down the hall. Chloe gives Eli, dozing soundly, a final look. *He deserves a better world than this,* she thinks, turning off the light.

Headed to the kitchen, Chloe suddenly hears vicious growls and violent scratching coming from the other end of the apartment—along with her mother's bloodcurdling screams.

"No, no!" Marielle is shouting. "Chloe, Jean-Luc, help!"

"*Maman!*" Chloe yells back, rushing to find her.

On her way down the hall, she notices that the guest room door is wide open...the pantry door is wide open...and to her horror, *the front door is wide open, too.*

Chloe understands immediately what's happened. In her stepmother's absentminded search for the bathroom, she has done the unthinkable.

She's just let in the animals.

CHAPTER 12

"MAMAN!" CHLOE SHOUTS AGAIN, rummaging frantically around the kitchen for anything she can use to fight back. "I'm coming!"

She uses one hand to grab the first blade she spots, a small paring knife, and the other hand to heave an old frying pan off the stove.

Not the ideal set of weapons, by any means, but they'll have to do.

Chloe rushes toward the gruesome sounds of the struggle emanating from inside the apartment's tiny bathroom. She charges in, desperate to save Marielle's life.

But she isn't at all prepared for the horrifying sight that awaits her.

A pack of feral foxes—the animals Chloe saw earlier climbing up the outside of the building—is literally tearing her elderly stepmother limb from limb.

They're attacking Marielle ravenously, ripping her bloody nightgown to shreds, wrenching whole chunks of flesh from her body as she cries and struggles and screams.

Chloe roars with anger and snaps into action.

She clobbers the nearest fox square on the head with the heavy pan, feeling his skull crunch inward from the impact like a hardboiled egg. She hits another fox, then sinks the paring knife into the furry back of a third.

A fourth fox, realizing Chloe is both a threat and a meal, turns on her, leaping up and clamping his jagged teeth into her thigh.

Chloe yelps in pain but manages to pierce her knife straight into the animal's eyeball, lodging it deep in the socket, before forcefully prying the creature off.

She pummels the animal with the pan, again and again, until finally it dies.

"Maman!" she yells, kneeling beside her horrendously disfigured stepmother, nearly slipping on the blood-soaked tile floor.

Marielle is mercifully slipping into unconsciousness. She reaches a trembling hand toward her stepdaughter's face and whispers, in a haze, "Chloe…*ma petite fille*…my sweet girl…"

Then her hand falls to her side. Her last breath escapes her lungs.

Chloe is too shocked to cry. Too staggered to make any sound at all.

But with so much adrenaline still pulsing through her veins, she is *not* too stunned to take action.

"Eli! *Papa!*" she screams, rushing out of the bathroom into the hallway.

She finds her father standing there in his underwear, shaking like a leaf.

"Your stepmother…I heard such terrible noises. Is she…?"

"Yes, Papa. She's—she is dead." Jean-Luc takes a step toward the bathroom to look for himself, but Chloe stops him. "Don't."

Jean-Luc looks past Chloe, into the front hallway, and his eyes grow wide.

Chloe turns around—and sees three pit bulls trotting into the apartment through the still-open front door.

"Come on, we have to hurry!" Chloe implores, trying to pull her father along.

But with surprising strength, Jean-Luc resists. He grips his daughter's shoulder tightly and looks her straight in the eye.

"*Non,* Chloe. I am a slow, old man. It is my time. You and Eli—*you* must go."

Chloe is left aghast by her father's command, and by the ultimate sacrifice he is insisting he make for his daughter and grandson. She wants to argue with him, *plead* with him, to reconsider, but she knows his mind is made up.

"I love you," is all she says, then turns and dashes back to Eli's room.

She makes it inside and slams the door shut behind her—just moments before she hears this second wave of animals begin brutally mauling her frail father.

She finds Eli awake in bed, cowering under the blankets, crying. Chloe rushes over and sweeps him into her arms.

"Eli, it's okay, sweetie, Mommy's here. We have to go!"

But how? Not through the front door: the apartment is now crawling with wild animals. But not through the window, either: even if she could break the boards, that metal grate is bolted on tight.

Are they trapped?

No. Chloe gets an idea.

She flings open the closet and pushes aside some of her old childhood clothes that are still hanging there, revealing a small trapdoor: a dumbwaiter, dating back to the turn of the century, when the apartment building was one single luxury home and Chloe's bedroom was part of the servant's quarters. She discovered this odd historical remnant as a girl and treated it as a secret cubby, a hiding spot for dolls and diaries.

Now, as she pries off the wooden plank she nailed over it only a few days earlier, she hopes it just might save their lives.

She opens the squeaky door and orders Eli to wiggle inside first. "I know you're scared," she says. "I am, too. But I'll be right behind you. You can do it!"

The boy bravely obeys. Chloe squeezes in after him and the two carefully climb down this dark, dusty chamber, using ledges and splintery boards.

They finally make it to the ground floor—a former kitchen converted long ago into a garage. Chloe kicks open the trap-door and she and Eli crawl out.

The space is cluttered and dark, and Chloe can't find the light switch. Taking Eli's hand, she gropes her way to the man-ual sliding garage door. She strains to pull it open a few feet, and together mother and son slip out onto the sidewalk—the first time either has stepped foot outside the apartment build-ing in almost two weeks.

Chloe's heart is thumping wildly as she scans the eerily abandoned, trash-strewn Paris streets. The occasional animal growl or human scream echoes in the distance.

Now what?

Her parents are both dead. Their apartment, her only refuge, is overrun with feral animals. Her husband is God knows where, returning God knows when. Her son is cold, tired, terrified. And so is she.

Choking back tears, Chloe scoops Eli into her arms and does the only thing she can think of.

She runs.

CHAPTER 13

"IT DOESN'T MAKE ANY damn sense!" Freitas exclaims, hurling a giant binder full of molecular charts and data graphs clean across our plane's cabin.

He's steaming mad, but Sarah and the other scientists and I are so exhausted we barely react. It feels like we've been discussing our recent findings and debating our hypotheses—make that our *lack* of recent findings and our *flawed* hypotheses—since the moment we left Bali. Hours ago.

We're not far from our next destination. But we're still light-years away from any kind of solution to the animal crisis.

"We should have stayed in Bali longer," Sarah says, "like I wanted to. Those jungles, that sea—they're home to thousands of different species. We ran experiments on less than one percent of them."

"That's still dozens of different animals," I say. "Not all of which, let me remind you"—I hold up my arms, showing some painful jellyfish stings and bandaged sea snake bites—"were as 'friendly' as we were led to believe."

Indeed, my own unfortunate episode in the water turned out to be just the beginning. Over the next few days, two other groups from our team fended off sudden animal attacks. First a swarm of so-called gliding lizards. Then a stampede of banteng, a breed of wild cattle. Can't say I'm sorry I missed it.

"We sequenced their DNA," I continue. "We ran brain scans. Conducted autopsies. If I remember correctly," I add sarcastically, "*somebody* even collected and ran tests on monkey droppings. And we found *nothing* out of the ordinary. No unusual radiation or electromagnetic patterns, either. No strange chemicals in the water or magic fairy dust in the air. Nil. *Nada.* We spent ninety-six hours in Bali and all I got was this lousy t-shirt. And, oh, yeah—I almost lost my life."

The other government scientists on board all mumble in agreement. Sarah folds her arms. She won't concede anything to me—I think out of spite. But she doesn't *disagree* with me, either. Which I guess I'll take as a sign of progress?

Freitas checks his watch and pensively rubs his beard. I've known the guy less than two weeks, but I'd swear there's more gray hair in it now than when I met him.

Sensing a lull in our endless discussion, I take out my international satellite phone and dial Chloe again in Paris. One of the perks of traveling on a government plane is that you get to use your government cellphone during the flight.

Not that it does me any good at the moment.

I've been calling the Tousignant apartment hourly since we took off, but no one's answering. Which happens again this time. The landline rings and rings, and then the answering machine kicks in. I've already left a few increasingly nervous messages, so I hang up. Just for the heck of it, I dial Chloe's old American cellphone number, which we shut off after moving to the Arctic. I'm not surprised when I get an automated message telling me the number's no longer in service, but it still feels a little ominous.

I close my eyes for a moment, desperate to calm my nerves and push the creeping fear I'm feeling out of my mind. There must be a simple explanation, right? Maybe the neighborhood's phone lines are down. Maybe the power's out. Maybe Chloe and her family left for an even safer location. Or maybe...maybe...

I guess I dozed off there for a little while, because when I open my eyes again I see Freitas, Sarah, and the others all buckling their seat belts for landing.

I look out my window. We're coming up fast on our destination: Johannesburg. A sprawling metropolis flanked by an enormous nature preserve to the south and teeming slums to the west.

We've come here, Freitas explained before takeoff, because unlike Bali, it's a major urban area facing a markedly *high* rate of animal attacks, and he wants us to conduct a series of parallel tests and experiments for comparison.

But I'm not sure I buy that. In fact, I think there's something he's not telling us.

Jakarta, Bangkok, Manila, Sydney—these are all big cities that *also* have high rates of animal attacks, and each is a much shorter trip from Bali than Johannesburg is. Flying all the way across the Indian Ocean to South Africa took us nearly fifteen hours. Freitas knows one of the most precious resources we have in our hunt for a solution to HAC is time. He wouldn't waste it without a very good reason.

Still peering out my window, I think I've just spotted it.

A massive, swirling flock of birds—they look like white-backed vultures, or maybe falcons—seems to be heading right for us like an airborne tornado.

Some of the other scientists notice it, too, and like me are gripping their armrests, bracing for an attack…

That never comes. Instead, as the birds pass close by our plane, I realize a few of them don't look like any I've ever seen before—except maybe in *Jurassic Park*.

Did I just glimpse some scales? Beaks lined with sharp teeth? Reptilian heads?

If I didn't know better, I'd say some of them looked positively…*prehistoric*.

CHAPTER 14

I'M HANGING ON WITH all my might as our convoy of SUVs weaves along this rough, badly potholed road. Our vehicle is topping forty, maybe fifty miles per hour, tossing us around inside like ice cubes in a cocktail shaker.

But I don't want to slow down one bit. In fact, I wish we'd speed up.

We're cruising along Bertha Street, a major downtown Johannesburg thoroughfare, and the chaos outside is some of the most appalling I've seen.

Gray-furred vervet monkeys are swinging from power lines, hooting and screeching. Leopards are leaping from abandoned car to abandoned car. A flock of goshawks is circling and cawing overhead. Giant baboons are scaling darkened skyscrapers. Military Humvees are overturned, hastily built barricades sit abandoned. Bloody, rotting human carcasses litter the streets. The few living souls I spot are crouched on terraces and rooftops, firing off high-powered rifles at any and all creatures they can—the final holdouts, desperately defending their homes, refusing to surrender.

The entire city center of Johannesburg has been overrun by wildlife. The phrase "concrete jungle" suddenly has a whole new meaning. I'm speechless.

Freitas is sitting in the front seat. "This place," he says with a wry smirk, "is a little different from Bali, wouldn't you agree?"

As if on cue, a vervet monkey drops down onto our windshield and starts frantically scratching at the glass.

Sarah recoils, but I'm transfixed. For a brief moment, I see a slight resemblance in him to Attila, a lovable chimpanzee I rescued from a medical testing lab years ago and kept as a pet when I lived in New York City. I cared for that little guy deeply…until he turned to the animal dark side, like all the rest.

"Get off of there, you damn stupid ape!" barks Kabelo, our local driver and guide. I can't help but snicker at what I assume is an accidental similarity to Charlton Heston's famous line in *Planet of the Apes*. Kabelo turns the windshield wipers on high and swerves back and forth a few times until the primate is thrown from the car.

"Yeah," I respond now to Freitas. "Ain't exactly another tropical paradise, that's for sure."

Sarah, sitting next to me, folds her arms. "I don't know how in the world you expect us to collect any specimens here," she says, an unusual level of agitation in her voice.

Not that I blame her. If this is what the city core looks like, I don't want to imagine what's happening in the nature preserve on the outskirts, which is where we're headed.

"The doctor makes a good point," I say. "There are just too many animals running around. Trying to capture and autopsy even one of them—that's suicide."

"Kabelo, be careful!" Freitas shouts as our SUV narrowly avoids getting T-boned by a charging stampede of big-horned Cape buffalo.

Our fearless leader takes a deep breath, then turns around to face Sarah and me and the other scientists in our vehicle. I can tell there's something on his mind, something he's debating whether or not to share.

"You're right. Trying to trap one of these animals? That *is* suicide. Thankfully, that's not why we've come to South Africa."

My told-you-so internal celebration is brief. I start to get nervous. Why *are* we here?

"There have been rumors," Freitas continues, "that the…'affliction'…has started spreading. To *humans*."

Huh? I glance around the vehicle at Sarah and the others. This is clearly the first time any of *us* are hearing that rumor.

"There have been unconfirmed sightings," Freitas says, "matching similar classified reports from elsewhere around the world—which I've convinced Washington to suppress—of a group of rabid individuals living in the Suikerbosrand Nature Reserve. Locals now consider *them* to be the most dangerous creatures in the area."

Freitas pauses solemnly. Then adds: "We're here to capture one. And prevent this global epidemic from entering an even more devastating phase."

My jaw is literally hanging open. Sarah and the others are stammering.

What the hell is this guy talking about?

For the past umpteen years, the planet has been battling HAC, Human-*Animal* Conflict. It's *animals* whose behavior has been going haywire, thanks to the abundance of petroleum-derived hydrocarbons in the environment being chemically altered by cellphone radiation waves. It's *animals* who have been rising up and attacking innocent people because human scents have been chemically altered, too, and are now perceived as attack pheromones. And it's animals—and *only* animals—who are susceptible to this because *Homo sapiens* lacks the highly sensitive vomeronasal organ almost all other creatures possess that detects airborne pheromones in the first place.

This isn't just some personal hunch of mine. It's *the* accepted theory about the animal crisis within the mainstream scientific community—and it has been for quite some time. It's been tested and duplicated in labs around the world.

Now we're talking about Human-*Human* Conflict? No. No way. It's anatomically impossible. Absurd. The fact that we're even chasing after this urban legend at all is a ridiculous waste of time and resources. If it's true, yes, of course, it would upend our entire understanding of what's been going on. But it *can't* be. Right?

"I understand this is a lot to process," Freitas says. "And frankly, I'm praying that the rumors turn out to be false. But you can understand why the government insisted we come and find out for certain. Because if the stories *are* correct, and if it spreads…"

He trails off and shakes his head. The doomsday scenario he's alluding to—millions, maybe billions of *people* suddenly turning on each other like vicious beasts—is too horrifying to even say out loud.

Through my window I see we've reached the outskirts of the city. The buildings are beginning to thin out and the landscape is looking more verdant.

Soon we'll be arriving at the nature preserve, so I take out my satellite phone and try calling Chloe and Eli in Paris one final time.

It's not that I won't have service inside the park. It's that apparently, I'll have my hands full trying to track and tranquilize a goddamn feral human being.

The line rings and rings. I've been calling for hours now and there's still no answer. Even for an optimist like myself, it's getting harder and harder not to worry.

Not just about my family. About the future of the human race.

CHAPTER 15

WE'VE BEEN TREKKING ALONG this jungle trail for less than fifteen minutes and already I'm drenched with sweat.

Kabelo and Dikotsi, and a few other local guides are at the head of our group, hacking away at vines and tree limbs with huge machetes to help clear our path. Still, the underbrush is dense and uneven. We're all lugging heavy gear and carrying firearms. The midday African sun is directly overhead, beating down on us without mercy.

Freitas puts a pair of high-powered binoculars to his eyes, awkwardly shifting the McMillan M1A assault rifle slung over his shoulder. The man may be a brilliant scientist, but he's clearly not very comfortable toting such a bulky weapon.

To be fair, neither am I. Especially since mine has a bayonet.

"Remember," Freitas says, addressing the team. "These are *people* we're after. Not animals. We have no idea how the sickness will have affected them. Whether they'll be savage or intelligent. Whether they'll attack unarmed or with weapons. Whether they—"

"Oh, give it a break, doc!" I exclaim. "I'm sorry, but I just can't listen to this nonsense. We're facing a serious global crisis here, and you're making us hike through a dangerous jungle in search of the living dead? This is nuts!"

"I don't disagree, Oz," Freitas replies. "After the order came in, believe me, I pushed back. But when President Hardinson calls you herself, it's not easy to say no."

Jesus. I've learned by now that Freitas isn't a very good actor. From his expression, I think he's telling the truth. So the *White House* thinks there's a real chance HAC might have spread to humans. Maybe it's not just a dumb rumor after all.

"Fine," I say. "Let's assume these feral humans really do exist. How do we possibly explain it—scientifically? We'd have to throw out the entire pheromone theory."

"Not necessarily," says Sarah. She's blotting her glistening forehead with a bandana. I've forgotten how hot she looks when she's, well…hot.

"*Yes* necessarily," I reply. "HAC is caused by animals misinterpreting human scents as attack pheromones, which triggers aggressive behavior. And they detect those pheromones through the VNO gland at the base of their nasal cavity. A gland that human beings don't possess."

"You're saying humans aren't affected by pheromones at all, Oz? Come on."

"Despite what the makers of Axe body spray might have you believe," I answer, "the scientific jury is still out on that one."

"Precisely," says Freitas. "Perhaps we perceive them in a different way. Perhaps these feral humans aren't using their olfactory organs at all. Maybe they're absorbing pheromones through mucous tissue in their lungs."

"Right, like how nicotine is absorbed from smoking," says Sarah. "Simple."

I exhale a long sigh—and suddenly can't help but wonder what scary, invisible airborne particles might have just entered my bloodstream. I hate to admit it, but Sarah and Freitas have the beginnings of a decent working theory. I just pray it's not needed.

"All right," I concede. "Maybe it's possible. But that still doesn't explain—"

"*Gevaar, gevaar!*" shouts one of our guides, suddenly dropping his machete and whipping out his Desert Eagle handgun. I don't speak Afrikaans, but I understand exactly what he's saying. *Danger*.

Our whole team freezes, and we scramble to ready our weapons.

Something is rushing frantically through the dense bushes to our left. I can't make out what—or *who*—it is, but it's heading right for us, fast.

Kabelo raises his rifle and unleashes a volley of shots in their direction.

"Don't shoot!" Freitas yells, grabbing Kabelo's gun. "We need them alive!"

"I need *me* alive more!" he huffs, shaking off Freitas's grip.

"There may not be many of them," Freitas pleads. "And they are your countrymen. Please, at least hold your fire until we see what they—"

"They're jackals!" I shout, almost relieved to glimpse some furry paws and pointy snouts through the leaves, instead of human hands and heads. "Let's take 'em out!"

I start shooting my Armalite AR-10 first, and the rest of the team quickly follows suit. We're bombarding the underbrush with bullets, but it's impossible to see how many jackals we've hit—or how many in the pack are still charging at us.

The remaining animals—about five or six of them—finally

burst out of the vegetation, all yipping and frantically snapping their sharp jaws. They're fast as hell and impossible to hit, even by over a dozen men and women with semiautomatic weapons.

Three jackals get close enough to attack. Dr. Chang gets a big chunk of his leg bitten off by one before stabbing it to death with a bowie knife. A second jackal lunges at Kabelo, who crushes its head with his rifle.

A final jackal leaps up directly at me—but I shoot it, midair, and it's dead before it hits the ground.

We all take a moment to catch our breath and regroup. Chang's injury is much more than a flesh wound, but he'll survive.

I wipe off the jackal blood that splattered onto my face when I shot the animal from such close range. If I'd missed? I wouldn't have much of a face *left*.

Then another thought enters my head. An even grimmer one.

If a pack of three-foot-long rabid jackals almost managed to kill us...just imagine what a pack of feral humans could do.

CHAPTER 16

CHLOE STEPS OUT INTO the wet Paris afternoon, holding Eli in her arms. She had hoped the rain might have let up by now, but the day is getting late and it's still coming down in buckets.

Screw it, Chloe thinks, draping a slimy plastic trash bag over her and her son's heads. She'd rather get a little wet than be out on the street after dark.

And they have a hell of a lot of ground to cover.

It feels like a lifetime ago, but it was only last night that she and Eli barely made it out of her parents' apartment building alive. She'd flagged down a gendarmerie Jeep, but there was little the exhausted soldiers could do to help. They gave her directions to the nearest emergency government shelter, only a few kilometers away, but warned it was already filled to twice its intended capacity.

It wasn't worth the risk. Chloe ducked inside the first suitable place she saw—an abandoned bakery—and hunkered down with Eli for the night.

Using napkins and pastry boxes as tinder, she started a small fire—not just for warmth, but in hopes that the flames would help hide her and her son's scents from any nearby creatures. Chloe also found a few ancient mille-feuille pastries still in the cracked display case, which she shared with Eli as a little treat.

They were hard as rocks but, given the circumstances, tasted absolutely *delicious*.

Early the next morning, the rain came. Chloe considered staying inside the bakery, where it was nice and dry, but decided against it.

Oz would likely be calling the apartment to check in, and he would grow sick with worry when no one answered. Chloe knew she had to let her husband know that she and Eli were all right. She'd memorized his satellite phone number, thankfully, but how could she—

No. First things first. Chloe had to get somewhere safe. That was the priority.

But where? She racked her brain. Government shelters were bursting at the seams, and she'd heard horror stories about the conditions inside. She still had a few old friends and distant relatives in the city, but no way of contacting them or even learning if they were alive—let alone if they'd take her and Eli in. She could try to get ahold of Oz, but even if he pulled every string he could at the highest levels of the American government, an evacuation would take too long.

There *was* one other option.

About a week ago, Chloe had overheard her stepmother speaking with a neighbor, a middle-aged political science professor named Pierre. He'd heard from a colleague that a few hundred people had built a shelter, or a fortified commune, at Versailles—not inside the famous palace itself but somewhere close by. It was open to all and apparently safer, cleaner, and better run than any government one.

Chloe has no idea whether this magical place really exists or not. But the Batterie de Bouviers, an old fortification built in the 1870s, is a few miles from the palace gardens and would make the perfect spot for it.

Versailles is over ten miles from the center of Paris, roughly where she is now. That's a grueling hike with a four-year-old on a perfect day. On a cold and rainy one, with feral animals stalking the streets? Forget it.

Chloe knows she might be insane for putting any faith at all into this too-good-to-be-true rumor. But, really, what other choice does she have?

Pulling the trash bag around the two of them like a shawl, Chloe sets out with Eli.

In the waning daylight, she certainly feels safer than she did last night. But she can finally see in full, stark relief just how hellish things have gotten in her beloved city. The shattered storefronts. The overturned cars and buses. The gutters flowing with human blood.

Clutching Eli even closer, she turns onto Boulevard Saint-Michel. Once one of the city's scenic tree-lined streets, it now looks like a deserted war zone.

Chloe is hurrying along the sidewalk, staying close to the buildings for cover…when she hears something. A low rumbling. Or growling. Speeding toward her.

She tenses. She says a silent prayer. She looks up.

But it's not an animal.

It's a gray Citroën Jumper, a boxy commercial van. It screeches to a halt beside her and its rear doors fly open.

"Mes amis!" says one of the young women inside, flashing Chloe a clownlike grin and holding what looks like a medieval dagger. "My friends! You must get off the street. It is not safe. Come with us, quickly!"

Like the other seven or eight people crammed inside the van, this woman's head is completely shaved, and she's wearing a flowing brown robe tied at the waist.

Chloe stands completely frozen—terrified, but trying desperately not to look it. She's never seen these freaks before in her life.

But she knows exactly who they are.

"You are…the Fraterre?" she asks nervously.

"*Oui!*" the woman happily exclaims. "Now hurry, we don't have much time!"

The Fraterre, short for La Fraternité de la Terre. The Brotherhood of the Earth.

Chloe has heard rumors about this group, an eccentric cult—part Greenpeace, part Heaven's Gate. It sprung up across France over the past few months in bizarre, quasi-spiritual *solidarité* with Mother Nature. No one knows much about them other than that they're a bunch of nut jobs who think HAC is a divine blessing. They have allegedly assaulted and even killed those who disagree with them.

And now a van full of armed Fraterre cultists are ordering Chloe and Eli to get in.

Chloe stutters. Her mind is racing. What about the fortification near Versailles? What about calling Oz? Then again, maybe this group can actually help keep her safe—at least for the time being?

"*Merci beaucoup,*" she says at last with a big, fake smile.

She climbs inside, Eli in her arms, her heart jackhammering in her chest. The doors are slammed shut and the van peels out.

"Where are we going?"

CHAPTER 17

MY BACK AND KNEES are killing me. Sweat is stinging my eyes. What I wouldn't give right now just to stand up straight for a few seconds and blot my brow.

But I know that would probably be a death wish.

Freitas, Sarah, the other scientists, and I have been crawling through the underbrush on our hands and knees for what feels like ages. We've been moving slowly, deliberately, painstakingly. We've been careful not to make a sound or get too close.

Why?

We've been following a small band of *feral humans*.

Yup. We found the bastards.

And they're freaky beyond belief.

Freitas spotted them first, though he didn't even realize it. After Chang's jackal bite, two of our guides offered to lead the scientist out of the jungle to get first aid. Less than ten minutes later, Freitas noticed a group of people out in front of us. Initially he thought they were members of our team who'd somehow gotten lost. He nearly called out to them—until I literally cupped his mouth with my hand, grabbed his high-powered binoculars, and took a look for myself.

All I managed to croak was, "Mother of God."

I counted five of them. Adults. A mix of men and women,

black and white, old and young. They were wearing clothes, normal ones, but dirty and tattered, as if they'd been living in the jungle for weeks. One was carrying a bolt-action rifle, the others a mix of knives, shovels, and other tools. They were walking upright but slightly hunched over, their arms swinging unnaturally, almost gorilla-like.

They looked, in a word, *primal*.

Even from so far away, I could see a scary deadness in their expressions. They were regular humans on the outside. But was there any soul left inside?

Freitas immediately gave the order for all of us to crouch down and follow. We crawled behind them, maybe fifty or sixty yards, tracking as the group lumbered deeper and deeper into the nature preserve.

At one point I asked Freitas in a whisper what our plan was. How much longer would we be stalking these "people"? How would we ever capture one? He admitted he didn't know yet. For now, he just wanted to observe them in their natural habitat.

Yeah, right. What we're looking at? Nothing "natural" about it.

Fine, I thought. Let's see where this goes. Let's see where they lead us.

Let's see what they do next.

That was almost half an hour ago. We're still crawling along after them, inching our way through the prickly vegetation. We pass a babbling brook. My hands and face are getting rubbed raw, but I push on....

When suddenly the five feral humans freeze. They prick up their ears. Their senses switch to high alert. They raise their weapons.

I trade nervous glances with Freitas and Sarah. Do they know we're behind them? Have they picked up our scent? Are we in danger?

The "leader" of the pack grunts something, and in a flash the five humans start running—*away* from us, farther into the jungle.

"Go, go!" Freitas commands. "After them!"

Too surprised to argue, we all leap to our feet and pursue. But, damn, are those rabid humans fast! Even our African guides are having trouble keeping up.

At last we reach the crest of a small hill. Gasping for breath, I spot the five humans in the valley below—and I gesture wildly at Freitas, Sarah, and the others to hang back and duck down again.

I've just realized why they've been running.

They're *hunting*.

But not us. Their target is a kudu, a grayish-white antelope they've managed to separate from its herd and surround.

I expect the animal to start attacking the humans any second. But instead, it nervously leaps and prances every which way, looking for an escape. Carefully, the lead human raises his rifle and fires a single shot—striking the antelope's hind leg. The creature falls to the ground, crippled but very much alive.

Now things *really* start to get weird.

The five humans encircle the animal and all place their hands around its neck. Slowly they tighten their grip, choking the helpless antelope as it wheezes and struggles, finally exhaling its last breath.

In unison, the humans bow their heads. They release a low, guttural moan, almost as if in prayer. I'm reminded of the waiter in Bali, who attributed the island's lack of animal attacks to the Hindu respect for all life.

Then they bare their teeth and sink them directly into the antelope's flesh.

They viciously tear through its fur, exposing the crimson muscle tissue and tendons underneath. They rip jagged chunks off with their mouths, like a pride of lions eviscerating a fresh kill. They gulp down the raw meat whole, without chewing. Their mouths and cheeks are covered in blood.

Freitas, Sarah, the scientists, our guides, and I watch this feeding frenzy with a mix of disbelief and revulsion. It's like something straight out of a horror movie, except it's happening maybe three hundred feet in front of us.

"Still want to try to capture one of 'em?" I whisper to Freitas.

He just flashes me a grim look. Of course the answer is yes.

But we both know the task just got a whole lot scarier.

Before long, the antelope carcass has been reduced to virtually a skeleton. The feeding is slowing down in speed and intensity. The meal is almost over.

We're all holding our breath. Waiting to see what these wild humans will do next…

When a digital beeping noise suddenly pierces the jungle air.

Jesus Christ—my satellite phone is ringing!

The humans all turn and look up in our direction. The leader lets out a deep, furious roar.

They've spotted us.

CHAPTER 18

"DON'T SHOOT!" FREITAS DESPERATELY implores, but it's no use. He's lost all control over our group. It's every man for himself.

And it's absolute bedlam.

Many team members have already run off, but a few guides and scared scientists stay behind. They use our elevated position to their advantage and let loose a torrent of gunfire at the feral humans in the valley below as they scatter in all directions.

I watch two of the humans get hit. But the other three don't—and quickly disappear into the dense foliage, dashing back up the hillside in our direction.

"Come on!" I yell to Sarah and Freitas as I turn around to run back the way we came. I see Sarah is on board, but Freitas is pointing somewhere else.

"I think if we cut across the hill, we can probably make it back—"

"Sorry, doc. You're on your own."

I'm already on the run for my life. I'm not about to risk getting lost on top of that.

I start hauling ass back through the jungle. Branches scrape my arms and face as I whip past. All around me I hear gunshots ringing and screams echoing.

Sarah's sprinting just to my left. But after I pass the bubbling creek I remember crawling past minutes earlier, she's suddenly disappeared. I've lost her.

"Sarah?" I call, slowing down the tiniest bit.

She doesn't respond. But I do hear *another* voice.

This one is deep and scratchy. With a South African accent. It comes from close by, but it somehow sounds distant. Haunting.

"We…are…human!"

Holy shit!

I do a quick 360-degree spin, searching for the source. My eyes dart everywhere, but I don't see a soul.

"Hello?" I shout. "Where are you? *Who* are you?"

"Do not…be afraid! We…will not…hurt you. Please, listen… to me!"

I turn now toward the direction of the voice and aim my rifle at it—not easy to do with my adrenaline pumping and my hands trembling.

For the briefest moment, I wonder if maybe this feral human is being honest. The way they ate that antelope was savage, but how they killed it was almost reverent. Maybe they do have respect for human life. Maybe they *aren't* vicious killers like the rest of the animal kingdom. Maybe we pre-judged them too quickly. Maybe—

"Arrrrrgh!"

One of the males lunges out of the tree line and charges at me, baring his teeth and brandishing a pickaxe.

I squeeze the trigger and pepper his chest with rounds. But he keeps coming, swinging his axe wildly.

At the last possible moment I crouch down and spear my bayonet up and into his chest—piercing him clean through the heart.

He releases his axe and flails. He gurgles blood. Finally he goes limp, and I shove him to the jungle floor.

"You…you sneaky son of a bitch!" I shout at his bloody corpse.

I'm livid. I can't believe I doubted for even one millisecond that he wanted to kill me. These savages are *worse* than the animals. They have tools at their disposal. I don't just mean guns and pickaxes. They have language. Cognition. *Trickery.*

I take off running again, equal parts furious and fearful. I yell team members' names—Sarah, Freitas, Kabelo, and some of the others—but I get no response.

I keep moving. I hope I'm still headed in the right direction, but I'm starting to feel light-headed. All the trees and shrubs are starting to look alike.

"Help, help me!" I hear a woman scream, from somewhere not too far away.

That voice is one I instantly recognize: Sarah's.

I switch course and sprint toward it. Not wanting to give up the potential element of surprise, I don't yell back.

And I'm very glad I don't. When I finally see her, she's being chased by a lone female feral human holding a pitchfork—who is quickly gaining.

I raise my rifle but can't get a clean shot, so I loop around to outflank her primal pursuer.

As soon as they reach a clearing, I plow into the woman like a linebacker and tackle her to the ground.

We roll around in the underbrush together, grappling viciously. For such a small woman, she's strong as an ox.

Grunting and straining—employing some of the moves I

learned on my JV high school wrestling team—I finally manage to flip her on her back and pin her down.

She starts speaking to me in that same eerie, scratchy voice the man had, in an African language I don't understand. I assume she's begging for her life. Or trying to trick me again somehow. *Not this time.* I swing my rifle around from behind my back and position the bayonet blade inches from her throat…

"Oz, don't!" yells Sarah, rushing over to me. "Remember? We need her alive!"

Damnit. She's right. After all that talk of how we were going to trap a feral human, I've just done it by accident. Still, staring into this woman's beady, almost ghostly eyes, the desire to end her miserable life is overwhelming. But I resist.

"Grab her legs," I order Sarah. "Until we can find the others."

"You mean us?"

I look over to see Dr. Freitas, Kabelo, and many others hurrying toward us.

They practically pile onto the thrashing woman, helping me restrain her. I'm grateful for the assistance—she's incredibly strong.

"Is everyone all right?" I ask Freitas, still trying to catch my breath.

"Dr. Langston…he didn't make it. His death was…ugly. And our guide Dikotsi was mauled pretty badly. Some of the others are tending to him now."

I ease myself off of the feral woman and help flip her onto her stomach, allowing Kabelo to zip-tie her hands. Freitas and the others just stare at her, seemingly numb.

"Very well done, Oz," he says, patting my shoulder. "We've got what we came for. I'll call our pilot and tell him we're ready to fly."

"Really, now," I say skeptically. "And how are you gonna do that?"

Kabelo looks up at me and flashes a crooked grin.

"The white man forgets *again* he is carrying a cellphone?"

Everyone laughs. Including myself. It feels good. A release. Even the feral woman starts to cackle.

CHAPTER 19

I'M TORN BETWEEN TWO women: the most important one in my life, and quite possibly the most important one in the world.

Getting the captured feral human onto our plane was no easy task. It took five of us—five grown men—just to carry this one petite, flexi-cuffed young woman out of the jungle and back to our waiting vehicles. Unbelievably strong, she kept kicking, thrashing, and trying to bite us the whole time.

She also ranted in her scratchy, eerie voice. One of our guides happened to speak a few words of Tswana, the indigenous language she was using. *"Someone help me!"* he translated. *"I am a person, not a wild animal!"*

Technically, I suppose she was correct. But I've worked on the HAC crisis for many years now and have faced down more deadly predators than I can count. And she is by far the most ferocious and terrifying one I've ever seen.

As we finally got the woman secured into one of our SUVs, Dr. Woodruff said, "I just figured out who this pain in the ass reminds me of." He has a wicked sarcastic streak. "Helen, my ex-wife."

Of course, the name stuck.

Our convoy sped back through the mayhem of Johannesburg to the airport. We buckled "Helen" into a seat in the rearmost row of our Boeing C-40 military transport plane, her arms and legs strapped in as if she were in an electric chair. An emergency oxygen mask around her face kept her from biting or spitting.

We got airborne as quickly as we could, and not just because time was of the essence. We all knew that what we were doing—kidnapping an innocent foreign citizen and transporting her overseas against her will—put us in a legal gray area, to say the least.

We'd been flying for nearly thirty minutes before I remembered—in all the chaos and confusion of the past hour or so, I'd completely forgotten about my satellite phone, and the ring that alerted the pack of feral humans to our presence.

When I finally checked it, I saw I had a new voicemail, from a blocked number.

Hearing Chloe's voice, my relief was indescribable—until I listened through to the end.

Sounding remarkably calm, my wife explained how their apartment had been overrun by animals a few days ago. How she and Eli had managed to escape after her father and stepmother were killed. How they'd spent a night in a shelter from the streets but now were safe.

"We'll be staying with some, uh, *friends* for a while," she said. "Friends of the Earth. I can't tell you where exactly. But I also can't wait to see you, Oz. So you can...*hold me in your arms*. Okay, I love you. Bye."

I knew immediately my wife was in trouble.

One night, years ago, "Hold Me in Your Arms," a painfully cheesy 1988 love song by Rick Astley, came on at a bar where Chloe and I were having one of our first official dates. We joked that being forced to listen to such an awful tune on an endless loop would be even worse than an animal attack. Since then, "hold me in your arms" has become a kind of inside joke between us, a code phrase we use anytime something is bad or corny or scary.

Or, in this case, I could only presume, *dangerous.*

My wife wouldn't say those words unless something wasn't right. I'm certain of it. And those "friends of the Earth" she's staying with—who the hell are they? What is she talking about? Why "can't" she say where she is? What is she scared of?

All I know is, I need to find her and Eli right away and get them out of there fast.

"Freitas!" I shout, marching up the aisle to his seat. "We're changing course!"

"What in God's name are you talking about?" he asks. "We're en route to INL."

That would be the Idaho National Laboratory, the federal government's largest research facility with a dedicated biological sciences unit, nestled in the state's secluded eastern desert. There we'll poke and prod Helen and use every known test in existence on her.

"First we're going back to Paris," I say.

I tell him about the voicemail. What Chloe said. The coded message. My gut instinct that something is very wrong. And that even if *I'm* the one who's wrong, my wife and son are still all alone in a foreign city overrun by wild animals.

"Oz, we can't go there right now. It's too far out of our way. We've got a feral human on board! Don't you understand that? We have to get her to the lab ASAP."

I can't believe what I'm hearing.

"There is no one in the world more committed to solving this crisis than I am," I fire back, my voice rising. Sarah and some of the other scientists are starting to look over at us. "But you're asking me just to forget about my family? Imagine if it was yours!"

Freitas sighs deeply. "I consider the entire *planet* to be my family."

As a fellow man of science, I know what he means. And I respect it.

But as a husband and father, I think it's absolute horseshit.

"You promised me—*promised*—that if I left the Arctic, came along on this wild goose chase of yours, and helped you people stop HAC once and for all, you'd ensure my family's safety. Remember that?" I'm nearly trembling with rage now. "I'm not *asking* you, Dr. Freitas. I am *telling* you. Before Idaho, we are going to France!"

Freitas rubs his salt-and-pepper beard, clearly torn. Maybe I'm getting through to him. Every eye in the plane is now on us—including Helen's beady, bloodshot ones.

"Oz...I'm sorry. I am. But, no, we simply don't have the time or resources to—"

I slam my hand against the cabin wall—and pull out my sat phone.

"Oh, really? Let's see how fast those resources dry up when word leaks to the press that HAC has started spreading to *people* now, too—and that Dr. Evan Freitas of the U.S. Department of Energy has been personally keeping that information under wraps!"

That's my trump card. I'm not bluffing, either. Hell, I'd give away the codes to the nuclear football if it meant saving Chloe and Eli. And Freitas knows it.

"Fine. But I have a better idea," he says at last. "I'll have the White House send a diplomatic security team from the embassy to find them. Your wife called your government satellite phone, right? That means we can track the location of the call. What would you do alone in Paris anyway, Oz? Let the highly trained men with guns save your family. You're a scientist. We need you in Idaho. To help save the *world*."

I'm steaming mad, but I have to admit, Freitas makes a compelling case. And short of barging into the cabin, there's not much else I can do to redirect our plane.

I slide my sat phone back into my pocket. All I can think about is how badly I want to see Chloe and Eli again. And "hold them in my arms."

CHAPTER 20

AS I HURRY DOWN the movable stairway that's been pushed up against our plane, I cover my mouth and nose with the collar of my shirt. A dust storm is brewing about ten miles away, and the air is starting to swirl with dust and grit.

A fleet of military and government vehicles is on the tarmac of Hill Air Force Base waiting for us: a few tan Jeeps, some black Suburbans, an ambulance, and a giant fluorescent yellow truck emblazoned with INL CRITICAL INCIDENT RESPONSE TEAM.

Sarah and our colleagues and I have barely stepped off the aircraft when a group of federal scientists wearing white full-body hazmat suits scamper aboard.

With Freitas directing them, they soon reemerge with Helen, strapped onto an upright wheeled gurney liked the kind used to transport Hannibal Lecter in *The Silence of the Lambs*. Except this one is covered with a clear plastic quarantine tent, and Helen is screaming and thrashing against her restraints worse than ever.

Even the stone-faced Marines there to protect us betray hints of fear.

After Helen is loaded into the rear of the hazmat truck, Freitas, Sarah, and I are directed to the lead Suburban, where I'm surprised to see a familiar face.

"Look what the feral cats dragged in," says Mike Leahy, extending a meaty hand, the wind tousling his wavy silver hair. A high-ranking section chief with the National Security Agency, many months ago he acted as my unofficial government liaison and security escort. And let's just say…we didn't always get along.

I grimace as we shake hands. "Good to see you again, too, Mr. Leahy."

Our convoy is soon tearing down I-15, an endless two-lane desert highway, toward the laboratory. We *should* be able to see the Teton Range rising to the east, but it's obscured by that approaching dust storm.

"I'll be honest with you," Leahy says from the front seat. "When word started to spread back in DC that you were bringing back an infected human? It gave us quite a chuckle. But no one's laughing now."

"I'm glad," I say, "but you're wrong. 'Infected' implies some kind of disease-causing organism. Like bacteria, or a virus. We don't think that's the case here. Our working theory is, Helen's prehistoric-like behavior is somehow being triggered by pheromones, just like the animals' is."

"'Helen?'" Leahy scoffs. "You actually named that thing?"

"That *thing* is a human being," Sarah snaps. "With a *real* name we may never know. Show a little respect."

Damn. I'm liking Sarah more every day.

We ride in silence, and my mind immediately drifts back to Chloe and Eli. Freitas let me listen in as he called President Hardinson's chief of staff from the plane and got his personal guarantee he'd send a team to track down my wife and son in Paris. Now there's nothing else I can do but wait and pray that Chloe and Eli are found.

"That sandstorm sure is moving fast," says Sarah, gesturing out her window.

I look over—and my eyes nearly bug out of my head.

A smaller cloud of dust seems to be rolling across the desert right toward us.

"What…what in the hell…?" Leahy stutters.

As the cloud gets closer, I realize it's not a weather phenomenon at all.

It's a charging herd of wild mustangs. Dozens of them.

CHAPTER 21

"AW, SHIT!" LEAHY EXCLAIMS, grabbing his walkie-talkie. "Be advised, we got horses on our flank!" he barks into it. "All units—shoot and evade, shoot and evade!"

I hang on tight as our Marine driver slams the gas, and the entire convoy swerves off the highway and begins to speed up.

A mustang's top speed can reach over fifty miles per hour, but I'm confident we can outrun them. I feel even more hopeful as I watch other Marines in each of the escort Jeeps slide their M14s out their windows and unleash a torrent of automatic gunfire at the galloping broncos, quickly felling one after another.

But it's still too little, too late.

The remaining horses blast right through our line of vehicles. Glass shatters, metal groans, blood splatters, and bones crunch as thousands of pounds of car and horse collide at highway speed.

Two Jeeps, the ambulance, and one Suburban are toppled immediately, tumbling in different directions.

Then the Suburban I'm riding in is hit—and spins wildly, doing donuts in the desert dirt. Our driver, a female Marine, struggles to regain control as we're thrown around the car's interior like clothes inside a dryer.

"Go, damnit, go!" Leahy yells as the Marine pounds the

accelerator, kicking up more dust behind us. He pulls her sidearm from her holster and fires frantically out the broken window at the mustangs as they regroup and charge again.

We can't get away fast enough. Neighing and snorting, the colts ram us again, head-on, with incredible force, first knocking the Suburban onto its side and then flipping it onto its roof.

Shattered glass rains down around me as I dangle upside down, pinned, suspended by my seat belt. Beside me, Sarah and Freitas are also hanging—it looks like the impact of the crash has knocked them both out cold.

I start to get woozy. Images of Chloe and Eli flash through my mind. If I'm dying, I definitely want those two to be my final thoughts.

My head flops over in the other direction. Through the dusty haze I can make out the yellow hazmat vehicle.

It's also been tipped over and is being pummeled just as mercilessly by multiple mustangs, its white-suited passengers as helpless as we are.

One of the horses manages to bash open the back doors—and the animal suddenly rears up on its hind legs in terror.

Helen is inside, still strapped to her gurney, but the plastic quarantine tent around her is badly torn, and she's screaming and baring her teeth at the horse.

Another mustang notices. Then another, then another. Before long, the colts have regrouped and are charging yet again—*away* from us.

The rest of the horses rejoin the fleeing pack and kick up another massive dust cloud in their wake.

When it finally settles, they're gone.

Wrecked vehicles and bloody horse limbs litter the desert ground. Human moaning wafts through the hot air, along with Helen's feral screams.

CHAPTER 22

MY SNEAKERS AND RUBBER-TIPPED cane squeak against the floor as I hobble down this long, sterile hallway. I'm late to one of our frequent all-hands meetings, thanks to a pit stop at the lab's infirmary to grab a fresh handful of painkillers.

Over the past forty-eight hours, I've been popping those little guys like candy.

I push open the door of the conference room, which isn't easy. The stitches in my shoulder are still sore, and my busted knee still aches. Not to mention my three chipped teeth, sprained wrist, and the cuts and bruises over my whole body.

Seated around the giant marble table, their meeting already in progress, are Freitas, Sarah, Leahy, and most of the other scientists on our team. I say "most" because, between the feral human attack in the jungle and the mustang stampede on the highway, we've lost six colleagues in half as many days.

As I gently, painfully, sink into an empty chair, I have to remind myself how much worse my fate could have been.

Dr. Marilia Carvalho, a neuroscientist from São Paulo, is showing a series of colorful MRI brain scans on the large display screen. Since we arrived at the Idaho National Laboratory, we've been meeting like this often to share our research.

"But as you can see, while the subject's neurological structure is still identical to that of a typical human's, the vast majority of her neurological *activity* is occurring in the cerebellum, the medulla, and the basal ganglia."

"The so-called reptilian brain," Sarah offers. "An anatomical holdover from our days in the wild."

"Precisely. The higher capabilities in Helen's mind, like emotion and reason, have somehow been switched off. She most likely sees us modern humans as threats because her brain is literally functioning like a Neanderthal's."

"But why?" booms Leahy, jabbing his bulky arm cast in the air for emphasis. "That's the question Washington is paying you all to find out!"

"Our working theory is still pheromones, Mr. Leahy," says Freitas, who has two black eyes and a broken nose covered with a thick beige bandage. "We believe that explains why, as soon as the mustangs 'smelled' Helen, they backed off."

"But why is it happening to some folks and not others?" Leahy demands. "Why in some *places* and not others?"

Those are all fair questions. But I have an even more pressing one.

"Why hasn't it shown signs of regressing?" I ask. My colleagues all turn to me quizzically. "And why aren't any of you more afraid of that?

"Think back seven months ago," I continue, "when the president signed that emergency executive order, and all those world leaders joined her, putting a global moratorium on cellphone use, power generation, cars, planes. While it lasted, nearly all electromagnetic radiation was removed from the environment, and animal attacks plummeted—within *hours*. Wildlife started returning to normal."

Nods all around the table. Happy memories from a more hopeful time.

"But look at Helen. She's been in a completely sterile environment, inside a Faraday shield that blocks all electrical signals, for almost two days—and she's as feral as ever! We know how to reverse the effects of HAC on animals. But on people? We're back to square one. Is there an 'antidote,' or is it permanent? Shit, maybe it *is* contagious after all."

For what feels like forever, no one speaks. I'm not happy I just sucked all the air out of the conference room, but I said what I felt I had to.

"It's almost as if...some kind of irreversible physical changes are happening in Helen's brain," Sarah says somberly. "Perhaps we've been approaching it all wrong."

"Perhaps we should hear the latest on everyone's research first," Freitas says, steering the meeting back on track.

And so the rest of the scientists present their latest, equally inconclusive findings. Then the group starts filing out. We all have an enormous amount of work to do.

Shakily, I rise to my feet and begin limping toward the door. Freitas pulls me aside, placing a paternal hand on my back.

"Oz, I have some news," he says, his voice solemn. "About your family."

"The French cellphone number Chloe called from was identified, along with its last location: an abandoned monastery near Chantilly. Apparently some kind of wacko animal rights cult has been squatting there."

I know right away they must be the "friends of the Earth" Chloe cryptically mentioned in her message.

"When agents arrived, the group itself was gone, but local police have some leads as to where they went next."

I can only pray Chloe and Eli are still with them. But I do have additional cause for hope. Among the other items they found in the monastery was our dog-eared copy of *A Tale of Two Cities*.

CHAPTER 23

"PLEASE HOLD FOR THE president of the United States."

I've met Marlena Hardinson many times before. I lectured her and other world leaders in the Cabinet Room of the White House. I even spent a few months living with her, the First Gentleman, and other high-ranking officials at Thule Air Base in Greenland after animals overran Washington and the government was temporarily evacuated.

Still, it's always pretty exciting to get a call from the leader of the free world.

Even when you know she's about to chew you out.

"Dr. Freitas, *Mr.* Oz," President Hardinson says pointedly as soon as she gets on the line, her husky voice brimming with frustration. "Can you please explain to me how an international operation costing over half a million dollars in travel, equipment, and logistical expenses *per day* has yielded no new breakthroughs on the animal crisis—or the growing *human* one—in almost four weeks?"

Freitas and I, along with just a few other colleagues (since most of our team, including Sarah, is still in Idaho hard at work), are back aboard our transport plane, this time flying across the Pacific. We're listening to this unexpected call on an encrypted speakerphone.

Freitas gulps, visibly rattled.

"I see you received the briefing packet we prepared for you, Madam President."

"Which might as well have been a stack of blank pages," she responds. "Except the part about the new human affliction being 'potentially irreversible.' Is that true?"

"We don't know for sure, ma'am," I cut in. "After all, we've only been able to examine one live specimen. That's why we're on our way to—"

"Tokyo. Yes, I'm aware. I spoke with Prime Minister Iwasaki this morning and informed him of your plans. He told me, in confidence, that there have been dozens of reported incidents involving feral humans in recent days, especially in the countryside."

"Have any been picked up yet by the Japanese press?" Freitas asks nervously. "Because if word gets out, we could be looking at a level of global pandemonium—"

"The prime minister, as *we* have, has been doing absolutely everything in his power to *suppress* any reporting on the feral humans. But if there's one thing I've learned after all my years in Washington, you can't keep a lid on bad news forever."

She's right. Especially of this magnitude. What was once just a silly rumor about bands of people "going native" in the game preserves of Africa has quickly proven to be a deadly reality all over, in places as diverse as Finland, South Korea, Egypt, and Japan. With most countries already teetering on the brink of anarchy, local governments have been trying desperately to sweep each incident under the rug. But it's only a matter of time before a cellphone video goes viral showing feral humans mauling innocent ones, and panic is unleashed around the world.

"Godspeed to you all," Hardinson says. "Oh, and Oz. My chief of staff informs me a security team in Paris has been making headway locating your wife and son?"

"Yes, ma'am," I reply. "Thank you again for all your administration's help."

"I'm not doing it out of the kindness of my heart, Oz. As I'm sure you know. We're only trying to save them because *you're* trying to save humankind."

I understand the president's veiled threat loud and clear: succeed, or else.

Seven billion lives are hanging in the balance.

Including the two I cherish most.

CHAPTER 24

OUR MITSUBISHI H-60 TRANSPORT helicopter thunders above the sprawling metropolis that is Tokyo. It's a stunningly dense city that seems to stretch on forever.

But even from such a high altitude, it's clear how badly the endless waves of animal attacks have ravaged Tokyo and its people.

It's midday, but judging by the lack of movement, it seems like huge swaths of the city are without power. Pillars of smoke dot the skyline. I can see flocks of striped sparrowhawks, ready to swoop down on human prey. Herds of something—wild boar?—flow through the streets like living, snorting rivers.

We bank southwest. Gradually the urban density becomes more suburban, then finally lush and mountainous. This tells me we're nearing our destination: semirural Yamanashi Prefecture, one of the most geographically secluded areas in the country.

Our chopper finally descends right in the middle of the main quad of Tsuru University, to the utter shock of the handful of students and faculty brave enough to be outside. Freitas slides open the cabin door and I see an elderly Japanese man hurrying toward us, shielding his face against the rotor wash.

He has a bushy white goatee, thick black-rimmed glasses, and wears a tan suit and red bow tie.

My first thought is, the guy resembles a kooky mashup of Mr. Miyagi and Colonel Sanders. He must be Professor Junichi Tanaka, the highly regarded naturalist Freitas has been in contact with, who'll be leading us into the highlands to trap a second feral human.

Great. At least our guides back in South Africa were strapping young men. If we're attacked with Grandpa here at the helm? I'd say it's pretty much every man for himself.

"Konnichiwa, Freitas-*san,"* Tanaka says, offering a smile and his hand to shake. But Freitas has already started bowing and doesn't notice this. Tanaka returns the bow, just as Freitas rises up and extends *his* hand.

My boss is about to bow again when I grab his shoulder and stop him. Another time, another place, this little culture clash might be amusing. But not now.

"How about we ditch the formalities and get down to business?"

Freitas introduces the members of the skeleton team we've brought with us as Tanaka leads us all to an idling van. One of his graduate students, a twenty-something geeky-looking kid named Yusuke, is behind the wheel.

"First we will take you to the place where they killed all those Americans," Tanaka says, directing us inside the vehicle. "Then we will track them down."

"Uh…come again, mate?" asks Dr. Bret Clement, an immunologist from New Zealand, arching an eyebrow in concern.

This is rather alarming news to me, too.

"You told us there were only *sightings* of feral humans around here, Freitas," I say. "What American dead is he talking about?"

Freitas sighs and looks away. I know immediately he has once again kept his team partially in the dark.

"Mormon missionaries. About five of them. They'd been living in a remote mountain village near Otsuki. One afternoon, they were outside, apparently repairing their well. Neighbors heard screaming. By the time the cops arrived, they were all dead. Police sealed off the scene and claimed the deaths were a religion-motivated murder-suicide. The handful of neighbors who claimed they saw a pack of filthy, screeching Japanese rushing back into the woods? Their stories were deliberately disregarded and buried, by direct order from the Japanese Ministry of Justice."

Unbelievable. I supposed desperate times call for desperate, semi-illegal measures. But still. It's a miracle that word of the human attacks hasn't spread. Then again, the world is in such a state of chaos, maybe not.

Yusuke drives slowly and carefully along the narrow, winding roads that lead up the side of Mount Gangaharasuri, which I appreciate. But I'm mindful of how low the sun has slipped in the sky when we finally arrive at the missionaries' former village.

We exit the van, duck under the blue-and-white Japanese police crime scene tape, and do a quick walkabout of the property. The wooden home is modest, even by local standards. The stone path surrounding the well is covered with dried blood.

"My best guess," Professor Tanaka says, inspecting a topographical map on his iPhone and scanning the dense, hilly forest that starts just a few yards from the house, "is the pack went *that* way. The terrain is still steep, but less so. And in about twenty kilometers, there is a small cave beside a freshwater creek."

"The perfect spot for a prehistoric human settlement," Freitas says. "Let's go."

He starts marching toward the woods, but I hesitate. As do some of the others.

"Are you serious?" I say. "It's already after five o'clock. Sundown's in less than an hour. By the time we reach that cave, it'll be pitch black. Just think about that."

Tanaka answers instead. "Oz-*san,* there is a saying. *Jinsei ga hikari o tsukuru hozon shimasu.* Save a life, and your path will always have light."

"That's a nice proverb and all, Professor, but—"

"Proverb? No. I just made it up. Now let's go."

I can't help but scoff as Tanaka and Yusuke head bravely into the woods. Freitas and the other scientists soon follow. Reluctantly, I do as well.

I'm all for saving a life. Just as long as it doesn't cost my own.

CHAPTER 25

NIGHT FALLS ON MOUNT GANGAHARASURI. In addition to our guns and gear, each member of our ten-man team is using a long-range, super-bright LED tactical flashlight to illuminate the way. But as the last rays of reddish-orange sunlight disappear behind the horizon, a cold and heavy darkness engulfs us for miles.

"We are nearly at the cave," Tanaka says. With his eyes glued to the GPS program on his iPhone, he nearly trips on a hidden rock. "Just a few more kilometers."

"Good. And remember," Freitas says to the rest of us, "if those feral humans *are* there? You all know exactly what to do."

He means that we're to carry out the plan of attack we carefully crafted. We might not have learned much about what's *causing* humans to turn rabid yet, but we're certainly more prepared to sedate and capture one than we were outside Johannesburg. I'm feeling confident but also tingly with nerves.

Suddenly, Tanaka stops in his tracks. He holds up his palm for us to halt.

We all stand still as statues for a moment—until we hear a frantic rustling coming from some distant trees.

Instinctively, many of us, including myself, aim our flashlights in that direction. We can't see anything yet through the branches, but whatever it is, it looks to be about five or six feet tall. It's moving fast. And there's more than one.

Looks like the feral humans are coming for us first.

As we start to spread out and get ready, I slowly reach behind me. Slung over my shoulder are two weapons I can choose from: one lethal, one not. Even though it goes against our plan, my assault rifle is sounding pretty tempting right about now.

The rustling gets louder and louder...until four upright creatures burst from the trees and stagger toward us—not feral humans but Asiatic black bears.

Our group flies into chaos. Tanaka, Yusuke, Freitas, and the scientists all drop their flashlights, scramble for cover, and grope for their *real* weapons.

Thankfully, I already have mine aimed and ready.

I pepper the approaching bears with bullets as best I can in the darkness. I think I've hit at least two, but they keep coming. They roar and prepare to charge, their first target apparently Tanaka...

When just as suddenly, they all stop, retreat, and scamper back into the jungle, whimpering, their tiny tails literally between their legs.

"What the hell was that?" Freitas asks, picking himself up from the ground.

"Same thing that happened with the mustangs on the highway," I say. "Except this time, they didn't get a whiff of a feral human. Just a bunch of normal ones—who I guess should probably try to shower a little more regularly."

With relieved chuckles, our group reassembles and continues on.

We know we're getting close when we start to smell smoke from a campfire. Crouching low, we follow a tributary of the creek Tanaka mentioned. Before long, it leads us directly to the cave.

And inside, there they are.

CHAPTER 26

THERE ARE EIGHT OF them, all squatting in a circle around the glowing embers, feasting on what looks like barbecued squirrel. Their skin and tattered clothes are filthy, their posture apelike. Once again, they seem to eerily straddle the line between human and animal, modern and primitive.

We all spread out in a semicircle, take our positions…and quietly slip on gas masks. Then we each ready the miniature pellet guns we've brought, loaded with rounds of a custom-designed nerve gas containing a mild paralysis agent. To put it simply, our plan is to defeat the feral humans by not fighting them at all.

Freitas gives the signal and we each shoot our little pellets toward our unaware fellow *Homo sapiens*. The odorless gas should take just under thirty seconds to dissipate enough throughout the air, undetected, to begin making them woozy.

Instead, the humans' nostrils flare before the pellets even hit the ground.

Oh, shit, I think, as it suddenly dawns on me: the gas was designed to be odorless to *normal* people. These half-human/half-Neanderthals very likely have a superior olfactory sense. Or at least their brains do, subconsciously.

In which case, we're screwed.

Alerted to a disturbance, the feral humans look around,

spot us, and let out a piercing battle cry. They leap to their feet, snatch up some of the prehistoric-looking weapons lying around the fire—spears, slingshots, tomahawks—and charge at us.

Freitas tries barking orders, but no one can hear him. And none of us cares. We're all scrambling to aim our weapons and stay alive.

One of them lunges at me with a "dagger" made of sharpened flint. She manages to slash my arm, but then I twist, parry, and shoot her in the chest point-blank.

More and more gunfire echoes across the mountain as our team fights back.

I can't see much of the "battlefield" through the fogged visor of my gas mask, but it seems like we've overwhelmed the feral humans with our modern firepower. Realizing they're outgunned, they actually start fleeing back into the jungle.

"You're not getting away that easy!" I shout, my voice muffled by my aspirator.

I pick the closest one to me—a middle-aged male—and charge after him. But he's fast and nimble as a cheetah and scrabbles up the rocky terrain with ease.

Realizing he's getting away, I make a risky decision. I stop running and kneel. I raise my rifle scope to my visor and try to line up the perfect, one-in-a-thousand shot, hoping to hit him in his leg and cripple him.

I squeeze the trigger—and yelp with joy as the man topples over into the brush.

I race over. Bleeding badly from his right thigh, he's now trying to *crawl* away.

But as soon as he sees me, the man stops and starts screeching and thrashing wildly, desperately struggling to punch and claw at me.

Even though he's wounded, watching his frenetic energy is still unnerving.

Which gives me an idea.

I take a few steps back, pull out my pellet gun again, and fire a little canister right at him. It bounces off him harmlessly and then begins releasing its paralyzing nerve gas. The man coughs and wheezes, kicks and writhes, but can't get away fast enough. Within seconds, he starts slowing down, finally collapsing on the jungle floor.

Satisfied that he's no longer a threat, I reapproach—this time readying the pair of handcuffs and leg shackles I've also brought.

I flip the unconscious man over, tug his arms behind his back, and slap on the cuffs, just like they do in the movies.

"You're under arrest," I can't help but say. "You have the right to remain human."

CHAPTER 27

"WHAT THE HELL DO you mean, her brain is *shrinking?*"

Freitas says it, but all of us are thinking it.

We're on our transport plane heading home to Idaho, in the midst of a heated video conference with Sarah, Dr. Carvalho, and the rest of our team back at the lab. Displayed on the other half of the monitor is the latest batch of MRI scans recently conducted on Helen's brain. And from the looks of it, her outer cerebral cortex isn't just inactive. Some of the tissue has actually started dying.

In feral *animals,* nothing like this has ever been seen before. Unless it's some kind of anomaly, it's a troubling development for all kinds of reasons—one giant one in particular.

It might mean whatever's happening to feral humans *can't be reversed*.

We know what's causing *animals* to go wild. And at least in theory, we know how to stop it. But Helen's been in electromagnetic isolation for a week and a half now, and her behavior has only gotten worse. And now her actual *brain* is wasting away? With more reports of rabid human attacks trickling in by the hour, from every corner of the globe, the number of possible permanent cases out there is staggering.

"That's why I think we need to change course," says Sarah,

"and start working to find some kind of antidote. Or vaccine. Right away."

"Agreed," says Freitas. "This thing is spreading faster than any of us could have imagined. Before long, we could be talking about hundreds of thousands or maybe millions of infected humans—all lacking anatomically correct human brains."

"Don't be absurd," says Dr. Tanaka, who's flying with us to the United States to help handle the rabid Japanese man I captured in the jungle. "There is still so much about this affliction we do not know. To attempt to formulate a cure so prematurely is a reckless waste of time!"

Clearly Tanaka feels very passionately about this. I notice his brow is glistening, his cheeks are ruddy, and he's digging his nails deep into the faux-leather armrest.

But as the discussion continues, I can't help but zone out. For one thing, I'm exhausted. Trekking miles up the foothills of Mount Fuji and fighting off a pack of prehistoric humans can really take it out of you.

But I'm also a little light-headed with anticipation, a welcome change from dread. Because in less than twelve hours, I'll be seeing Eli and Chloe.

I got the call on my sat phone just as we were boarding in Tokyo. It came from a 202 number—a Washington, DC, area code—that I didn't recognize: the personal cellphone of President Hardinson's chief of staff.

"Mr. Oz, I wanted to tell you myself as soon as I heard. We found your family."

I nearly broke down and wept right there on the tarmac.

Diplomatic security agents, working with local French police, had tracked Chloe and Eli to an abandoned warehouse about forty miles outside of Paris, where they were hostages of the bizarre animal cult. My wife and son were rescued amid a shootout and put on the next plane out of there. Knowing that they're finally safe—it's indescribable. They'll be arriving at the Idaho National Laboratory just a few hours after we do.

Our video conference with the lab ends, but the debate over next steps rages on. Freitas and Tanaka are really starting to get into it. As for myself, I stifle a yawn. It's pitch-black over the Pacific and my eyelids are getting heavy.

"You'll all have to carry on without me," I tell them. "I'm gonna head down below for a little shut-eye."

I walk to the rear of our plane, toward the hatch that leads to the lower level, stuffed with our gear and equipment. I pass our captured Japanese feral human, Reiji. Tanaka had picked that name for him, explaining with a chuckle that it means "a well-mannered baby." The man is strapped to a gurney under a hard plastic shell like a newborn in an incubator, thrashing against his restraints like crazy. Watching him, I can appreciate the irony.

I'm about to head downstairs when I notice something about Reiji from this close up.

His brow is dripping with sweat. His cheeks are splotchy red. And he's shredding the thin mattress with his sharp-tipped fingers.

The sweat, the complexion, the nails—it's a more extreme version of everything I just saw Tanaka doing.

No…my God…does that mean…?

"Aaaaargh!"

CHAPTER 28

A VICIOUS ROAR COMES not from Reiji but from behind me. I spin around to the front of the cabin just in time to see Tanaka leap up from his seat and lunge at Freitas. Before Freitas can react, Tanaka's got his hands around his neck, nails digging deep into the flesh.

The other scientists, caught completely by surprise, scramble to yank the madman off, but he easily knocks them away with one hand, the other clutching Freitas's windpipe, blood gushing like a sprinkler. His sudden strength is incredible.

"Dr. Freitas!" I yell, dashing back up the aisle to help.

Tanaka turns around and sees me charging. He drops Freitas's limp body and rushes into the open cockpit—where our two pilots are just as stunned and even more helpless.

Tanaka grabs one of them from behind. In an instant he places her in a brutal chokehold and violently snaps her neck.

I'm just stepping over Freitas's writhing body, racing toward Tanaka, as he attacks the second pilot. While they tussle, Tanaka intentionally presses down the yoke with his knee— and the plane tilts into a steep nosedive.

I'm hurled forward and tumble around wildly. Everyone does—along with an avalanche of loose papers and cellphones and laptops, each of the latter two now a deadly projectile.

Somehow I manage to get onto my hands and knees. Hanging on with all my might, I painstakingly crawl the rest of the way toward the cockpit, where Tanaka and the pilot are still fighting—and of course the feral human is winning.

Dizzy from the rapid altitude drop and throbbing with pain, I spot a fire extinguisher hanging by the cockpit door. *A weapon.*

I stagger to my feet, grab the heavy metal canister, and with every ounce of strength I can muster, swing it directly at Tanaka's skull.

Thunk. I can feel his cranium splinter. Tanaka cries out in pain, stumbles, but remains standing. "You bastard!" he shouts—as he turns to attack *me.*

I swing again. This time…I miss.

Tanaka springs toward me, but I crouch low and slip out of his grasp. Just as he spins back around, I take one more shot and nail him right in the middle of his face. His nose shatters, and three of his front teeth fall out of his mouth to the ground. Then he drops.

But my relief is brief. We're still plummeting toward the Pacific.

I yank on the yoke with trembling hands and desperately try to pull up. The plane levels off a bit, but I can feel we're still dropping fast. The instrument panel is blinking like a Christmas tree. Warning alarms are beeping wildly.

And both pilots are dead.

I have absolutely no idea what to do, except buckle in and pray.

I unbelt one of the pilots, shove him aside, take his bloody seat, and strap in.

I use all the strength I have left to keep tugging up on the yoke—especially when I see the dark, choppy water getting closer and closer. In my mind, I get glimpses of Chloe and Eli.

I can't die, I tell myself. *Not like this. Not without saying good-bye.*

And then, impact.

The noise is thunderous as the airplane smashes into the water. The cabin shudders and groans.

The plane finally comes to a stop. Almost immediately, I feel it start sinking.

Shaking off the stunned euphoria I'm feeling at having survived, I unbuckle my seat belt and stagger back into the cabin, which has been severed nearly in half and is quickly filling up with both water and smoke.

"Can anyone hear me?" I shout, coughing, wading through a flood of human carnage. "Is anyone okay?"

Silence. I can see that most of our team is dead, their bodies mangled and bloody.

But then, incredibly, I hear quiet mumbling. *Someone's still alive.*

Freitas!

"Hang in there, doc!" I say, splashing over to him. I sling the barely conscious man onto my shoulder. "We gotta get off this plane!"

I unlatch an emergency exit and a giant yellow slide-raft automatically inflates and extends into the water. *Thank God.* I put Freitas onto it, then give the sinking cabin a final look.

I see Tanaka floating facedown. Reiji, too, is long gone. His gurney is on its side, the plastic covering is shattered, and a giant shard has decapitated him.

Damnit—after all that. So much for bringing either of *them* back to the lab.

But there's no time for wallowing. I climb into the raft myself, disconnect it from the plane, and we immediately start to drift away in the choppy current.

I've barely gotten Freitas rolled onto his back so I can examine his wounds when, with a final, awful groan, our burning aircraft splits in two and disappears underwater.

CHAPTER 29

QUICK: HOW LONG CAN the average person last without water? A week? Five days? Three?

It's one of those scary stats you've heard a hundred times but never thought you'd need—until you find yourself floating on a raft in the middle of the Pacific.

I couldn't tell you how many hours it's been since the crash. If I had to guess, only about eighteen or so. But they've been long. And hellish.

Throughout the cold, pitch-black night, I tried to stabilize Freitas and stop his bleeding, ripping strips of fabric from our clothes to make crude bandages and tourniquets.

As the sun came up, I got a clearer view of his injuries. Mine, too. But when morning turned to afternoon, the sun's rays turned hot and punishing. With nothing at all to use for shade, our skin quickly started to burn.

I still had my satellite phone in my pocket, but it had been smashed to pieces. I thought about trying to paddle—with just my hands; why didn't they put oars on this thing?—but had no idea which direction to go. I figured it was better to save my strength anyway. *And* stay close to the crash site. I mean, a military transport plane on a critical government mission just crashed into the sea. Surely *somebody* saw that on the radar and sent help.

Right?

Now it's night again. The temperature is dropping. Salt is crusted around my eyes. My mouth feels like sandpaper, my skin like it's on fire. Freitas is slipping in and out of consciousness again. He's still breathing, but barely.

Having hardly slept in three days now, I feel the gentle bobbing of the raft start to lull me to sleep. I know I should keep my eyes open, to monitor Freitas, to keep watch for a passing ship to flag down. But I feel so weak. Bone-tired.

I think again of Chloe and Eli, who I pray have made it safely to the Idaho lab by now. And I know I have to keep going, keep fighting. They need me. The *world* needs me, I think, feeling myself start to drift off. *To survive dozens of animal and feral human attacks on land, only to die on the open water…*

The blare of a foghorn startles me awake.

It's just before dawn; the sky is an incandescent blue. I don't see anything in front of me. Painfully, I turn around—and behold a glorious sight.

A gray navy destroyer, off in the distance, steaming our way.

"Dr. Freitas!" I exclaim, gently shaking him awake. "They're coming! We're saved!"

He groans in acknowledgment. And I think I detect the tiniest smile on his bruised, bloody face.

A black Zodiac raft is soon lowered from the destroyer into the water. It speeds toward us, carrying about eight men in dark-blue camouflage uniforms. A few of them are wearing white armbands bearing a red cross: medics.

The highest-ranking sailor calls to me as they get near: "Are you Jackson Oz?"

"Yes!" I croak. "And I'm all right. But Dr. Freitas is in serious condition. The rest of our team...and our specimen... *both* of them...they're dead."

Their boat comes to a stop near our yellow raft. Medics quickly rush aboard, carrying a stretcher over to Freitas. "You're safe now," the officer tells me.

Am I? I wonder, as I'm wrapped in a silver thermal blanket and guided onto their craft. Twenty-four hours ago, I witnessed a seemingly normal human being turn into an unrecognizable beast. Without explanation. Without warning.

We speed back toward the looming destroyer, bouncing up and down in the waves, the cool ocean mist spraying my face.

As I glance around at all these young sailors, I can't help but wonder: Could any of them be next? Could their commanding officer? Could Freitas?

Could I?

CHAPTER 30

JOINT BASE PEARL HARBOR-HICKAM. In 1941, it was the site of one of the most devastating surprises in American history.

Across all the main islands of Hawaii, wild animal attacks are as bad as anywhere. But there have been exactly zero feral *human* ones. Ever.

At least that's the word from Captain Paul Fileri, the stern, buzz-cut commander of the vessel that rescued me. My de facto escort since we arrived on base, he's standing next to my bed in the infirmary as a nurse drains my wounds and changes the dressings.

"That's good news," I say, adding, "or I suppose it is. But what I *really* want to know—"

"You *suppose?*" Fileri asks, almost offended. "Oz, a third of the president's Animal Crisis Task Force—from what I understand, the leading international experts in this matter—was just killed. The team leader is down the hall in a medically induced coma. Maybe you don't quite grasp the severity of the situation, but—"

"With all due respect, Captain," I say, clearly irking this career military officer who isn't used to being interrupted, "I've devoted *years* of my life to this 'situation.' I've traveled to every corner of the globe looking for answers. Shit, I just captured one feral human in the wild, then killed a second with my bare hands! So I think I grasp its 'severity' very well, thank you. But right now, all I care about is my family. Are they all right? Please. Tell me. Did they arrive safely in Idaho?"

Fileri frowns. "I don't know anything about that. My orders came directly from the Pentagon, as soon as they learned your plane had gone down. Full-steam to its last known position, rescue any survivors, bring them back to base—"

"I understand that. And I'm very grateful. But what I'd be even *more* grateful for right now is an encrypted satellite phone."

Fileri's eyes narrow. So I explain.

"To speak to the White House. They're expecting my call. To tell me, now that Freitas is out of commission, how the *commander in chief* would like us to proceed."

As I'd hoped, those were the magic words.

Even if they were a big fat lie.

Of course I'll try to get ahold of somebody close to the president, maybe her chief of staff again, to find out how I'm supposed to get back to the rest of the team running the show now, and what the hell we're supposed to do next.

But obviously my first call is going to be to the Idaho National Laboratory.

Captain Fileri exits the room. He reappears a few minutes later with a bulky black wireless phone, promising to check in on me again shortly.

As soon as he's gone, I tap the arm of the friendly nurse still tending to me. "Sorry, I know you're busy, but you must have a smartphone on you, right?"

Thankfully, she does. Even more thankfully, cell service on

the island is still working. Within seconds she's done me a huge favor: she's googled the Idaho lab's main number. I can't dial it fast enough.

It rings.

"Come on, pick up," I whisper under my breath.

The line rings again. Then again.

I'm bursting with anticipation now. I can't stand it.

Another ring. Then another.

By the eighth ring, my cautious excitement has been replaced by a sinking feeling in the pit of my stomach.

I'm calling the main switchboard, in the middle of a workday, at a major federal scientific facility. There should be someone there to answer the damn phone!

CHAPTER 31

"SHE'S COMING! RUN!"

Clutching Eli in her arms, Chloe follows the command without question as screams and gunshots ring out nearby.

She quickly falls into step with a stream of other scientists and lab personnel all racing down a long corridor tinged with the smell of smoke.

Running for their lives.

All across the biological sciences wing, red lights are flashing and a shrill alarm is blaring. The warning system was designed to be used if a poisonous chemical or deadly pathogen was accidentally released into the air.

Today it's sounding for an even more terrifying reason.

A feral human being—captured in South Africa and brought here for study, nicknamed "Helen"—has just escaped.

The chaos began only minutes ago. As a distracted researcher was preparing to conduct a brain biopsy on her, Helen somehow managed to swipe a scalpel off the instrument tray, cut through her restraints—then slice open the scientist's jugular vein.

A rabid woman on the loose with a surgical blade would be scary enough. But Helen is scary *clever,* too. When armed guards charged into the research lab, she leapt out from a hiding spot, overpowered one, stole his pistol, and gunned down the rest. Then she took to stalking the halls, shooting at anyone and everyone she saw.

Chloe can feel her heart thudding in her chest. Eli is crying and clutching onto her tight. People are pushing and shoving. It's chaos.

And the smoke and gunshots are getting closer.

Chloe had first heard rumors while she was still living as a virtual prisoner among those freakish cult members in France that the animal affliction had begun spreading to people. Given her science background and all she knew about HAC, she dismissed it as utter nonsense, scientifically impossible. Just more of their crazy ranting.

But soon after she and Eli were rescued by American security forces and put on a plane to be reunited with her husband, she learned that Oz was on his way back from Japan, where he'd just captured a feral human.

Suddenly it didn't sound so crazy after all.

Chloe rounds a corner, which leads to an indoor courtyard of sorts, one that branches off into four separate corridors.

The scientists scramble every which way, but Chloe wants to be smart. She wants to run to an exit—not run in circles. She's only been at the lab for a few days and doesn't know her way around. Standing paralyzed, she debates where to go…

"Chloe, this way!" A familiar voice.

Dr. Sarah Lipchitz—a young biologist Chloe met when they first arrived. She'd tried to bond with Chloe over their shared "love" of Oz. At first Chloe was put off by this younger, perhaps prettier, woman who wouldn't shut up about how wonderful her husband was. Of course Chloe believed that Oz had remained faithful, and it was clear that Sarah was just feeling sad and lonely and scared. Chloe had begun to warm up to her.

And thank God she did. That woman might just save their lives.

With Sarah in the lead, the group dashes down the center-left hallway. Sure enough, they soon spot a bright red EXIT sign above a door that clearly leads outside.

Suddenly, a bullet streaks by and ricochets off the wall, just inches from Chloe's head.

She screams and glances behind her. Helen must be looking for a way out, too: half-screaming in some African language, half-roaring in rage, she's coming up behind them!

"Keep running, don't stop!" Sarah urges. Chloe runs, pulling Eli at her side.

They finally reach the exit and burst outside into the hot desert evening.

"One of the Jeeps!" Sarah yells. "They leave the keys in the ignition. Go, go!"

The women and Eli scurry over the asphalt in a parking lot filled with official laboratory vehicles. They make it to one of several tan SUVs. Sure enough, it's unlocked.

They all pile inside: Sarah behind the wheel, Chloe in the front seat, holding Eli on her lap.

Helen, still running after them, fires twice more—shattering the rear windshield—as Sarah starts the engine and burns rubber.

The Jeep is heading straight for a metal checkpoint gate that is both unmanned and closed tight. They're picking up speed—but so is Helen.

Right above those ominous little words OBJECTS IN MIR-
ROR ARE CLOSER THAN THEY APPEAR, Chloe sees the feral
woman starting to sprint—fast enough to leave Usain Bolt in
the dust. She's gaining on them.

"Now what?" Chloe shouts. "We're trapped!"

Sarah keeps the pedal to the floor. "Just hang on!"

At the very last second, she cuts the wheel away from the
checkpoint and the Jeep barrels straight through the chain-
link fence.

At least they've made it out of the burning facility, but
Helen has, too.

She continues chasing them, getting terrifyingly close. She
fires the last few bullets in her pistol, striking the back bumper
and popping a rear tire. The Jeep keeps going, picking up more
and more speed, Sarah finally putting some real distance between them.

Chloe spins around in her seat just in time to watch the
feral human reach a point of frustration and slow down—
then abruptly change course and run instead toward the vast
desert surrounding the blazing, smoking lab.

"*Mon dieu!*" is all Chloe can whisper in relief. Panting heavily, her pulse racing, she adds, "*Merci,* Sarah. You saved us."

The two women trade a look and glance back at Helen.
She's already disappeared into the dry expanse.

CHAPTER 32

AFTER FAILING TO REACH a single soul inside the Idaho lab, I've started freaking out. A *lot*. It seems more and more likely that something awful may have happened there.

And that Chloe and Eli might be in danger. *Again*.

So I change tack. Googling the number on the iPhone the nurse lent me, I call the Department of Energy's main switchboard. Finally I speak to a human being…in media affairs. All he'll tell me is that, yes, there's been a recent "incident" at the lab and "multiple persons are still unaccounted for."

Unaccounted for? Not what a guy wants to hear when he's three thousand miles and half an ocean away, and his wife and son might be involved.

"Get dressed, Mr. Oz," says Captain Fileri, marching back into my room. He tosses me a pair of sneakers, khakis, and a blue button-down to replace the flimsy hospital gown I'm wearing. "We're wheels up in thirty minutes."

Fileri explains he's just spoken with the White House. Despite the recent loss of nearly two-thirds of the Animal Crisis Task Force scientists, Washington is scrambling to keep the team's critical work moving forward. They're assembling a whole *new* group of experts, and they're ordering me to return to DC via military plane to be among them. Immediately.

"That all sounds fine and dandy, Captain," I say, "right after we make a quick pit stop to pick up my—"

"That's a negative," Fileri snaps. "The command is to evac you and Dr. Freitas off the island and back to the capital. No detour, no delay. There just isn't time."

It's very clear to me that the captain isn't going to budge on this. I know he's just following orders. And I know the country—the world—still does need my expertise.

But I also know that Chloe and Eli need me more. And the last time I put my work ahead of my family, I nearly lost them forever. I am *never* going to do it again.

So I put on my best poker face and say: "All right, sir. I'll be ready in a minute."

As soon as Fileri leaves, the clock starts ticking.

For me to make my escape.

CHAPTER 33

I THROW ON THE fresh clothes, grab my still-damp wallet from the meager personal effects on the table, pocket the iPhone (sorry, nurse!), and quietly lock the door to my room. Then I hobble over to the window.

I pry off one of the wooden boards meant to keep out animals and see I'm on the third floor—way too high to risk jumping down safely.

So I decide to do what I've seen in old movies so many times. I'll use my bed linens to make a rope.

Nuts, I know, but what other choice do I have?

I strip the bed and hastily knot two sheets together as tight as I can. I tie one end to the railing, toss the other end outside, and carefully start to climb down.

I'm about halfway down when, damnit, one of the sheets rips.

I fall into some bushes, intentionally rolling and tumbling to soften the impact of the fall. I may be a little scuffed up, as if I wasn't already, but I've made it.

Now I just have to slip aboard the next commercial flight to the mainland…just as soon as I figure out where the hell the airport is.

I search in Google Maps, but the screen doesn't move. I try again. Still nothing. Seriously?

But then I hear a loud rumbling overhead—and see a jet-liner flying dangerously close to the ground. Is it going to crash? No. It's coming in for a landing. Which means the military facility and the airport are just blocks apart.

Keeping an eye out for both wild animals and military police, I race across the base. A lot of the chain-link fence along its perimeter looks damaged by—what else?—attacks from feral creatures, so I find an opening, slip through, and keep running as fast as I can until I reach the airport. It's not hard to find it, since hundreds, maybe thousands, of people are cramming into the terminal, desperate to get off the islands. Which won't be easy. Since the animal crisis has dragged on, the number of flights all around the world has gone down dramatically, while the cost of flying has skyrocketed.

I get in a long ticket line and wait. I'm terrified that any second, Captain Fileri will burst through the doors and drag me back to the base.

Finally it's my turn to speak to an agent. I breathlessly explain my situation and how badly I need to get to Salt Lake City—the closest major city to the lab—to make sure my wife and son are okay.

But the agent barely lets me finish. The next available direct flight to anywhere in the Rockies, she tells me, isn't for four days.

My heart sinks. My eyes tear up. I beg and plead. Isn't there *any* other option?

The agent purses her lips and types rapidly. Maybe I've gotten through to her.

"There's a plane leaving for Vancouver in twenty minutes, if you can make it. From there you can connect to San Francisco. Then to Chicago. Then double back through Phoenix to Salt Lake. You'll be traveling for over thirty-six hours straight but—"

"I'll take it!" I exclaim, slapping a credit card down on the counter. By some miracle, my cards were undamaged in my wallet.

And I need all *three* of my credit cards to split up and cover the whopping price: $29,487. Insane, but worth every penny.

The agent hands me my ticket and I take off like a rocket through the packed terminal. I somehow manage to make it through security and reach the gate seconds before the boarding doors close.

CHAPTER 34

I SCREAM IN TERROR as I'm jolted awake in my seat—and grab the unfamiliar hand just inches from my throat.

But then I relax and let it go. And turn beet-red from embarrassment.

It was just the flight attendant tapping me on the shoulder, asking me to bring my seat to the upright position. We'll be landing soon in Salt Lake City.

The past forty-plus hours have been a blur of exhaustion, stress, and actual pain. The meds I was given at the military hospital in Hawaii have long since worn off, and my entire body is throbbing. Add to that multiple layovers and multiple delays in multiple airports, each more chaotic than the next...plus the constant threat of a feral human attack at any moment and...well, you get the idea. Not exactly a pleasure trip.

Seeing all the other passengers whip out their smartphones after we landed in Vancouver, it dawned on me. I felt so stupid for not thinking of it sooner. My wife doesn't have a cell I can call, but of course I still know her email address.

Using the nurse's iPhone, I logged into my personal account for the first time in weeks and fired off a quick note, praying that Chloe would think to check her email, too.

About six hours later, when I landed in San Francisco...no response.

But then, *another* six hours later, after we touched down in Chicago...I dabbed away tears of joy at the sight of my wife's name in my inbox. Still more tears came as I read about the terror that went down at the lab and their harrowing escape.

As soon as the plane's wheels make contact with the tarmac and my journey finally ends, I leap up out of my seat, race down the jet bridge, sprint through the busy terminal, and burst outside into the hot Utah afternoon.

The curbside pickup area is total mayhem. Cars honking, cops shouting.

My iPhone died hours ago, before I could arrange any kind of specific meet-up time and location with Chloe. I need to charge it, badly, but first I want to find some ground transportation. I've come so far, and my family is *still* so far.

Then something catches my eye: a handmade sign with the words JACKSON OZ.

It's being held up by Chloe, standing in front of a tan Jeep as if she were a chauffeur, a megawatt smile plastered across her beautiful face.

Eli is clinging to her leg. "Daddy!" he yells, letting go and bounding up to me.

He leaps into my arms. I squeeze the boy so tightly I'm afraid he might pop. Covering his messy hair with kisses, I carry him to Chloe and wrap her in the hug as well.

And the three of us just stay like that. Half-laughing, half-crying.

No words. Just unimaginable relief.

And infinite love.

Finally we pull apart, sniffling, wiping our eyes.

"So, how was your little vacation, *mon amour?*" she asks with her trademark smirk. I've missed that so much. To answer, I give her a long, deep kiss.

The front door of the Jeep opens and out steps Sarah. Like my wife and son, she looks tired and stressed and grimy but also relieved to see me. The feeling is mutual, especially since Chloe told me in her email that Sarah helped save their lives.

"I don't know how to thank you," I say as we embrace.

"*I* do," Sarah answers, pulling away to look at both Chloe and me. "No more crazy expeditions to far-flung corners of the globe. No more unnecessary tests. No more big government agencies telling us what to do. And no more delay."

Chloe understands where Sarah's going with this and picks up the thread.

"*Oui!* Feral human attacks are on the rise. And with the president's task force in ruins…yes, we will need equipment and a laboratory and new specimens…but the three of us— working *together* this time, Oz—may be the best shot the world has at finding a cure."

I smile, feeling a real sense of hope and optimism I haven't in weeks.

"I couldn't agree more. And I think I know where we should start."

CHAPTER 35

NOTHING LIKE FLYING FORTY hours on five different planes, then taking a six-hour road trip through the sweltering Nevada desert.

But, hey, I'm not complaining. I'm alert and fired up and feeling great. I've got my wife by my side, my little boy dozing in the backseat, and the beginnings of some actual working theories about the feral humans and how to cure them.

"I agree with you, Oz," says Sarah, "that the pheromones that feral humans give off must be different from normal humans'. When animals get one whiff, they all go running. But how do you explain the tissue death we saw in Helen's brain? Pheromones affect behavior, mating, aggression. Not brain damage. It's impossible."

"Actually, it is not," Chloe offers. "Research has shown that cells can die in response to pheromones if response pathways are lacking."

"Fine," Sarah concedes. "But the more pressing question is, how do we stop it? And reverse it in the people already affected? How in the world do we regrow human brains?"

"Easy," I reply. "Stem cells. They're like cellular free spaces. With the potential to grow into any kind of cells in the human body—including brain tissue, as long as we program them right. Toss in a high-octane antihistamine to block phero-mone absorption, and we'll be in business!"

Chloe and Sarah consider my suggestion, both clearly in-trigued by it.

"We all know stem cell therapy is still a new field," I con-tinue. "The idea I'm proposing is radical. It's hard. But—"

"You're wrong, Oz," Sarah replies. "It's simple. It's elegant. It's…genius."

Chloe chuckles good-naturedly. "Careful now, Sarah," she says. "My husband's head is full of great ideas. But we don't want it to get so big it explodes."

We continue driving down this long, deserted stretch of I-15. Dirt and shrubs are all around us, as far as the eye can see. A highway sign says we're only about sev-enty miles out from our destination: Las Vegas. An old friend of Sarah's from grad school is an adjunct profes-sor of biochemistry at the University of Nevada. With his expertise—not to mention the use of his lab space and equipment—we just might be able to pull off my "genius" idea. Emphasis on *might*.

"Of course, the *real* challenge," Sarah says, "is going to be finding some feral human test subjects. If history is any guide, that won't be—"

"Oz, look out!" Chloe shouts.

Before I have time to react, a pack of rabid coyotes lying in wait along the highway shoulder leap up to the road—easily a dozen or more, all yipping madly—and onto the Jeep.

I swerve wildly—to try to shake them off, since none of us has a weapon, and because I can't see a damn thing.

The animals scratch at the windshield like fiends. They snap their razor-sharp fangs at the shut windows. The smart little bastards even claw at the tires to try to pop them and slow us down.

Trying to kill us.

Eli is crying. Sarah is screaming. Chloe is just hanging on for dear life.

Me, I keep jerking the wheel side to side, accelerating fast and then braking sharply, trying desperately to shake them off.

And it seems to be working. One by one the coyotes lose their grip and tumble off onto the hot asphalt. So I keep it up.

Until I *mess* it up.

There's a highway sign I don't see until it's too late.

I sideswipe it. Direct hit. The passenger window next to Sarah shatters.

The Jeep goes spinning wildly out of control.

Most of the coyotes are thrown off, but once our car comes to a helpless stop, they regroup and charge at us. I stomp the pedal, but it's too late.

At the broken window, I see two coyotes approach to leap in…

But instead of piling inside, they begin howling.

They jump away from the car just as fast and scurry away. Within seconds, the entire pack has disappeared into the desert.

Jesus, another close call! All that talk about rabid humans, it's easy to forget there are still *animals* out there who want us dead just as much.

Slowly Chloe, Sarah, and I all catch our breath. We're relieved. We're safe.

But then, we begin to trade nervous glances.

Sarah is turning pale with shock. We're all having the same chilling thought.

The reason the coyotes ran away the second before they jumped through Sarah's window...

Is because she must be on the verge of going feral.

CHAPTER 36

UP UNTIL NOW, THE stakes of the feral human crisis had been huge but impersonal.

I knew thousands of people around the world had been affected, but I didn't *know* any of them. Helen and Reiji were total strangers to me. I'd only met Tanaka a day before our fateful flight over the Pacific.

But now, with Sarah about to join their ranks, this damn plague has come to my doorstep. She's a colleague. A friend. A good person who saved Chloe and Eli's lives at the Idaho lab. A good scientist whose help we need to discover a cure.

"But she could kill us, all of us!" Chloe anxiously whispered to me the first night we spent inside the UNLV lab. "If she *changes* before we discover the antidote—"

"Incentive for us to discover it even faster," I replied. "And on the bright side, now we have a rabid human guinea pig to test it on."

I tried to downplay my wife's fears, but of course I felt them tenfold.

I shared with her, Sarah, and Dr. David Stapf—Sarah's biochemist friend from grad school—what I saw happen to Tanaka in the minutes before he went rabid. I wanted us all to be on the lookout for similar warning signs: sweaty brow, red face, clenched fists, arguing, and aggressive behavior.

And just in case we miss them somehow, Sarah's given us permission, if she starts acting dangerously, to put her down. Like an animal.

I respect her bravery, but, God, do I hope it doesn't come to that.

Except now, it's looking like it might.

We're wrapping up day six locked in the bowels of the University of Nevada science complex, trying to program the stem cell genetic sequence that will bring dead white blood cells back to life in a petri dish. So far, we've crammed about two months of research into one grueling week. And I feel it. My back aches from hunching over my microscope eighteen hours a day. My eyelids are heavy, my mind foggy.

I glance over at Eli, on the floor in the corner, playing with a collection of lab equipment serving as toys. Rubber gloves, plastic funnels, safety goggles. Just watching his innocent smile is enough to keep me going.

Next I look over at Chloe, working furiously at her lab station, pipetting solutions into test tubes. Her dedication makes me love her even more.

Then I notice Sarah, also working hard…but with more intensity somehow, almost with an anger in her eyes. Could this be the first sign of aggressive behavior? I watch as she subtly dabs some sweat off her forehead. It's hot and stuffy down in this lab; I'm sweating, too. But maybe that's another symptom of her impending change?

"You guys, check this out!" David exclaims, leaping off his lab stool.

Chloe, Sarah, and I head over and take turns peering into David's digital microscope.

"Oh my God," Sarah says, seeing it first.

"Incredible," Chloe adds after she looks.

Finally, it's my turn—but I don't have any words. Just silent joy.

I'm watching thousands of previously dead white blood cells regenerate right before my eyes! I clap David on the back with excitement.

"Amazing, right?" he says. "Obviously there's no way to know if this nucleotide chain will have the same effect inside a feral human brain. I *think* it should, but—"

"David," I say, "we don't have time to 'think.' We need certainty. Now."

Chloe suggests we share our results with the new DOE team, with whom we've been in sporadic touch the past few days, so they can run with it themselves.

"For sure," I say. "But first, get these stem cells into a nasal spray canister. When Sarah starts…transforming…at least we'll have *something* to try on her."

Everyone soberly agrees, and David eagerly sets to work. We all do. That was just the kind of moral boost we needed. Maybe we'll cure this thing after all.

But then, barely two hours later, everything changes.

Every single light and device and computer in our lab flickers off.

"*Incroyable!*" Chloe shouts, enraged. "We are on the brink of saving mankind and we lose electricity?"

"It's all right, honey. Relax. I'm sure it's just…"

In the near distance, we can hear glass being shattered. Guns being fired. And humans screaming, grunting, roaring.

Feral humans.

We all immediately realize we're no longer safe here.

I turn to David. "How many nasal injector serums did you make?"

"Just...just one," he stutters. "For Sarah."

Great.

"Make sure you bring it," I say. "I have an awful feeling we're going to need it."

CHAPTER 37

ALL FIVE OF US—Chloe, Eli, Sarah, David, and myself—race up the stairs and outside. It's the first time we've stepped foot out of the lab in days. The sun is setting and the mostly empty campus is bathed in eerie, shadowy orange light. *Only* eerie, shadowy orange light. It looks like the entire school has lost power.

Scratch that. Glancing around in every direction, I see that the blackout stretches across *the entire city of Las Vegas.*

I also see the source of those feral war cries.

A band of rabid humans is stalking across the campus—a dozen, at least, maybe more, chasing and ferociously attacking everyone they encounter. They're also a distorted reflection of Vegas society. One is wearing the black vest and green visor of a blackjack dealer. Another, the heavy makeup and skimpy dress of a cocktail waitress or maybe a prostitute. Another is a Vegas cop, in uniform, firing his sidearm.

"What do we do?" asks Sarah, panicking.

The truth is, I have no goddamn idea.

We can't just stand here, but we don't have a plan, either. We don't have a new safe destination. And we don't have any weapons.

All we've got is a wrecked government Jeep with a quarter

tank of gas. A single nasal injector with an antidote that *might* work. And each other.

The most important thing of all.

"What do we do? We run!"

Scooping up my son and pulling my wife along by the hand, we rush to the Jeep still parked not far from the lab entrance. We pile inside and peel out.

By the time we get off campus, we spot another cluster of feral humans coming from the other direction—the Strip, its famous casinos and hotels all scarily dark. One of them wears the uniform of a hotel housekeeper. Another, a burly bald man wielding a shotgun, has on the shiny black suit of a casino bouncer.

They catch sight of our speeding Jeep and decide to pursue. As they pick up speed, the bouncer fires at us, spiderwebbing our rear windshield with buckshot.

"Go faster, Oz!" Chloe shouts from the backseat.

So I do. And soon we're whizzing down one of the city's wide boulevards, littered with trash and abandoned cars and the occasional non-feral person running for his or her life.

We seem to have lost the second pack of rabid humans, but more keep popping up around every corner. A Chinese tourist hurls a concrete cinder-block at us with incredible strength, leaving a divot in the hood. Even a feral Elvis impersonator leaps in front of the Jeep and bashes one of the headlights with a baseball bat.

"*Merde!*" Chloe exclaims. "Goddamn you, Oz! I said faster! Why can't you ever do anything right?"

"Hey, I'm trying my best here!" I call back to her, almost

more freaked out by her angry tone of voice than by the rabid humans we're trying to avoid.

When I suddenly realize…holy shit…

I turn around in my seat to look at Chloe. Her forehead is drenched. Her cheeks are deep crimson. She's holding Eli in her lap, but clutching onto him so tightly that his skin his turning white—and she's digging her nails into his flesh a bit, making him cry.

Please. God, no…it can't be…

Chloe lets loose a bloodcurdling primal roar and grabs me from behind.

She—not Sarah—is the one who's been going feral!

Our car fills with screaming and mayhem as Chloe attacks me like a maniac, clawing at my face and neck from behind, quickly drawing blood.

Stunned, Sarah and David scramble to yank her off while I try to keep the car moving and under control. We swerve wildly—sideswiping a telephone pole, scraping the roof of an overturned tour bus, just narrowly avoiding being hit by a flaming Molotov cocktail hurled by a feral human on a rooftop I can't even see.

As the fight continues—me resisting and struggling and gurgling on my own blood—I see David pull the nasal injector from his pocket. He rips off the cap with his teeth, yanks Chloe's head back by her hair, jams the injector up her nostril, and depresses the trigger.

Chloe gasps and screams. She starts to writhe and seize, shaking horribly and frothing at the mouth. It's an awful, agonizing sight…

But it's over in just a few seconds.

Chloe releases her grip on me and slumps back in her seat. Slowly, her breathing and complexion return to normal. Her muscles relax.

Before our eyes, *she becomes a healthy human being again!*

"What…what just…did I…?" is all she can manage to croak.

"It's okay, Chloe," I whisper, tears of relief streaming down my bloodied face.

Sarah, David, little Eli—they're overwhelmed as well.

I refocus on the road ahead. I press down on the gas even harder and squeal onto a highway on-ramp.

Behind me, through my rearview mirror as we drive farther and farther away, I can see columns of smoke rising. Sin City's been turned into a war zone.

But at least we saved my wife.

And thanks to our antidote, *we might save humanity, too.*

"It's okay, baby," I say again. "Everything's going to be okay."

EPILOGUE

"AS OF TODAY, MADAM PRESIDENT, the vaccination rate stands at seventy-three percent. That includes all major urban populations of one million or more—"

"What about the *remaining* twenty-seven percent of Americans, Dr. Freitas?"

President Hardinson glares at Freitas, who's one of the many advisors, military leaders, and scientists—Chloe and I among them—seated around this giant polished conference table. He gulps.

"We're working on it, ma'am."

He can say *that* again.

Over the past three months since we developed the antihistamine antidote to human pheromonal rabidity, or HPR, as I've dubbed it, in that musty Las Vegas lab, I've been helping the government mass-produce and disseminate it as quickly and widely as possible. Given the strained state of the country—and the world—the progress we've made has been remarkable, even for a cynic like yours truly.

But I hear the president's concern loud and clear. A quarter of the country has yet to be inoculated.

That's eighty million new potential feral humans. A staggering thought.

Clearly we have our work cut out for us.

The meeting of the newly re-formed and renamed Animal & Human Crisis Task Force ends, and Chloe and I start to leave. We find ourselves exiting alongside Freitas, who's pushing himself along in his wheelchair. The plane crash left his face badly scarred, and he's still too weak to walk—but he's alive, miraculously.

"Chloe, Oz, I meant to ask you both," he says. "How are you finding the accommodations?"

"This isn't the first time we've lived in seclusion with the leader of the free world," I say. Just a few weeks ago, the White House was evacuated for the second time in eight months. The threat of feral human attacks was just too great. "It ain't the Ritz," I continue. "But living underground sure beats living in the Arctic."

Chloe and I walk down one of the mountain compound's long, dim central hallways toward the daycare center. Eli now spends most of his waking hours there, learning and playing with kids his own age—instead of being alone with his frazzled parents or running away from animal attacks or witnessing his mother turn feral. We've only been at Raven Rock a few weeks, but already the kid is thriving. Which warms my heart. And gives me hope.

But as we near the daycare center, I can tell that there's something on Chloe's mind. I stop walking and take her hand. I stare deep into her gorgeous eyes.

"What is it, Chloe?" I ask tenderly.

She avoids my gaze and gently runs a finger along one of the deep scars on the side of my neck—a mark from when, just a few months ago inside that Jeep in Vegas, she tried to kill me. She's still upset about the whole episode, even though I've tried to convince her it wasn't her fault. And that I still love her more than anything.

"I don't know," she answers softly. "I am just…afraid. HPR is under control. All three of us are together again. We're living in the safest place on Earth. And yet…I don't know how to describe it. It's just a feeling. An uneasy one."

I pull my sweet, beautiful wife into a warm embrace. "I know," I say. "I'm afraid, too. But there's nothing to be…"

I stop talking—because I hear something.

A faint, distant *scratching* sound. Almost a burrowing. But it's not coming from one particular spot. It's emanating, almost echoing, all around us.

Chloe and I share a look. We both hear it. We're both concerned.

And then, we're both shocked—as *a swarm of cockroaches emerges from the cinder-block walls all around us,* pushing through every nook and cranny, thousands of them, black and shiny, squirming and wiggling…

And coming right at us.

THE
PRETENDER

JAMES PATTERSON
with ANDREW BOURELLE

PROLOGUE

I SPEED THROUGH THE desert along a dirt road, my Jeep leaving a cloud of dust in its wake. The setting sun gives the desert landscape a reddish hue. The only thing visible in any direction, besides sagebrush and cacti, is a run-down shack up ahead. Marco's car is already parked outside.

I have the feeling I'm walking into a trap.

On my passenger seat sits a black satin sack about the size of a sandwich bag, containing a few million dollars' worth of diamonds. Other than that, I have only a gas station cup half full of soda. I have no gun. No knife. I bet Marco has one or the other.

Or both.

I'd been telling Marco for weeks that I was going to quit after this heist—what we'd called "the job to end all jobs"—and Marco had not been happy about it. He'd even joked that he wasn't going to let me leave. I didn't think much of it, but then Marco insisted that we rendezvous here, in the middle of nowhere. We had always met in public places before.

I stop the Jeep about a hundred yards from the shack and let it sit, idling in neutral. I take a drink from my soda. I think about shifting the Jeep into gear and taking off. Then I get an idea.

I wedge the Styrofoam cup between my legs and pull off the lid. I pick up the satin bag and pour the diamonds into my soda. The stones, ranging in size from grains of sand to corn kernels, collect in a pile on top of the ice. They shimmer in the sunlight, and then they sink without a trace into the brown liquid. I put the lid back on and hold the cup up, weighing it. The cup is heavier, but everything about it still looks normal.

I park my Jeep next to Marco's Dodge Charger. There's a film of desert dust over both our cars.

The shack looks like something left over from a nuclear war. The windows are all broken. The front door is missing. Most of the shingles have been yanked off the roof by wind. The walls are full of holes and covered in graffiti, as if teenagers had come out here and taken turns with sledgehammers and spray paint.

As I approach the building, I drink from the cup as if it's an ordinary soda. My feet crunch on glass and other debris as I step over the threshold. Marco is sitting on a metal chair at a table missing one of its legs. He is idly carving a piece of wood with a serrated folding knife. Rays of sunlight poke through the walls, illuminating the dust floating in the air.

"Logan!" Marco says, his face lighting up when he sees me.

He's dressed as he always is, in dark slacks and a gray sport coat over a black T-shirt.

He jams the knife into the table and stands. He extends his hand to shake mine, but instead I lean in to give him a hug, hoping to figure out if he's got a weapon inside his sport coat. He looks surprised, but he hugs me back.

My chest bumps against a pistol tucked into a shoulder holster.

"We did it," I say, clapping him on the back.

"We sure did, old friend," Marco says. "We sure as hell did."

I settle into a wobbly chair across from Marco's seat. I set the cup of soda on the table.

Marco sits across from me. His steel-gray eyes bore into me.

"So?" Marco says.

"So," I say, smiling and acting as if nothing is wrong.

"So," Marco repeats, "where are the rocks, man?"

"I've got them," I say, being deliberately vague.

"I want to see them, dude."

"There's time for that."

"Are they in the Jeep?" Marco says.

I shrug.

"Stop fucking around," he says jokingly—but I can see in his eyes he's not kidding.

He rises and takes a step toward the door, but then hesitates and grabs his knife off the table. I watch him through the window as he opens the Jeep door and looks around inside. Behind him, the sun is an orange blob in the distant haze, seconds from disappearing below the horizon.

Marco comes storming back, holding the empty satin bag. He flings it at me.

"What the hell are you trying to pull?" Marco says.

"What the hell are *you* trying to pull?" I say, rising out of my chair. "You set up a rendezvous in the middle of nowhere. You brought a gun. I'm not stupid, Marco. You were going to kill me as soon as I showed you the diamonds."

Marco stares at me for a moment, and then reaches into his jacket and pulls out the pistol.

"Congratulations," Marco says. "You've got it all figured out."

"You couldn't just let me go, could you?"

He looks at me like I've insulted him. "What did you think you were going to do?" he says. "Pretend you're just like everybody else? Meet a girl and settle down? Live a normal life?"

"That sounds about right."

"I won't let you just ride off into the sunset, old friend," he says, and he aims the Beretta M9 at my face.

I take a sip from my soda. "You can't kill me, Marco. If you shoot me, you'll never know where the diamonds are."

"Don't mess with me, Logan. Tell me where the diamonds are or I'll put a bullet through your goddamn brain."

"Go ahead," I say. "Flush the diamonds down the toilet."

I would happily give Marco his half of the diamonds, but I can't do that, given the predicament. I would be dead the moment Marco saw the first diamond come spilling out of the cup. My only chance of survival is the hope that Marco won't kill me because he knows that if he does, the diamonds will be gone forever.

I step backward toward the door.

I can see Marco considering his options, realizing he hasn't thought this all the way through. He has the gun, but I hold all the cards. He is, at his core, a businessman. And no businessman would light a match to millions of dollars. If there's any chance he can get the money later, he'll take it. After years of working with him, I know how patient he can be. He never rushes a job. And if I walk out that door, I become his next job.

"There was no need to do this," I say. "There was plenty for both of us. I never would have betrayed you."

"Don't kid yourself," Marco says. "There's no honor among thieves."

"There should be."

I turn my back on him and walk to the Jeep. The sun is gone now, casting a dying orange afterglow into the darkening sky.

"Good-bye, old friend," I call over my shoulder.

"Good-bye," Marco says. "For now."

CHAPTER 1

Two Years Later

HANNAH STARES OUT AT Lower Echo Lake, a long, feather-shaped sheet of blue glass with forested mountain peaks rising up around it. In the early morning, the lake is calm. The still water reflects the brilliant blue sky like a mirror. The land is silent.

She steps out of her car and inhales deeply, filling her lungs with the cool mountain air. Hannah's lived in the Lake Tahoe Basin for a year now, but she's never hiked here.

There is a path that runs four miles along Lower Echo Lake and Upper Echo Lake, twin alpine bodies of water lined with vacation cabins. Then the trail ascends into a remote area called Desolation Wilderness, a beautiful terrain of pine forests, granite rock formations, and ice-cold lakes. Her destination today is Lake Aloha, which, she's been told, gets its name from a series of islands resembling Hawaii that brave hikers can swim out to.

She doesn't expect to do any swimming today. It's mid-September, and there's already a chill in the air. And she's never gotten used to the cold water in this mountain community. Even on the hottest summer day, she will barely dip her toe in Lake Tahoe. But she wants to see Lake Aloha for herself.

As a reporter for the *Lake Tahoe Gazette,* she works long

hours and doesn't get out nearly enough to enjoy the place she lives in. She has no real friends—no boyfriend—and as her first summer here draws to an end, she recently realized she wasn't actually getting out and doing enough in her spare time. She knows numerous people in town, but they're all coworkers or sources for her articles. She's decided her lack of friends shouldn't stop her from trying to have fun.

This short hike is an attempt to do just that.

She pulls her daypack from her backseat and double-checks to make sure she has everything she needs: water, food, sunscreen, first-aid kit.

The parking lot is empty, but suddenly a Jeep Wrangler pulls into a nearby space. She recognizes the driver, a man she's seen at the gym. He is cute, probably in his early thirties like her, with sandy blond hair and the body of an athlete. She doesn't know his name. They've never spoken. But as he steps out of his vehicle, his eyes meet hers, and he offers her a smile. His expression is friendly, maybe even a little flirtatious, and it seems to say, *I know you from somewhere, don't I?*

Hannah returns his smile, but then she feels self-conscious. She turns away, throwing her pack over one shoulder. She saunters down to the general store, wondering if the mystery man is watching her.

Her plan is to take the water taxi across the two Echo Lakes, cutting four miles off what would otherwise be an eleven-mile one-way hike. There is a kid, probably no more than twenty, with a patchy beard and acne bumps on his forehead, waiting behind the counter.

She asks him about the water taxi, and he explains that he can take her. She pays and then goes outside to wait in the taxi, a long wooden motorboat with benches along the port and starboard sides for passengers.

Today, it looks like she's the only passenger.

The guy from the gym has one leg propped up on the bumper of his Jeep, and he's rubbing sunscreen onto his muscular legs. He's obviously going to hike around the lakes. No shortcut for him. Hell, Hannah thinks, he might *run* the eleven miles to Lake Aloha. He looks like he could do it.

The kid comes out and hops into the boat. He grabs the starter cord to start the motor but hesitates.

"Hey, man," he calls up to the guy from the gym. "You want a ride? It's twelve bucks."

The guy looks up and seems to think about the offer.

"Sure," he says. "Be right there."

Hannah's heartbeat accelerates. She has a strange suspicion that the guy agreed simply for an opportunity to spend time with her. She tells herself she's being silly, but when he jogs down the pier and steps into the boat, he sits only a few feet from her.

"Hi," he says, flashing her an electric smile and extending his hand. "My name's Logan."

CHAPTER 2

HANNAH'S EDITOR ONCE TOLD her that most people in the news business tend to be introverted. Journalism is a job that forces otherwise shy, socially awkward people to step out of their comfort zones and talk to other people. Hannah never thought much of the theory, but now, sitting next to Logan, she wonders if her editor is onto something.

Under the protective cloak of her job title, Hannah never has any problem talking to complete strangers, even asking them intimate personal questions. She can handle complaints from the public about her coverage of an issue. She can go into her editor's office and demand better positioning for one of her stories. But, if she's honest with herself, she knows her confidence is really an act. Here she is sitting next to a cute guy, and she feels completely tongue-tied.

They are both quiet. As handsome as he is, he might be just as introverted as she is.

The boat zips along the water, giving them a wonderful vantage of the scenery on both sides of the lake. They pass one vacation home after another. Accessible only by boat or hiking trail, the cabins line the lake, each with their own private pier. Most of the cabins look empty, closed up for the end of the season. There are a couple of girls in bathing suits goofing around on a dock at the far end of the lake, probably daring each other to jump into the ice-cold water but neither taking the plunge. Otherwise, no one is around.

Hannah checks her phone, just to give her hands something to do, and sees that there's no service out here.

Finally, she takes a deep breath and says, "I think I've seen you at the gym."

Logan smacks his knee. "I knew you looked familiar."

Hannah mentions that she's seen him in the afternoon spinning class, the least crowded of all the classes because it's in the middle of the afternoon when most people are working.

"I sometimes go there to get the blood flowing before I'm on deadline," Hannah says. "I work at the *Lake Tahoe Gazette*."

He starts asking questions about her job, and then their conversation seems to become more and more natural. Relief washes over her like a warm wave. Why was it so hard to start talking to him? There's obvious chemistry.

She reaches into her daypack and pulls out a business card. She hands it to him, suddenly feeling awkward again. She's giving him her number in the guise of professional courtesy, but she hopes he'll see through her pretense to know her real intention: she wants him to call and ask her out.

He asks if she has a pen and an extra card, and the next thing she knows, he's writing down his telephone number on the back of one of her business cards.

"If you ever want to go to a class together," he says, "give me a call. You know, for motivation."

She stares at the card. He's written his full name, first and last—Logan Bishop—and his cell phone number.

Hannah smiles. She can't help herself. Logan's green eyes

are telling her that he's looking for more than a gym buddy. She looks away, feeling her cheeks flush.

"So, what about you?" she says. "What do you do for a living?"

He looks away, his embarrassment palpable.

"I don't really like to say," he says, squirming visibly in his seat. "I have a little trust fund that I'm living on right now."

"Oh," Hannah says.

She realizes she hasn't hidden her surprise very well. She wants to say something to recover from it, to show him that this doesn't bother her. But the truth is she's never known anyone with a trust fund. Someone from a family rich enough that he doesn't have to work. Perhaps the news shouldn't have come as a surprise to her. But she's from a blue-collar, working-class family—she was the first to go to college—and the thought of someone who simply has enough that he doesn't need to be employed is so foreign to her that she can't quite even grasp what that kind of life would be like.

Especially since she's a journalist, one of the lowest-paying jobs there is for a college graduate. She works really hard—fifty to sixty hours a week—for her meager wages.

"I'm not exactly rich," Logan says, backtracking. "It won't last forever. It's just temporary while I figure some things out."

"Sounds great," Hannah says. "No need to be ashamed."

She can tell from his face that things have changed between them.

Stop being a snob, she tells herself. *Just because he's rich doesn't mean he's a bad person.*

"So, how do you spend your days?" she asks, trying to move the conversation along and get past this awkwardness.

He shrugs. "Hiking, swimming, skiing. Depends on the weather, I guess."

"Wow," she says. "That must be nice."

Now he looks even more embarrassed.

The weird thing about him is that he doesn't seem like some rich asshole living off Mommy and Daddy's allowance. He seems like a down-to-earth guy. He is nice and he has a certain boyish charm. He doesn't seem smarmy or pretentious. He seems like the kind of guy she could really enjoy spending time with.

The boat zips along, and they are both silent. The end of the first lake is approaching. She wants to start over, change the subject.

I've still got a little time to salvage this situation, she thinks.

Then she notices one of the girls on the pier. Probably fourteen or fifteen, she is jumping up and down on the dock, yelling and waving her arms. Hannah can't make out what she's saying because of the whining boat motor.

"What's that girl doing?" she says to Logan.

He turns, noticing the girl for the first time.

"Hey," he says to the pilot, "let off the motor for a second."

The pilot does as he's told, and the boat slows to a crawl. The motor idles, still audible but much quieter.

"Help!" the girl on the dock screams. She points into the water. "My sister!"

The message is clear: her sister is drowning.

CHAPTER 3

"GO!" LOGAN YELLS TO the pilot.

The kid does as he's instructed. He presses down on the throttle, and the propeller digs into the water, the bow lifting into the air. The boat surges forward, rising and falling, chopping into the water. It makes up the gap to the pier in seconds. The pilot cuts the engine at the last instant and yanks the rudder so the boat swings parallel to the dock.

Before the sidewall even touches the dock, Logan leaps out and dives into the water. He cuts the surface with hardly a splash. His action is so sudden that Hannah gasps.

The boat rocks in the waves it created, but the water is incredibly clear, and Hannah can see Logan under the surface, a blur swimming toward another blur.

The water must be glacially cold. Fed entirely from snowmelt, the lake is frigid all summer long, but this late in the season and this early in the morning, swimming would be like jumping into a bucket of ice water.

Hannah feels suddenly very helpless. This is an emergency, and she wants to help. What can she do?

You're a journalist, her inner editor's voice says. *Cover what's happening.*

Now Hannah has a purpose. She hops out of the boat onto

the deck, next to the girl. Hannah pulls out her phone, turns it to video mode, and begins to record.

A second after the camera begins to record, Logan bursts from the surface with the drowning girl in his arms. He begins swimming toward shore, holding one arm around her. The girl, maybe eleven or twelve, is completely limp. Her hair floats on the surface like strands of seaweed.

Hannah walks down the dock, filming Logan the whole time. She is on the bank when he comes up out of the water, holding the lifeless girl.

This footage is unbelievable, Hannah thinks. Then she feels ill at the thought. This girl is dying, and all she's doing is filming what's happening.

But she doesn't stop. Her editor's voice is in her ears, spurring her on.

Logan sets the girl down in a patch of grass and kneels next to her. He puts two fingers on her throat, checking for a pulse, and puts his head over her face, his neck turned so he can watch for her chest rising and falling and feel her breath on his cheek.

"There's a pulse," he says, his voice unbelievably calm. "But she's not breathing."

Hannah's heart slugs in her chest. She doesn't stop filming.

Logan tilts the girl's head back and tries to give her rescue breathing. The girl's chest doesn't rise. No air is getting in. Logan puts his hands together, palms down, and presses on the girl's abdomen.

Water bubbles up out of the girl's mouth, and Logan quickly turns her on her side. Lake water faucets from her mouth and nose.

"She's breathing," Logan announces, "but she's still unconscious."

Hannah thinks this seems like a good place to stop filming. She presses the red button and pockets her phone.

Logan puts his arms under the girl and lifts her. She's in a one-piece suit, and her arms and legs flop like pale, boneless noodles. Logan rushes past Hannah and the girl's sister. He places the girl down in the boat.

"Everybody in," he says, taking the sister's hand and helping her into the boat. He takes Hannah's hand, and before she knows it, she's sitting in the boat next to the unconscious girl.

"I'm going inside to call an ambulance," Logan says. "Hopefully they'll meet you at the parking lot."

Hannah opens her mouth to say they'll wait for him, but then stops herself. As if he can read her mind, Logan says, "You'll waste valuable time if you wait for me. I'll run down the path and meet you there."

The boat pilot needs no more instruction. He yanks the starter cord and the motor fires up. He presses the throttle and spins the boat in a tight arc, aiming it back the way they came.

As the boat speeds away, Hannah cranes her neck and watches as Logan runs into the cabin.

CHAPTER 4

THE PARAMEDICS LIFT THE unconscious girl and place her on a stretcher. Hannah and the older sister watch from the dock. The pilot of the boat stays in his seat, out of the way.

"My dad told me to take care of her," the sister says to Hannah. "But when she didn't come up, I just panicked. I didn't know what to do."

"She's going to be okay," Hannah says.

The girl looks up at her with puffy, tear-filled eyes and says, "Is she?"

Hannah puts her arm around the girl. It's not a gesture Hannah would normally be comfortable making—always the professional asking questions, not the friend providing comfort—but it seems to be what the girl needs. She collapses into Hannah, beginning to sob.

The paramedics roll the stretcher down the pier, toward the parking lot and the waiting ambulance.

"Come on," Hannah says, and she keeps her arm around the older girl as they follow.

The paramedics put the girl inside and begin to work on her: putting an oxygen mask over her mouth to help her breathe, placing an IV in her arm. When they're about to close the doors, Hannah says, "Can her sister go with her?"

The paramedics look at the girl under Hannah's arm skeptically.

"How old are you?"

"Seventeen," the girl says.

For a moment, Hannah thinks the girl must be lying. She barely looks old enough for high school.

"I'll call my dad when we get to the hospital," the girl says. "He's in town already."

"Okay," the paramedic says, relenting.

The girl climbs aboard, and the doors slam shut. The sirens come to life, and the ambulance pulls to the edge of the parking lot, hesitates for an instant at the intersection, and then races away at high speed.

Hannah takes a deep breath. She can't believe what just happened. She hopes the girl is going to be okay, and she has a good feeling she will. The girl was breathing and was in good hands.

Hannah turns toward the lake. Everything seems incredibly vivid—like her senses are heightened. The colors of the trees and the water seem to stand out. The fresh air is delicious. Every sound—every birdcall, every bug chirp—seems to vibrate with discrete clarity.

The pilot of the boat comes walking toward her. He's carrying her daypack, as well as Logan's.

"Some morning," he says, with a grin on his face telling her that he's feeling the same intense adrenaline rush.

He asks if she wants a ride back across the lake to the trailhead.

"No thanks," she says. "I think my plans for the day have changed."

She glances toward the path along the lake, expecting Logan to come jogging up. But there's no sign of him.

The boat pilot offers her daypack to her, and then he holds up Logan's pack, as if unsure what to do with it.

"I can put this behind the counter inside," he says. "Or I can leave it with you."

Hannah thinks for a moment and then tells him to put it behind the counter.

Before the kid walks off, Hannah tells him that she's a reporter for the *Lake Tahoe Gazette*.

"Can I ask you a few questions?" she says. "For an article."

He agrees, and he gives her exactly what she's hoping for: lively, pathos-laden quotes about what they witnessed.

When the interview concludes, Hannah leans against her car and waits for Logan to come walking down the path. He has a two- or three-mile hike to get back, and she's surprised he hasn't made it yet. He's had plenty of time.

She pulls out her phone and watches the video. The images are incredible. She's no professional videographer, but the camera is in focus, and she was in the right place at the right time. When Logan carries the girl out of the water, he looks like a movie hero. His shirt sticks to his chest. His arm muscles are taut. His expression is calm, yet determined.

She watches it again, mesmerized.

Now she feels antsy. She wants to get to the newspaper. The art department can extract an image from the video—a picture of Logan looking heroic—and put it next to her story in tomorrow's paper. They can also have the article up on the website by this afternoon, along with the full video.

"This thing's gonna go viral," she mutters to herself as she watches the video a third time.

She looks up and still there's no sign of Logan. Is it possible he went ahead and hiked up to Lake Aloha? She doubts it. He has no water, no food.

Hannah knows her article will be much better if she has an interview with the hero himself. But she also knows how the news business works, and a story like this will demand follow-up articles. She can do an interview with the girl and her family. Another interview with Logan. Not getting a quote from him in the first article won't be a big deal if she's able to interview him tomorrow. Or the next day.

And if she's honest with herself, she knows this will give her an excuse to call him. All of her misgivings about him being a rich trust-fund baby are erased. She saw the real Logan in action. Money or no money, he's a good person.

As she climbs into her car and starts the engine, she looks again to the path. Still no sign of him.

After she drives away, when no one is watching, there's movement from the shadows of a cluster of pine trees near the trailhead.

Logan steps out of hiding.

CHAPTER 5

I SLEEP IN LATE, and when I do get up, I'm more stiff and sore than I expected to be. I'm in good shape, so I didn't think the dive into the water and the jog back up the trail would have taxed my muscles. Certainly, summiting Mount Tallac or snowboarding all day at Heavenly Mountain Resort is more exhausting. But there must be something about the intensity of saving someone's life, the adrenaline of the experience, and the stress it puts on the body.

I check the time on my phone and see an unfamiliar number called me twice. It's a Lake Tahoe number. Maybe Hannah? I'll listen to the messages later.

I walk through my small two-bedroom house in my boxers, rolling my neck from side to side. My house is furnished modestly, with most of the furniture purchased at thrift stores. No paintings or photographs hang on the walls. I might have a few million dollars in diamonds at my disposal, but I've always preferred an austere lifestyle.

My place could use a woman's touch, though.

I look through the refrigerator and decide a big helping of protein is what I need. I pull out egg whites, sliced turkey, and shredded mozzarella cheese to make myself an omelet.

As I cook, I think about the day before. After I called 911

and answered all their questions, I ran back down the path toward the general store and the parking lot. I knew there was nothing else I could do. More than anything, I was jogging because I was cold. The air was chilly in the morning, and I was wearing wet shorts and T-shirt. My shoes squished water with every step.

When I approached the store and could see the paramedics loading the girl into the ambulance, I stopped and then crept into the trees, climbing up the mountainside, looking for a place to lay low.

I wasn't sure why I'd hidden.

I'd liked Hannah from the moment we started talking. But in my mind, some kind of warning bell was going off. Like the feeling before my last encounter with Marco, my old partner, some sixth sense said to me that I should refrain from stepping out into the spotlight.

Maybe it was that Hannah is a journalist. I don't see how what happened could be much of a news story. Maybe a brief blurb on page four. But still I don't quite trust Hannah, which I realize is a strange contradiction—I like her, but I don't trust her.

I think it comes down simply to the fact that I'm someone who wants—no, *needs*—to stay hidden. Hannah is someone who works in the public eye, whose job it is to reveal what's hidden. I don't want the world to know where I am or even who I am.

I set my steaming omelet down on my table and pour myself a glass of orange juice. I eat quickly, voraciously, and feel better immediately. Now all my worries about yesterday seem like paranoia.

It is a cloudy day, nothing like the clear, beautiful weather yesterday, and the gloom of the sky seeps through the windows and gives my house a depressing air. I still need to make a trek up to Lake Aloha before the weather turns too cold. But today just isn't an inviting day to do it.

Nevertheless, I don't want to be cooped up all day. I check the time and see that I could make it to the afternoon spinning class at the gym. I might run into Hannah, but I don't quite feel the same worry I did the day before. That had just been the old Logan, the cautious Logan, the guarded Logan. The Logan who had to look over his shoulder all the time.

Now, with a fresh mind and full stomach, I think it wouldn't be so bad to run into Hannah.

I dress and then jog to the gym, which is just a few blocks away along a path that runs parallel to the lake. Lake Tahoe— twelve miles wide and twenty-two miles long—is known for its amazing clarity. The surface reflects the color of the sky. It's ordinarily an intense cobalt blue, but today, under a foamy gray sky, the water looks opaque and gray and choppy. The beach, which was packed with tourists all summer, is empty.

When I get to the gym, I say a quick hello to the employee working the front counter, and then I head back to the spinning room. There's a stack of newspapers in a rack by the door, but I don't even think to glance at them. It doesn't occur to me that my picture might be on the front page.

CHAPTER 6

I STAKE CLAIM TO a bike in the back of the room and begin adjusting the seat and pedals. A minute later, a pretty young woman comes in and chooses the bike next to mine. She smiles at me, and I smile back—a shared smile, like yesterday with Hannah. I've been living in Lake Tahoe for two years and never once had a date. Two days in a row now I've had pretty girls smile at me.

The class starts. There are a few other people in the class, going through the motions, their bodies on autopilot, but I push myself hard. I'm feeling a little frustrated—my inability to get to Lake Aloha yesterday, today's crappy weather keeping me from it again—so I try to take my annoyance out on the workout.

Out of the corner of my eye, I see the woman next to me pushing herself just as hard. She sees me and smiles. I grin, and we both turn up the resistance, fighting the pedals. We're communicating without words, motivating each other.

Sweat beads on my forehead and my T-shirt starts to cling to my wet chest. She wipes her brow with a towel, takes a quick drink, and gets back to work. The instructor is speaking through his headset and fast-paced rock music is playing, but I'm not paying attention to anything but her. She's my inspiration.

I catch myself thinking about Hannah. Nine out of ten guys would probably say this girl next to me is more attractive. She is somewhere in her mid-twenties, with an athletic frame and blond hair that, even pulled back in a ponytail, is luxuriant. She has a pretty face with sharp cheekbones and a ski-jump nose.

Hannah, on the other hand, is a little bit more like the girl next door. She has plain brown hair, cut in a no-nonsense bob, and most guys might say she needs to lose a few pounds, although I found her curves quite sexy. What struck me about Hannah that other guys might overlook were her dark-brown doe eyes and her genuine, heartfelt smile.

But this girl next to me has an incredible smile too—shining and bright, like a sunrise. I've always felt you can tell a lot about a person from her smile.

When the class is finished, I dismount my bike and wipe my face. My shirt is soaking with sweat. My hair feels like I just stepped out of the shower. The girl is sweaty too, her arms slick with perspiration, her hair damp at the temples.

"Wow," she says, "that was fun."

It's the first time I've heard her speak, and I love the soft elegance of her voice.

"I'm Claire," she says, extending her hand.

"Logan."

Her hand is small and smooth, and holding it is like touching electricity.

We wipe down our bikes and start talking. She's lived in Tahoe for a only few weeks now, having moved from Ohio.

"Getting away from a bad job," she says. She hesitates, as if unsure whether to be this forthcoming, then adds, "And a bad relationship."

I tell her I've lived here for two years and love it: hiking, swimming, skiing. It's an outdoor enthusiast's paradise.

"That's why I moved here," she says.

I feel a pang of guilt, like I'm cheating on Hannah. But, I tell myself, we've never gone out. And, besides, something about Hannah was telling me to be cautious. Maybe I should listen to that voice in my head.

As Claire looks up at me with eyes as blue and deep as Lake Tahoe, I can't help but marvel at my good fortune that, after two years of being alone, I've met two good-looking women in two days.

I've been told I'm handsome, but I have a tendency to be introverted. And my previous line of work always compelled me to be antisocial and paranoid, to never let anyone get too close. So I wouldn't normally make the first move. But today I feel emboldened, and I ask her if she wants to exchange numbers.

"Maybe we can go for a hike before it gets too cold."

She smiles, and we program each other's numbers into our phones. We walk together as we head toward the door.

I figure I'll walk Claire to her car, but as we're passing by the front desk, one of the employees, a teenager in a San Francisco Giants ball cap, says to me, "Hey, man, I saw your picture in the paper. That was totally awesome. Way to go, dude."

"What?" I'm thinking the kid must have me mixed up with someone else.

"Yeah," the young guy says, pointing to the stack of *Lake Tahoe Gazette*s by the door. "Front page."

I grab one of the papers and stare at it. There's a huge photo above the fold of me coming up out of the water with the girl in my arms. My hair is wet and my expression is serious—but my identity is unmistakable.

The headline says, HERO SAVES DROWNING GIRL.

The byline says, BY HANNAH RYAN.

Claire crowds in next to me and looks at the picture. Her mouth turns into an O.

"Oh, my God," she says. "That's *you*. You're going to be famous!"

CHAPTER 7

HANNAH IS SITTING AT her desk trying to write about an uneventful city council meeting when she gets a call from the receptionist telling her that a man named Logan Bishop is in the lobby for her.

"He's cute," the receptionist whispers into the phone, then adds, "Holy shit. Is that the guy on the front page?"

"I'll be right there," Hannah says.

The newsroom is a large open-air office space, with the reporters wedged into cramped cubicles. Hannah strolls over the gray stained carpet as if she's gliding on mist.

When she opens the door to the lobby, the receptionist points outside and says he's waiting for her there. She can see him through the glass double doors, pacing as if nervous. His hair is damp and his T-shirt is sweat stained, as if he came straight from the gym.

Hannah steps outside with an enormous smile on her face. She can't help it. But then she looks at him more closely—his face pinched, his teeth clenched, his skin strangely flushed—and her smile vanishes.

"You're mad?" she says.

"Hell, yes, I'm mad," he says, holding up the paper and pointing to his picture. "What the hell is this?"

"I'm sorry," she says. "I was just doing my job."

Logan can barely contain his anger. "Your fucking job?"

Hannah feels suddenly very defensive. She was shy yesterday, but on the job, she has the utmost confidence. "Yes," she snaps. "I report the news." She points to the paper. "That is news, whether you like it or not."

"This is no one's business," he says. "You don't understand what you've done."

"Help me understand," she says. "Tell me."

"Why? So you can put it in the fucking paper?"

Hannah doesn't respond. The two of them are standing in the grass outside of the building. The air is chilly, and the gray sky creates a melancholy ambience. This isn't how she wanted their next meeting to go.

Logan takes a deep breath. It seems like much of his anger has drained from him. He's still upset, but the anger has turned to something else. Resignation. Helplessness.

"I tried to call you," Hannah says. "You didn't answer."

"Would it have made a difference?" Logan says. "If you'd reached me and I'd asked you not to run the story?"

"Probably not."

There's a bench in the grass for people to sit and read the paper. Logan flops onto it and holds his head in his hands.

"Look," Hannah says, sitting next to him. "I'm sorry, but this is a good story. 'A hero passerby saves a young girl from drowning.' People complain all the time that newspapers only report the bad news. Here is a feel-good story—someone doing something good, something heroic. I'm sorry you don't like it, but I'm glad I wrote it."

She wants him to see that he did a good thing and that people should know about it. This is the kind of news people *like* to read about, not the wars and murders and government corruption that always dominate headlines.

She tries to place her hand on his shoulder, but he jerks away. She has a sick, sinking feeling in her stomach. Yesterday, they were practically ready to make out. Today, she can't even lay a comforting hand on his shoulder without him flinching. It hits her then: they're never going to go out on a date. They'll probably never even be friends. Her chances of any kind of relationship with him have vanished like a ripple on a pond.

"Aren't I entitled to my privacy?" Logan says.

She shrugs. "You did something in a public place where there were witnesses. You're entitled to say no to an interview, but if there are other people I can interview, then there's nothing you can do to stop me from talking to them and reporting on what they say."

"Is there ever a time when you wouldn't report something you thought was newsworthy?"

"No."

Logan takes a deep breath and seems to relax a little with the exhalation.

"How is the girl, by the way?" he asks.

Now Hannah beams again—a big, genuine, heartfelt smile. "She's doing great."

Hannah explains that the little girl's name is Patricia—everyone calls her Patty—and that her father, a doctor from San Francisco, had rented the cabin for a few weeks to spend time with his two girls.

"He said he'd happily pay you a reward for saving her," Hannah adds. "It's the least he could do."

Logan dismisses the idea with a wave of his hand.

"You know," he says, looking down at the picture of himself, "I don't even remember you taking that picture."

Hannah opens her mouth to speak, and he cuts her off.

"I'm sorry I got so mad," he says, "but I'm a private person. I don't like a lot of attention."

"Well," Hannah says, reluctantly, "I've got some bad news for you."

Logan stares at her, waiting.

"There's more than just a picture," she says. "I actually took a whole video. It's up on our website right now. It's gotten a lot of hits. It's gone viral, actually."

Logan squints at her. "What does that mean?"

"It means news channels all over the country are showing it."

"Goddamn it!" Logan says, bolting to his feet, his anger back in full force, like a smoldering campfire reignited by a sudden gust of wind.

"It's a great video," Hannah says. "Very moving. Very inspiring."

Logan begins to stomp off and then turns back. "Do me a favor, Hannah. Just leave me the fuck alone."

"There's something else," she says, but he's already halfway across the parking lot.

She isn't able to tell him that someone claiming to be an old friend stopped by the paper that morning asking about him.

CHAPTER 8

I HARDLY SLEEP, AND when I get up, it's still dark outside. I sit on my deck and look out over the lake, waiting for the sun to rise. I can't decide whether I should skip town or stick around.

If that video is being played on national news programs, there's a chance Marco will see it and come looking for me. The safe play would be to leave Lake Tahoe and never look back. But I'm probably just being paranoid again. How many dozens of videos like that go viral each week, earning a thirty-second spot on some national broadcast before they're forgotten again? The odds of Marco seeing it are slim at best.

As the sun rises and the sky turns from black to blue, I think about the life I've made here. I have no close friends, no girl-friend—yet. But it's a new life, very different from the one before. Living in Los Angeles, plotting jobs with Marco. There was always the fear of getting caught. Or being betrayed.

I feel like a new person now. I left that life only two years ago, and Lake Tahoe is only about four hundred fifty miles from LA. But that world seems like it was a lifetime ago. Those memories seem like something that happened to another person, on another planet entirely.

If I run, I'll feel like I never left that life at all, like I've been playing pretend the last two years. But if I stay, keep putting down roots, maybe this life will continue to feel more and more like *my* life.

Yesterday's clouds have broken up. Sunlight reflects like golden scales off the water. It looks like it's going to be a nice day to go hiking. I go back inside and begin to get my gear together. One thing is for sure: regardless of whether I decide to stay or go, I need to hike up to Lake Aloha.

That's where I've hidden the diamonds. I was heading to their hiding spot two days ago before Hannah spotted the girl in the water.

When I first moved here, it seemed like a good idea. I'd broken away from all my contacts in LA, so I didn't have a fence who could sell the diamonds. I would only ever be able to sell one or two at a time without drawing attention to myself, which was fine for me since I wanted to make the money last the rest of my life anyway.

But I needed a place to keep them. Hiding them in my house seemed like a bad idea, no matter how well hidden they were. If anyone ever investigated me—or came looking for me—I didn't want the diamonds to be anywhere close.

So I found the perfect hiding spot in the wilderness, and I go up there a couple of times a year to grab a few stones that I can take to Reno or Sacramento to sell.

As fall approaches, the first snow could be only weeks away. I have to get up there and get a couple of diamonds to last me through the winter. Or if I'm going to split town, I need to grab the whole bag. Either way, the hike is a must. I'll have eleven miles of trail to decide what to do.

I fill up the water bladder of my daypack and throw in some granola bars, trail mix, and sunscreen. I dress in cargo shorts, a T-shirt, and a sweatshirt. I lace up my Merrell hiking shoes.

As I'm about to leave, my phone buzzes with an incoming text. I expect it to be Hannah, and I'm prepared to delete it. But it's not from her. It's from Claire.

The text reads, It's a beautiful day. Want to go for a hike?

I stare at the words and consider inviting her. What would it hurt to bring her along? After seeing the intensity of her workout yesterday at the gym, I know she's not going to hold me back. And once we're up there, it shouldn't be difficult to slip away from her to get the diamonds.

As much as I enjoy hiking alone, I've been doing that for two years now. It would be nice to have a beautiful woman to keep me company.

I text back, Getting ready to hike to Lake Aloha. Want to come along?

I think briefly about the possibility that I'm putting this girl in danger, but I picture her smile and her sapphire-blue eyes, and I push any concern I have out of my head.

CHAPTER 9

AT THE PARKING LOT, Claire is waiting for me, sitting on the tail-gate of a beat-up Toyota Tacoma. She waves and smiles as I pull up, and I feel a tingling inside. She's wearing a pair of hiking shorts and a tank top over a sports bra, a very practical outfit that is still sexy as hell, showing off her long legs and tanned, toned arms.

The place is busier this morning, with about a dozen cars in the parking lot and people going in and out of the general store. There are a handful of passengers loading into the water taxi. I wonder if the news coverage has caused the sudden in-flux of visitors. Maybe people want to see where the so-called heroism occurred.

The same kid is piloting the taxi today, and when he spots me, he yells, "Hey, man, you want a ride? It's on the house to-day!"

I explain to Claire that the taxi can bypass four miles of the hike.

"Nah," she says, "we came here to hike, didn't we?"

My heart warms at her words. It's obvious she's better suited for me than Hannah ever would be.

I tell the pilot that we'll pass, and he says that we can always get a ride on the way back.

"There's a telephone at the dock at the other end," he says. "The number is taped to the phone. Just give us a buzz and we'll come get you."

For a second, I think he's going to tell everyone in the boat who I am, but he—unlike Hannah—keeps my identity a secret, and I'm thankful for that.

Claire and I buy a couple bottles of Gatorade at the general store, and then we head out. The miles go by in a blur as we talk nonstop. I try to ask as many questions as I can, hoping to keep her from asking me too many details about my past. When she does ask me about what I do, I don't tell her that I have a trust fund. I've learned from my mistake with Hannah. Instead, I tell her that my parents died, and I'm temporarily living off the insurance money.

"It won't last forever," I say. "But for now I'm just trying to figure out what's next for me."

"I'm so sorry about your parents," she says, and she puts a comforting hand on my shoulder.

I feel a pang of guilt about pretending that I have money because of my parents' death. My parents are dead, but there was certainly no insurance or inheritance. I can't tell her the truth. What would I say? That I'm a retired thief living off a stash of stolen diamonds?

The trail is flat and shaded as we walk along the two Echo Lakes. We pass the dock at the far end and spot the pay phone the pilot was talking about, then the trail ascends and begins to get rockier. We hike in the shade of red fir and lodgepole pine, but they begin to thin the higher we climb. The trail is made up of rocks that are bleached white from the sun. The temperature begins to rise and soon we are both slick with sweat like the day before in the spinning class.

We hike for hours. When we get close to the lake, the landscape is made up almost entirely of granite, with the trail interweaving around boulders bigger than cars. The trees that do survive this high are twisted and gnarled by the wind and winter snow.

When we arrive at the lake, Claire says it's gorgeous, which makes me like her even more. Lake Aloha isn't beautiful in any traditional sense; it's stunning because its appearance is so unusual. When you imagine a mountain lake, you might think of a bowl of water that's more or less circular, its banks lined with pine trees and patches of green meadow. Lake Aloha is a misshapen body of water lying in a desolate granite valley, with strings of rock islands rising up out of the clear water. There are hardly any trees, barely any vegetation at all. The elevation is so high that dirty snow patches cling to the mountain peaks around us. The blue water seems to glow against the backdrop of barren rocky slopes.

I tell Claire I know a good place to stop, and I lead her to a granite-sloped bank about halfway around the lake.

Claire dips her hands into the lake and splashes water on her face. She gasps and says, "Holy crap, that's cold."

"You want to go for a swim?" I ask.

"Seriously?" she says. "That water's like ice."

"You mind if I take a dip?"

She stares at me as if I've just suggested something truly outrageous.

I kick off my shoes and pull my T-shirt over my head.

Her eyes drop to my bare chest and then she says, "Before you go getting all wet, there's something I want you to do."

"What's that?"

"Kiss me," she says.

She puts her hands—still wet and cold from the lake water—on my shoulders and pulls me down to kiss her. She opens her mouth, and our tongues touch. I wrap my arms around her and pull her body into mine.

It's in this moment that I realize there is no way I'm skipping town now.

Consequences be damned.

CHAPTER 10

AFTER WE'VE MADE OUT, and then eaten lunch, and then made out some more, I realize that I still need to get to the diamonds. It's midafternoon, and we should probably head back soon. I can't put it off any longer.

"I'm going to take that dip now," I say.

"Maybe I'll go with you," she says.

I'm worried for a moment, but I don't think she'll actually go through with it. The lake is pure snowmelt. Even in the warmest summer months, the water probably never gets above seventy degrees.

Claire kicks off her shoes, and we wade out into the water together. Cold engulfs my feet, and pain crawls up my legs, as if the chill is a living thing creeping through my bloodstream.

Claire inhales sharply and makes it as far as her knees, and then she splashes out of the water and back up onto the bank.

"No way," she says, hopping up and down. "That's impossible."

Her legs are red up to her knees, as if she stepped into boiling hot water instead of cold.

"You're crazy," she adds.

"I'm just more acclimated than you are," I say.

With that, I turn and dive forward under the water. I swim

for about twenty yards and come to a rock island about the size of a Volkswagen Beetle. I climb up on top to rest, but the air against my skin is even colder than the water. I wave at Claire and then dive off the other side.

The lake is as clear as drinking water. Sunbeams shine down through the water as I swim over and around boulders.

I bypass a couple small islands and finally arrive at an island a hundred yards from shore. It's rounded and about the size of a small backyard, rising up like the back of a white whale. I recognize it because of one gnarled tree that's growing out of the rock like the twisted, arthritic hand of a skeleton, beckoning me to my buried treasure.

The stone bank angles into the water, and I crawl up on the rock and lie on my back. My chest heaves. My body feels like it's glowing. After a minute, I rise, my limbs trembling. I wave at Claire, who is sitting on the bank.

I walk across the island, my wet feet slapping the granite. I find the crack I recognize, a point where two slabs of rock come together, and follow it to the edge of the water. There is a sheer drop-off on this side of the island.

I take a deep breath and dive straight down. The water is colder the deeper I get, like ice packed around my body. I keep my eyes open, and the cold seeps into my sockets. My ears ache from the depth.

A few feet from the bottom, there is a seam where two veins of rock come together. I run my hands along it and find the spot: a crevice about six inches wide. I reach my arm inside the crack, nearly to my shoulder. I pull out a small cloth satchel, then swim to the surface and catch my breath.

There's an underwater shelf about a foot wide that I can balance on, where the arc of the island keeps me hidden from Claire. I untie the satchel and pull out a plastic sandwich bag, packed full of diamonds. Even through the plastic bag, they glint in the sunlight.

I take three diamonds about the size of peas and shove them down into the pocket of my cargo shorts. I think about it and then grab a couple smaller ones. The smaller they are, the easier to sell. I zip up the bag and hesitate again. I pull out several more—a combination of big ones and little ones.

"Okay," I say aloud, "that's enough."

After I dive back under and replace the bag, I swim back toward shore. My arms and legs feel like they're strapped to twenty-pound weights. My lungs strain to pull in enough air.

At the bank, I flop down on top of the sun-warmed granite and try to get my breathing under control. Claire sits next to me and gives me her brightest, most beautiful smile.

"You disappeared there for a minute," she says. "What happened?"

"I was looking for sunken treasure," I say.

"Find any?"

"Nope," I say. "It was back here waiting for me all along."

"Yeah?"

"Yeah," I say, and I pull her down to kiss me.

When we're finished making out for the third time today, we sit up and stare out at the lake, enjoying the view one last time. The sun is starting to sink in the sky, and I tell Claire that we probably ought to take the water taxi back.

"We don't want to get caught out here in the dark," I say. "Besides, I'm pooped from that swim."

"That's too bad," she says, giving me a flirtatious smile. "I was hoping you'd still have some energy when we got back to town."

"Oh," I say. "Don't worry. I'll get my second wind."

I begin to lace up my hiking shoes. My eyes wander back out to the lake. The island where the rest of the diamonds are hidden is easy to spot. The tree's skeletal hand marks the location like an X on a treasure map. Or a grave marker.

I feel a twinge of fear, like I'm making the wrong choice. The smart thing would have been to tuck the whole bag into the pocket of my cargo shorts and then leave town first thing in the morning.

I realize now why I grabbed the extra diamonds from the bag.

I wanted some insurance in case I do have to run after all.

CHAPTER 11

HANNAH'S EDITOR CALLS HER into her office, which is unusual. Ashley Decker is a veteran journalist who worked at several metro papers before taking the editing job at the *Gazette,* and she believes in coming out into the newsroom to talk to her staff, not bringing them into her office. A call to the office usually means you are in trouble, which is something that happens to the other reporters every now and then, but never to Hannah.

"Sit," Ashley says, gesturing to an uncomfortable chair with orange foam stuffing spilling from cracks in the vinyl.

Ashley is in her mid-forties and attractive, but tired-looking. A high-pressure job and the long hours that come with it have taken their toll on her. She has crow's feet at the edges of her eyes, and filaments of silver have begun to highlight her silk-black hair.

She is someone who can command the respect of her staff and who can stand up to the publisher whenever they butt heads. She can do every job in the newsroom—reporter, photographer, copyeditor—better than the staff members paid to do them. And she can put on a dress, run a curling iron through her hair, and schmooze with Lake Tahoe's elite at any high-society function.

Hannah has always had great admiration for her. And

they've gotten along famously—Ashley recognizes a talented protégée when she sees one.

"So, what's happening with the profile of Logan Bishop? You know, the hero." Ashley adds this last part as if Hannah might have forgotten who he was.

"I don't think I can do the story," Hannah says. "He won't cooperate."

Ashley stares at her disapprovingly, a look Hannah has seen leveled at practically every other employee, but never herself.

"You can't convince him?" Ashley says. "Come on, this is a *good* story."

Hannah frowns and shakes her head. "Sorry, I think I've just about milked this one for all its worth."

It's been almost a week since she wrote the story about Logan saving the girl, and since then, Hannah has followed it up with an in-depth feature on the girl and her family; an article about the dangers of drowning; and even a day-in-the-life profile of what it's like to drive a water taxi on the Echo Lakes, for which she interviewed the kid who'd been with them that day along with a handful of his coworkers.

The only thing missing from this collection is an article about Logan.

Ashley leafs absently through some paperwork on her desk. Every surface of the desk is covered with notes or old copies of the *Gazette*. She finds what she's looking for—a copy of the front page with Logan's photo—and considers it.

"What's this guy afraid of?" she says.

"I think he just wants his privacy," Hannah says.

"Well, just because he doesn't want to talk doesn't mean there's no story there."

"I beg your pardon?"

"Find out what you can," Ashley says. "Talk to his friends. Find out where he works. See where he's from. It's possible to write a profile on someone even if they don't participate."

"I don't know," Hannah says. "That doesn't feel—"

"And who knows," Ashley says, pretending she didn't hear Hannah's objections, "if you tell him you're doing the story with or without his input, maybe he'll cooperate."

Hannah feels sick to her stomach. As a journalist, she's never had a problem asking hard questions. She's interviewed the family members of murder victims, people who'd lost their homes to wildfires, public figures embroiled in controversy. But she's always respected a person's right to say no. She's never tried to manipulate someone into speaking to the press when he didn't want to.

"I think we should just let the story go," Hannah says. "He saved a girl's life. I don't think we should punish him by plastering his face all over the newspaper if he doesn't want that."

Ashley stares at her, and Hannah thinks for a moment that the two of them might have their first real conflict. Hannah has always admired Ashley's ability to fight for what she feels strongly about, and now she psychs herself up to do the same—although it feels weird to prepare to fight with the person she's modeling her tenacity after.

A tense few seconds pass. Then Ashley shrugs and says, "I'll tell you what: just do some digging. See what you can find. If you still think there's no story, we'll bag it. I trust you."

A compromise, Hannah thinks. *I can agree to that.*

"Who knows?" Ashley adds. "Maybe this guy's hiding something. Maybe that's why he won't talk to you."

"Maybe," Hannah says, rising from her chair.

But Ashley's suggestion is ringing inside her like a struck tuning fork. *You don't know what you've done,* Logan had said. He'd mostly played himself off as a normal guy who simply wanted his privacy, but she suspected there was more to his secrecy than he'd let on.

"Wouldn't that be some shit?" Ashley says, cracking a smile. "What if our hero turns out to be some criminal?"

Hannah returns to her desk, thinking about the possibility.

What does she know about him? Not much. Just that he's independently wealthy and likes his privacy.

If he is hiding something bigger, that would actually make sense. She never quite thought the trust-fund story fit him. But does being a criminal on the run fit him either?

Hannah opens up her laptop and begins to dig.

CHAPTER 12

A WEEK AFTER MY hike to Lake Aloha with Claire, she and I are in a spinning class at the gym, sweating and laughing and motivating each other. It's the early-morning class, not the midafternoon class. This has become our routine, kicking off each day with a good workout. In the last week, we've spent every minute together that we can. She's pretty much moved in with me. We both agreed it would be temporary until she finds her own place, but I think, in our hearts, we both know this is permanent. She's made no effort to move and I certainly haven't pressured her to. I like having her around.

She has been looking for a job, though, taking her truck each day to drive around town to fill out applications and do interviews. She's been encouraging me to do the same, since she's under the impression that my insurance money will run out. I'm thinking about doing it, getting a real job of some kind. I haven't had much time alone to take a day and drive to Reno or Sacramento to try to sell some of the diamonds. And it might be nice to think of that money, my stash, as supplemental income.

When I turned my back on Marco, I wanted a normal life, didn't I?

What's more normal than working a regular job?

For now, though, I'm just trying to relish the moment. I've been alone for a long time. I want to enjoy being with someone.

These are the things I'm thinking about as we're finishing up the class, wiping down our bikes and taking long drinks of water. When Claire and I come walking out of the gym, I see Hannah waiting in the parking lot. She's wearing regular clothes: jeans, blouse, cardigan. She is wearing sneakers, but she clearly hasn't been working out, which tells me she's here for only one reason: to see me. And the fact that we're in the morning class, not the afternoon class where I used to see her, tells me that she's gone out of her way to find me. She's probably afraid I wouldn't answer her phone call.

When she sees us coming out of the building, she offers a bashful smile and lifts her arms up as if to surrender.

"Truce?" she says.

I smile and say hello. Obviously I was just being paranoid when I blew up at her about the article.

"I want to talk to you about something," she says. "Can I buy you a cup of coffee?" She gestures toward the café next door to the gym. "Off the record," she adds. "Not for publication. I just want to talk—as friends."

Claire eyes her suspiciously. My heart swells a little—she looks cute when she's jealous.

I tell Hannah that I'll meet her over in the coffee shop. Then I ask Claire if she minds going back to my house and waiting for me. It's just a short walk along the beach path. Today is a warm day—maybe the last of the season—and I don't think she'll mind.

"Should I be worried?" Claire says, gesturing toward the coffee shop as Hannah steps inside.

"Not at all," I say. "Hannah and I are just friends."

I give her a long, reassuring kiss, and then I head to the coffee shop. Hannah is waiting in line, and I join her. She buys a regular coffee and I opt for a soda instead. I'm more of a sugar junkie than a caffeine addict.

Hannah insists on paying.

In our seats, she smiles at me, and I can tell there's something on her mind. I wonder for a moment if she's going to declare that she has feelings for me, and I realize I'm not quite sure how I would handle that. I'm falling for Claire—hard— but sitting across from Hannah, I'm struck with how much I like her. With the sunlight through the window catching her hair and bringing out the depth in her chocolate-brown eyes, she's every bit as pretty as Claire.

In another life, I think, maybe she and I would have been meant for each other.

"Was that your girlfriend?" Hannah asks.

"I'm sorry I didn't introduce you. I guess you caught me off guard."

I tell her that I met Claire the day after I met her. Hannah has a melancholy look on her face, like she knows she missed her chance.

"There's something I need to talk to you about," she says. "I don't want you to get mad and storm off. I just want to talk. As friends."

Now I'm nervous.

She reaches into her purse and pulls out a piece of paper folded in half. She unfolds it and slides it across the table to me.

It's a photocopy of a warrant for my arrest.

CHAPTER 13

"SHIT," I SAY, AND I flop back in my seat. I tilt my head back and run my fingers through my sweaty hair. I think about how much trouble I'm in.

The problem isn't the warrant. The warrant is old. It's from an armored car job that Marco and I did a few years ago. The police brought me in after the warrant was issued, but they ended up releasing me. No charges were filed. Not enough evidence.

I'm sure Hannah knows all of this. Like I said, the problem isn't the warrant: the problem is that if Hannah knows about the warrant, then she probably knows a lot more. If she dug deep enough to speak to someone in LA's robbery division, which is what she would have had to do to get this outdated warrant, then she probably knows about a lot of the crimes I'm *suspected* of committing.

And if she writes about any of it, then Marco *will* find me.

Last time, I'd surprised Marco when I'd refused to show him the diamonds. Now he's had two years to think about that scenario, to reconsider how he would handle the situation if given a second chance. The next time he sees me, I won't be able to refuse. He'll kill me no matter what.

I take a drink from my soda and say, "Can we walk along the beach? I don't want to talk in here."

She looks out the window, as if considering whether she wants to be alone with me. There are plenty of people on the sand, out en masse for one of the last decent days of the season. Forecasters are predicting the temperature will plummet in the next couple days. It might even snow.

"Okay," she says.

We walk along the path back toward my house. There's a slight breeze, and it chills me because I'm still in my sweat-soaked clothes. The breeze pushes Hannah's hair back, and she walks without speaking.

"So, how much do you know?" I say.

"You've never been arrested," she says. "There's no valid warrant out for you."

"But?"

"But you're a suspect in a number of old robbery cases. Banks. Jewelry stores. Businesses that keep cash on hand. One detective I talked to called them 'mid-level jobs,' but he said your name had been kicked around in connection with the theft of some particularly valuable diamonds."

I'm quiet.

"He thought you graduated to the big leagues," she says. "Then you disappeared. They figured you were probably dead."

"I would have liked it if they kept on thinking that," I say.

We're not far from my house now. I can see it. We're going to be there before we know it, so I suggest to Hannah that we sit on a nearby bench.

"When you wouldn't let me interview you," Hannah says, "my editor asked me to find out more about you. It wasn't too hard to find this stuff."

"I should have used a fake name," I say. "I thought if I didn't have a bank account, didn't use a credit card, paid cash for my rent, didn't sign up for Facebook or anything stupid like that—I thought if I did all those things, I could fly under the radar."

"The thing is," Hannah says, "no one's actually after you. The police found you before and couldn't make the charges stick. You're not actually a wanted man."

I look into her deep brown eyes and am struck again by how pretty she is.

"It's not the police I'm running from, Hannah."

Her expression seems to change as she thinks about what I might be suggesting.

We're silent for a moment. I stare out at the water. When I was a kid growing up in San Francisco, my parents would bring me here each summer, and I fell in love with the brilliant blue water, the pine forests, the frosted mountain peaks. When I was pulling jobs with Marco, I thought about Lake Tahoe often, wondering if I could be a different person here. Step back in time and try to be the person I could have become, instead of the one I did.

"Last week," I say, "I asked you if you'd ever refrain from putting something in the paper you thought was newsworthy."

Hannah nods.

"Well," I say, "I'm going to tell you everything. Throw myself on your sword. You have to decide what to do with it."

She waits.

"I'm a thief, Hannah. Or I was. All those crimes I'm suspected of, I did them. My partner was a pretty bad guy named Marco. When I told him I was quitting, he tried to kill me. If he ever finds out where I am, he'll come for me. He'll cut my throat and pull my tongue out through the hole."

Hannah swallows.

"I came to Lake Tahoe to start over," I continue. "I don't want to be the person I was. I never killed anyone, Hannah. I was never that kind of criminal. But I stole from people. I hurt people. I don't like who I was."

It feels good, in a way, to get this information off my chest. I've been pretending for so long, it's nice to finally tell the truth to someone.

After a moment of silence, Hannah says, "So the story about the trust fund? That was all bullshit?"

I laugh. "Total bullshit." I'm not sure how much to tell her, but I've already started so I decide to see it through all the way. "I've got a stash of 'particularly valuable diamonds' hidden at Lake Aloha," I say, making quotation marks with my fingers. "I go up there a couple times a year to grab a few stones that I can sell and live off of."

Hannah seems mortified at the thought that the day we met, the day I saved a little girl's life, I was on a mission to retrieve stolen jewels.

She shakes her head, as if to clear her thoughts, and says, "I never thought 'trust fund baby' fit you." Now it's her turn to make air quotations. "That just didn't seem like you."

"What about now?" I say. "Does *thief* fit me any better?"

She looks at me carefully, as if really considering the question. "A little bit," she says. "But I'd like to think 'hero who saves little girl' fits the best."

"Me too," I say softly, not sure if that's true.

CHAPTER 14

"DOES SHE KNOW THE truth?" Hannah asks. "Your girlfriend."

"No," I say, looking away from her and out at the wavelets lapping at the shore. "But I should tell her before it gets more serious, shouldn't I?"

"If she's smart," Hannah says, "she'll run away from you as fast as she can."

"If I were smart," I say, "I would have run away from Lake Tahoe the moment I saw my picture in your newspaper. We don't always do what we're supposed to."

"No," she says, "we don't."

I try to figure out if there's a subtext to her words. Is she saying she won't write about what I'm telling her? Or at least thinking about it?

"For what it's worth," I say, standing up and tossing my soda into a nearby garbage can, "I'm sorry about all this."

"*You're* sorry?"

"Yeah," I say. "When you met me on that boat, I'm sure you didn't expect me to turn out to be a criminal."

I almost add, *A criminal who picked another girl over you.*

I don't need to say it. I can tell she gets the message.

"Look," she says. "I'm glad we met on that boat. You saved a little girl's life. Don't forget that. I'm the one who should say she's sorry. You didn't ask to have your picture in the paper."

I shrug. "You were just doing your job," I say, echoing her words from our fight a week ago.

I ask her if she decides to publish what she knows about me, will she warn me ahead of time?

"So you can split town?" she says.

I nod.

"I'll give you a heads up," she says.

"Well, I guess this could be good-bye," I say.

I open my arms, not sure if she'll hug me, but she steps in, and we hold each other for longer than decorum would suggest is necessary. I feel her warm body pressed against mine. I inhale deeply and smell her hair.

Ah, I think, *in another life…*

When we break, I point and show her which house is mine. I'm not sure why. I guess I just don't want this to be the last I ever see of her.

But as I watch her walk back down the beach path, I think it probably will be. She's a journalist in her heart, and when there's news, she reports it. I think she'll call this afternoon and let me know the paper is going to print the story. I can picture news anchors around the country saying to their respective audiences, "Remember that viral video we showed you last week about the hero saving the girl from drowning? New information has come to light, and you'll never guess what it is."

I figure I'll have about twelve hours to get out of town.

Which means that if I want any sort of life with Claire, I need to tell her the truth.

It occurs to me that if I left, I'd miss Hannah as much as Claire. This doesn't make any sense to me. Claire is perfect for me—and the last week has been wonderful. But the heart doesn't work the way the head does.

Hannah is far from perfect for me, but if I'm honest with myself, she's the one I would prefer to be coming home to right now.

I'm not sure what to do. Break up with Claire? Ask her to run away with me? I take the final steps to my house, going through the words I should say, playing different scenarios in my head.

But when I walk in the door, Claire is tied to a chair, duct tape strapped over her mouth. There are two men holding guns to her head.

One of them is a hairless gorilla with tattoo-coated arms.

The other one is Marco.

"Hello, old friend," he says, his lips spreading into a broad, sinister smile.

CHAPTER 15

I STEP FORWARD WITH my fists raised, and the hairless gorilla comes at me, ready to fight.

"Stop," Marco says, his voice sounding annoyed.

He presses the barrel of his gun into Claire's cheekbone. She tries to squirm away, but he keeps the gun hard against her skin.

"Okay, okay," I say, raising my hands.

"Don't move," Marco says. "Keep those hands raised." Then he nods to his partner. "Now, Jasper, you can have your fun."

The big guy, Jasper, walks toward me. He's a good two inches taller than me, making him at least six five. He's wearing jeans and a Motörhead T-shirt, both pulled tight over a husky, freakishly muscular frame. There isn't an inch of skin on his bulbous arms not covered in tattoos.

"I can't tell if you spend more time at the gym or the tattoo parlor," I say. "But I can tell you don't spend much time read-ing books."

Jasper smirks and tucks his pistol into his jeans. It's a bulky revolver ill-suited for being stuck into jeans, but that's where he keeps it.

He circles around behind me and then swings his big fist underneath my raised arms. Pain explodes through my ribs, and air rushes from my lungs. I fall to the floor, holding my side and trying to catch my breath.

Jasper squats down and drives his sledgehammer hand into my face. I see stars. Blood trickles from one nostril and my lips are bleeding into my mouth. I blink back tears and feel a wave of nausea.

"Don't knock him unconscious," Marco says. "Stick to the body."

Jasper does, thundering me with blows to my ribs, stomach, and back. I roll and squirm and try to cover myself, but if I can't fight back, there's little I can do.

"That's enough," Marco says, stepping forward to stand over me. I sit up, trying to breathe shallowly so I don't inflame my bruised—or broken—ribs.

"You know why I'm here?" he says.

"To kill me," I say. "So why don't you go ahead and get it over with?"

"I'm here for what you stole from me," Marco says.

His hair has grown longer and is pulled back in a ponytail, but otherwise my old partner is unchanged. He's dressed in a sharp outfit: black shirt and pants, gray sports coat, expensive dress shoes.

"Marco," I say. "We both know this was never about the diamonds. You just got your feelings hurt because I was quitting. You didn't want to be left alone, that's all this is. You're a jilted little schoolyard bully, petulant because your best friend dissed you."

Marco considers this. "Maybe so," he says. "But I still want those fucking diamonds."

I spit a glob of blood and mucus onto his shoe.

"Fuck you," I say, a string of blood hanging from my mouth.

He takes the butt of his gun and pistol whips me in the forehead. I fall back onto the floor, dizzy and lightheaded, fighting not to pass out.

"Hey," Jasper whines. "You said not to hit him in the head."

"Do as I say," Marco says, "not as I do."

Blood crawls down my forehead from a fresh gash.

"Tie him up," Marco orders.

Jasper rolls me over and duct-tapes my hands together behind my back. Then he yanks me onto a kitchen chair and wraps my feet to the legs and my arms to the back. He positions me facing Claire, who is tied in the same way except for the added swatch of tape over her mouth.

They haven't hurt her as far as I can tell, but she's clearly traumatized. Her hair is a mess and her eyes are red from crying. Her skin is pale, as if she might be sick at any moment.

Marco pockets his Beretta inside his shoulder holster, and he pulls out a folding knife with a rubber grip and a curved serrated blade. He kneels next to Claire. He presses the point against her cheek, not quite hard enough to draw blood, but close.

"Don't, Marco," I say.

"She's got pretty eyes," Marco says. "It would be a shame to have to cut them out."

"Don't fucking touch her!"

Marco turns to me, keeping the blade against her skin. "You see," he says, "this is what I didn't have last time we met. Leverage."

"Let her go, and I'll tell you where they are," I say.

"No," Marco says. "Tell me or I hurt her. I won't kill her, Logan, not yet, but I will hurt her."

Last time Marco and I had a standoff, I had all the cards. This time, he does.

"I hid them at Lake Aloha," I say, reluctantly. "It's a lake outside of town. You have to hike there. She and I went up there last week and I got a few." I gesture with my head toward the bathroom. "They're in a bottle of ibuprofen in my medicine cabinet."

Marco gives Jasper a nod, and the big guy goes into my bathroom. He comes back with a bottle of Advil. He shakes it and the tablets rattle around inside. He opens the bottle and pours maroon pills into his palm. He inspects them and dumps them on the floor. He pours another handful and sifts around in it. He holds his palm for Marco to inspect.

"Ah," Marco says, digging two pea-sized diamonds from among the pills. He inspects them, staring obsessively as if he's caught in a hypnotist's trance.

"Here's another," Jasper says, and Marco plucks a smaller diamond from Jasper's meaty hand and holds it up to his eyes.

"This one would be perfect for an engagement ring," he quips, ruffling Claire's hair.

"The whole bag is up there," I say. "Three million on the low end. Five if you've got the right buyer. Let Claire go, and you can have them all. I'll take you right to them. You just have to let her go."

"No." Marco shakes his head. "That's not how we're going to do this. We're going up there together, all four of us."

CHAPTER 16

THE VAN PULLS INTO the parking lot and rolls to a stop in an empty space facing the lake. I sit in the passenger seat, my wrists tied with duct tape. Behind us in the van, Claire sits with her hands and feet bound and tape over her mouth. She is trying not to cry, and failing. Jasper is twirling a lock of her blond hair with his finger.

"Don't worry," I say to Claire, craning my neck to see her. "We're going to be okay."

"That's true," Marco says, looking in the rearview mirror. "You're going to be just fine—*if* your boyfriend does what he's told."

Marco pulls out his knife. He leans toward me and pauses.

"Try anything," he says, "and she dies first. Got it?"

I say nothing.

"I want to hear you say it," Marco says.

"Got it," I say.

Before we left, they cleaned the blood off my face, but there's still a bruised gash on my forehead, and my lips are swollen and crusted red. They ransacked my hiking equipment, throwing together enough daypacks and water bottles for all of us. I was able to pick a few ibuprofen off the floor with my mouth and dry-swallow them. I have no idea if they're doing any good. My ribs feel like they've been pounded with a meat tenderizer.

Marco cuts the tape from my hands and yanks it off—and my arm hair with it. Behind us, Jasper is doing the same with Claire. She gasps as he yanks the tape off her face.

"The rules are very simple," Marco announces to the whole vehicle. "Logan, if you run off, we kill Claire. Claire, if you run off, we kill Logan. If either of you try to call for help or signal a hiker or ranger or anything like that, we kill both of you. And we kill whoever you try to signal."

Marco fixes me with his steel-gray eyes. "Do you believe we'll do it, old friend?"

"Yes," I say. "I believe you."

The parking lot is nearly empty, with only a little hustle and bustle from a few employees coming and going from the general store and working on the dock. It looks like the hoopla caused by the newspaper article has already passed.

The four of us pretend to be friends getting ready for a day hike. Claire is the worst at pretending. She's shivering, holding her head down, and sniffling. She's wearing no makeup and looks terrified, but she is still beautiful. Her blond hair is coming loose from being pulled back, and strands hang down around her face.

It's true that an hour ago I was considering breaking up with her, thinking about how I might like Hannah more, but she doesn't deserve to be going through this.

"It will save us about four miles if we take the water taxi," I tell Marco.

Marco looks down at the lake and the trail running alongside it.

"How long without it?" Marco asks.

"About eleven miles."

"One way?"

I nod. Claire and I are the only ones dressed for hiking. Before we left my house, I insisted that Marco let us change into comfortable cargo shorts, boots, and lightweight polyester T-shirts. Marco, who is only one shoe size smaller than me, was able to put on a pair of my running shoes, but otherwise his slacks and jacket are completely impractical for hiking. Jasper, in combat boots and jeans, looks more appropriately dressed for a rock concert than a day hiking in the wilderness.

"We'll take the boat," Marco declares. "But if either of you try anything," he adds, looking back and forth between Claire and me, "we'll kill the driver and dump him overboard."

The driver is a different person this time, a chubby twenty-something with a trucker hat and big stud earrings. We are the only ones in the taxi. When we load onto the boat, I keep expecting the driver to spot Jasper's gun. Marco's is well hidden in his shoulder holster, but Jasper's is only stuck into his jeans with his shirt pulled over. Still, the kid doesn't notice and doesn't seem to care that half our group isn't dressed for hiking.

As the boat skims across the surface of the lake, the air is colder. Clouds are moving in, covering the sky in murky gray. Claire holds her arms tightly around her body. I can see goose bumps on her legs and arms.

The boat speeds past the docks of the cabins perched on the granite banks.

"Can you get to these houses only by boat?" Marco asks me, as if we're pals and I'm taking him to a new place to hike.

THE PRETENDER • 321

"Or by foot," I say.

Marco frowns. "What about in the winter?"

"No one lives here year round," I say. "The lakes are frozen and you've got to use cross-country skis to get in and out."

The cabins appear to be vacated for the season, except for the one where the girl was drowning. A man is sitting on a deck chair at the edge of the water, reading a book. The father, I assume. He looks up at us and gives a friendly wave.

At this distance, there's no way he could recognize me as the man in the newspaper photograph.

I'm going to die because I saved your daughter, I think. I would be okay with that—to trade my life for hers. The problem is I don't want Claire to die because of me.

The boat slows as the driver navigates through a narrow channel to Upper Echo Lake. The water is so clear that we can see trout swimming beneath the boat. A few minutes later at the dock, the boat pilot points to the pay phone.

"If you guys want a ride back, give us a call," he says. "The number's posted. There's no cell service out here."

"We'll probably hike back," Marco says.

There is a subtext to these words. Marco and Jasper will hike back because they don't want any witnesses to say the boat pilot transported four people into the wilderness but only two came out.

CHAPTER 17

THE BOAT SPEEDS ACROSS the water, leaving us alone on the lake's edge. Claire starts crying, as if she'd been holding out hope that something would happen to keep us from going through with this.

"I'm sorry," I say to her, putting all the earnestness into my voice that I can. "I hate myself for putting you in this position."

She says nothing, but her eyes communicate all of her emotions: anger, confusion, fear, sadness, and—rising through all those to the surface—a feeling of betrayal.

Marco insists that I lead and he follow behind. Claire will be between him and Jasper, who will bring up the rear. If we pass another hiker or a ranger, we are supposed to act normal, like we are just four friends out enjoying the day.

"Don't forget," Marco says before we start, "no matter how fast you think you can run, our bullets are faster."

We begin hiking uphill. When we pass the wooden sign stating that we are entering Desolation Wilderness, Marco quips, "Sounds ominous."

We hike in silence for an hour, and then Marco says, "So, where'd you find the girl, old friend? She's cute."

I don't answer the question. Instead I say, "Where'd you get your new partner? Mercenaries-R-Us?"

From the back of the line, I hear Jasper chuckle.

"Is it love?" Marco continues. "Back when we were pulling jobs, I never figured you for the settling-down type."

"Back when we were pulling jobs, I never figured you for the betraying-your-partner type," I say. "Looks like neither of us ever really knew the other."

"I sure as hell *don't* know you," Marco says. "You've got millions of dollars in diamonds and you hide them out here in the woods? You live in a shithole when you could be living in a mansion. What the hell are you thinking?"

Instead of answering, I pick up the pace so Marco will be too out of breath to keep asking questions.

We hike for two more hours, and then Marco insists we stop at an overlook to rest. The sky is completely overcast now, and the temperature is dropping. There's a real autumn chill in the air.

We sit on a fallen tree in the order we hiked, with Marco between me and Claire.

Marco turns to Claire. "What about for you? Do you love him?"

She is quiet for a moment and then says, "I did."

Marco laughs. "Did you hear that? She *did*. That's gotta hurt."

I say nothing.

"How did you meet?" Marco asks Claire.

"Leave her alone," I say.

Marco ignores me and goes back to questioning Claire. "Did you ask him out or did he ask you out? I bet you asked him out. The Logan I knew back in Los Angeles never had the balls to talk to a girl. He's got movie-star good looks, but he's got no game with the ladies." He nudges my arm. "I know you better than you think, old friend."

"That's enough," I say.

"He wasn't good with girls," Marco says, "but I once saw him beat a guy twice his size unconscious with his bare hands. Your boyfriend was something special back in the day."

"That person doesn't exist anymore," I say quietly.

Marco laughs hard.

Jasper clears his throat and hocks a thick glob of snot and saliva out into the trees.

"The thing I don't get," Marco says to Claire, "is how you never suspected anything. Some strange guy living in Lake Tahoe. No job. A comfortable stream of money. Probably no real friends. None of that struck you as odd?"

"Leave her alone," I say again.

"He really had you fooled, didn't he?" Marco says. "Are you dumb or was the sex really that good?"

I rise. "I said leave her alone, Marco."

Marco looks up at me from the log, grinning, then he rises slowly. He pulls his Beretta from its holster. He points the barrel at Claire's head and she twists her face away and puts her hands up, as if they could stop a bullet.

"Hurt her and I'll kill you," I say.

Marco chuckles. "You're good, old friend, but there are two of us, and we've got the guns."

I step back, raising my hands.

"If you want to save your honeybunch," he says, "you've got to give me those diamonds."

"Well, what are we waiting for?" I say. "Let's get moving so we can both get what we want."

CHAPTER 18

I BRING THEM TO the same granite slope where Claire and I first kissed a week ago.

"We're here," I say.

Marco looks around curiously. "Okay, so where are the diamonds?"

I turn toward the lake and point. "Out there."

"You've got to be kidding me."

I shake my head. "I'll swim out and get them. When I get back, you let Claire go. Deal?"

"You're not going out there alone," Marco said. "Jasper, go with him."

I smirk. "Do you have any idea how cold that water is? It's pure snowmelt. It's probably not even sixty degrees."

Jasper walks to the edge of the water, bends over, and sticks his hand in. He holds it under for four or five seconds and then pulls it out. His hand is red, as if sunburned.

"No way," Jasper says, shaking his arm and flinging the water off his hand. "That hurts all the way to my elbow."

"Don't be such a pussy," Marco says. "I don't care if they pipe the water in straight from Antarctica, you're going with him."

Jasper shakes his head. "I ain't such a good swimmer in normal conditions."

Marco rolls his eyes. "All right," he says to me. "Don't you forget for a second that we got your girl. I don't care if you drown out there, if you don't come back, we're gonna kill her deader than Bruce Lee. And she's gonna wish she was dead long before I pull the trigger. Got it?"

I take a long drink from my CamelBak and then drop the pack on the ground. I kneel and untie my shoes. I pull my shirt off and stand barefoot in front of the others. The rock is cool under my feet. The air is chilly against my skin. Goosebumps rise on my chest.

I want to tell Claire that I will probably not survive after all of this, but that I will do everything I can to make sure she will.

Instead, I say, "I'm sorry. The last few days have been among the best in my life."

"I think I need a box of tissues," Jasper says.

Claire is looking hard at me, her eyes bloodshot, her skin pale. "I don't even know who you are," she says.

"Yes you do." I gesture to Marco. "It's this guy who doesn't know me."

"Oh, I know you," Marco says. "You're just pretending to be someone you're not."

I don't respond. I'm not sure who the real Logan is. But I need the old Logan if Claire and I are going to get through this.

I look across the lake, not turning my head but scanning the shoreline for other people. I see no one: no tents, no fishermen, no one. We haven't seen a soul since the boat driver dropped us off. We are all alone out here. There is no one to hear gunfire.

"What are you waiting for?" Marco says. "We ain't got all day."

I step into the water, taking deep breaths. When I am waist deep, I dunk my head and swim outward. The water is so cold that it feels hot, burning my skin.

I skip the Volkswagen Beetle island where I usually stop to catch my breath, and I go directly to the island with the skeleton tree.

I swim down and pull out the small cloth satchel. On the ledge, with the arc of the island keeping my actions hidden from the others, I untie the satchel and pull out the plastic sandwich bag. I let the satchel float away and tuck the bag into the pocket of my cargo shorts. Then I take a deep breath and swim back down to the crack where the diamonds were hidden.

This time, when I stick my arm into the crevice, I come out with another hidden treasure inside a waterproof plastic bag.

This one isn't a bag of diamonds.

It's a .45-caliber pistol.

CHAPTER 19

THE GUN IS A lightweight, titanium-framed pocket pistol, built for people with conceal-and-carry permits. Only five inches long, it fits inside the sandwich bag easily. The brand name of the gun is DoubleTap because it holds only two bullets. I'll need to make them count.

I tuck the gun into the other pocket of my shorts and climb up onto the island.

Claire is standing on the shore, with Marco and Jasper flanking her. I take a moment to catch my breath and dive back into the water.

I climb up onto the Volkswagen island twenty yards off shore to rest for a moment. My cargo shorts cling to my body and sag from the weight of the water and the contents of the pockets. I don't think the gun is visible. The diamonds make a bigger bulge. The pain in my ribs is gone now, smothered by the adrenaline pumping through my veins.

I jump into the water and swim for shore. When I can touch the sand under my feet again, I take my time walking forward, trying to slow my breathing. Marco and Jasper hold their guns in their hands. Claire's hands are clutched in front of her chest, like she is praying.

When I'm in two feet of water, I pull the package of diamonds out, open the bag's zipper, and then hold out my arm as if I'm going to pour the diamonds in the water.

"If I dump these," I say, "you'll still be able to find some of them. But it will be a giant pain in the ass in this cold water."

"Don't try to be clever," Marco says.

"Let Claire go."

Jasper takes her by the arm and raises his revolver and presses it to her head. She is breathing fast, almost to the point of hyperventilating. Tears stream down her cheeks.

"Come on," Marco says, "do we really have to do this?"

"Let her go," I say. "When I feel like she's a safe distance away, I'll turn over the diamonds."

"What, so she can run down to that pay phone and call the cops?" Marco says. "I've got another idea. I shoot you. We make Claire wade out into the water and gather up the diamonds from around your dead body. Then we beat the shit out of her until she begs us to kill her. Then, and only then, do we put her out of her misery." His voice rises as he speaks. "How's that sound to you?"

I tilt the bag, pretending I'm ready to pour it out. "I know I'm not getting out of this alive, Marco. But I'm not going to make it easy for you unless she goes free."

Marco's face is turning red. He grits his teeth and growls, "Logan, give me those goddamn diamonds."

"Suit yourself," I say.

I toss the open bag into the air. Diamonds spill out as the bag sails toward Marco. Marco tries to grab the bag with his free arm, but only slaps at it, knocking it to the ground. Diamonds rain down into the water and skitter on the rock like hailstones.

"You son of a bitch!" Marco roars, bending over to collect the diamonds. "Jasper, kill this motherfucker."

I'm already surging forward, pulling the gun out of my shorts. Jasper's eyes narrow, as if he is trying to figure out what I'm doing, then his eyes grow large with recognition. He turns the gun from Claire to me. I punch my finger through the plastic bag, take aim at the center of Jasper's face, and fire.

The gunshot echoes off the granite all around us.

I turn even before Jasper's body falls to the ground.

Marco rises. "What the—"

I swing my gun on Marco. He throws his arm out just in time, slapping the pistol aside. The bullet hits his shoulder. Marco gasps and tries to bring his own gun up, but he is holding it in the injured arm. I drop the two-shot pistol and grab Marco's wrist. With my other hand, I grasp a handful of his hair and wrestle him toward the bank. We fall in about eight inches of water, clawing and struggling. I gain leverage and put my knee on Marco's chest. He cranes his head to bring his mouth out of the water, and I press down harder.

Marco is trying to speak. All I can make out is "shoot" and something that sounds like "Jill"—maybe "kill"—and then I hold him under. An eruption of bubbles comes out before Marco closes his mouth and holds his breath.

I twist the Beretta out of Marco's hand—with the bullet wound, there is very little strength in his arm—and point the gun an inch above the water where Marco's face stares back at me. The gun has gotten wet, but I think it will probably still fire.

I'm right.

Marco's body goes limp.

I rise up, my chest heaving. A cloud of smoke hangs over the water. The gun lies on Marco's chest, still in his hand, partly submerged in water so opaque it looks like red paint.

"Good-bye, old friend," I say.

I start to turn and then pause. What had Marco said?

Shoot Jill?

Shoot, Jill!

I spin around and feel an explosive burning in my abdomen. I stagger back into the water, only then hearing the shot echoing around me.

Claire—or Jill—stands with Jasper's revolver in both hands. She points the gun at me and fires again.

CHAPTER 20

THE BULLET GOES WILD, so close I can hear it whining next to my ear like a supersonic insect. I dive into the water and swim, pumping my arms and legs as fast as I can. A geyser of water shoots up next to my head where another bullet hits. The revolver is louder than the other pistols had been, and the shots sound like canon fire bouncing off the rock.

She shoots three more times, the bullets twanging into the water nearby, and then the gun clicks empty. She might be trying to find extra shells, but I'm soon out of range. I swim to the island where I'd hidden the diamonds, and I crawl up onto the rocks. I drag myself to the lone tree, leaving a trail of blood, and lean against the trunk. My stomach lurches and I retch up hot liquid. I think for a moment that I must have swallowed water, but then realize how naive that idea is: my vomit is red and tastes like copper.

I inspect the wound: a dark hole the size of a dime to the left of my navel. There's no exit wound, meaning the lead slug is sitting somewhere in my belly. My body starts to shiver violently.

The woman on the shore, the woman who said her name was Claire, is on her hands and knees, gathering the diamonds. I might be able to wait her out. When she leaves, I can swim to shore. I might be able to make it to the telephone at the dock. It's possible.

As I wait, I put together their plan. It isn't hard to figure out.

Marco had known I would never give up the diamonds to him. If I gave up the diamonds, I would die. So no amount of threats or torture would get me to cooperate. But he knew me—in the end, he really did—and he knew I would give up the diamonds for someone I cared about. Marco had been working with Claire—or whatever her name is—from the start.

Marco must have seen the video as soon as it went viral. Within twenty-four hours of the video appearing on the internet, Claire was sitting in my spinning class, charming me. They probably hit the road from LA the night the video was released and then, first thing that morning, stopped by the *Lake Tahoe Gazette* to ask the article's author if they knew where they could find me. Now that I'm thinking about it, that day Hannah and I had a fight out in front of the paper, there was something else she wanted to tell me as I was storming off. Could it have been a warning?

When Marco showed up with Jasper today, I had assumed he'd been in town a couple days and as soon as they found me they'd rushed into my house brandishing guns, finding Claire there instead of me. But that wasn't the case. Marco and his team must have been here all week. Claire was his real partner, and he'd been patient as he put her to work. I remember when Claire sat down on the bike next to me at the gym and flashed me a sweet, friendly smile. It was all a performance, from that day to this one. I kept a secret from her, but she's the one who was a different person. She was the pretender.

Was any part of her real? Was she Marco's girlfriend? Marco had told her to shoot me, so she probably could have saved his life. Instead, she let me kill him before shooting me. Maybe she had conned Marco from the start as well.

Remembering meeting Claire in the spinning class—the way I'd fallen for her con like the world's most naive mark—makes me think of meeting Hannah the day before. I trusted the wrong girl. I wish I could go back in time and somehow make things work with Hannah. If I had stepped out of hiding after saving the girl and just talked to her, I could have asked her not to write the article. And even though she did write it, I shouldn't have gotten so mad at her. I never should have given Claire the time of day. I should have called Hannah and said, "Hey, I'd like to get to know you." I let myself imagine this alternative reality as I wait for Claire, or whatever her name is, to leave.

After about an hour, the woman finally rises to her feet and heads back down the trail. She walks along the boulders with a gait that seems entirely unfamiliar, as if she really is a different person altogether. Before she reaches a bend in the trail that will take her out of my sight, she looks over at me, and even though she is far away, I can see her blowing me a kiss.

I've stopped shivering. My entire body is enveloped in a warm numbness. I was wrong; I couldn't wait her out. I don't have the strength to swim to shore, let alone make it down the mountain to the telephone. All I can do is sit in the puddle of my blood and wait for the sun to go down. Or pass out. Whichever comes first.

Either way, once the darkness comes, I know I'll never see the light of day again.

CHAPTER 21

HANNAH SITS IN FRONT of her computer monitor. The whole article is there on her screen, perhaps her finest piece of investigative journalism to date. It's a twenty-inch story giving an unbiased and thorough account of who Logan is, from his various run-ins with the law to his recent heroism.

Hannah's editor is leaning over a nearby desk, talking to the designer who will be laying out the A section tonight. She looks over at Hannah and says, "Any progress on that feature article about the hero? We need a good story to anchor tomorrow's front page."

Hannah looks again at her article. It's a great story.

It's also Logan's death warrant.

She shakes her head no, and Ashley gives her a look that says she doesn't quite believe her. Then she goes back to her conversation with the designer.

Hannah highlights all the text of the article. Her finger hovers over the Delete key for a moment, then she presses it. The article disappears.

She rises from her desk and heads to the parking lot. She drives over to Logan's house, feeling a compulsion to tell him in person. A phone call won't do. She knows he has a girlfriend. She tells herself she wouldn't want to be his girlfriend anymore anyway, not after knowing what she knows. But that's probably not the truth, if she's being honest with herself. She wants to see him. She wants to look him in the eyes and say, "I believe the real Logan Bishop is the man who jumped into the water to save that girl. I don't care about what you've done in the past. I know who you are."

But Hannah's heart sinks when she walks up Logan's front walk. She can see his girlfriend's blond hair in the window, moving about the kitchen. When Hannah first met the girl, she hadn't trusted her. Claire showed up at the paper as soon as the article was published, telling Hannah she was an old friend of Logan's and wanting to know how she could find him.

Hannah had told her where Logan worked out, and she'd regretted it immediately. She didn't believe the girl was an old friend. She looked like an opportunistic little slut hoping to hook up with the handsome hero in the newspaper.

Hannah bangs on the door.

No one answers.

"I saw you through the window," Hannah calls out. "I know you're in there."

Claire swings the door open. She's wearing rubber gloves on her hands, and the stink of cleaning products emanates from the door.

The look she gives Hannah is far from friendly.

"Is Logan here?" Hannah says.

"No, he had some friends come into town and they went hiking."

"Do you know where they went?"

Claire shakes her head. Her put-out expression sends the clear message that she'd like for Hannah to leave so she can get back to whatever she was doing.

"You and Logan weren't really old friends, were you?" Hannah says. "You just saw a cute guy in the newspaper and wanted to meet him, didn't you?"

Claire stares at her with ice-cold eyes, and then her face finally breaks into a smile. "You got me," she says. "It doesn't matter now though. Logan and I broke up."

"You broke up?"

The corner of Claire's mouth curves up, as if she's holding back a grin.

"I'm just picking up the last of my things," Claire says. "Then I'm out of here. As soon as he gets back from his hike, he's all yours if you want him."

Hannah pulls her car onto Highway 50 and heads back toward the newspaper. At a stoplight, she dials Logan's number with her phone, but the call goes straight to voicemail. Her limbs buzz with a mixture of excitement and nervousness. Then she thinks about the whole encounter with Claire, how weird it was.

First of all, if Claire had been collecting her belongings, why was she cleaning Logan's house? That seemed like a generous thing to do in the aftermath of a breakup, and Claire didn't strike her as the kind of girl who would be that altruistic. It seemed more like she was scrubbing away any trace of her presence in Logan's house.

More important, given what Logan told her that morning, Hannah can't believe friends from out of town came to go hiking with him. Logan's been hiding from anyone who knows him. There's no way friends just showed up from out of town and he took them hiking.

Logan had said he'd hidden a cache of diamonds at Lake

Aloha. If "friends" had come from out of town, then that's where they'd gone. And not for some recreational hike.

Hannah slams on the brakes and whips her car in a tight U-turn. She speeds out of the city toward the trailhead where she first met Logan.

CHAPTER 22

THE SUN IS ABOUT to set when Hannah finally comes jogging up the path to Lake Aloha. This is her first time seeing the lake, and the setting sun and overcast sky give the desolate area a gray, gothic look. The lake is still, like a slab of steel, and the whole area is as silent as a cemetery.

She thinks about shouting Logan's name, but if he's in trouble, she doesn't want to alert his companions.

Her heart is pounding. One week ago, she took the water taxi because she thought the eleven-mile hike might be too much for her. Today, she practically ran the whole way. When she arrived at the parking lot, the employees informed her that the boat had just left and wouldn't be back for thirty minutes. She'd taken off running down the path.

It's amazing the energy that adrenaline can give you.

She takes off jogging along the path that circles the lake, not sure what she's looking for. Over a distant mountain, the moon begins to rise, peeking out through the clouds in a bright, eerie glow.

She looks around constantly as she moves, trying to maintain her footing while still looking for any sign of Logan. She nearly runs into a body lying on the rocks.

She lets out a scream and then claps her hand over her mouth.

The man is clearly dead. His vacant eyes catch the moonlight, and the blood on his face looks black.

Hannah looks around wildly. There's another body in the shallow water. The person's face is submerged. She thinks for a moment that it might be Logan, but the clothes are all wrong.

Then she spots a pair of hiking shoes that look like Logan's. And his daypack.

Tears spring to her eyes. Her airway constricts. She doesn't know what to do.

Then, barely audible over her own breathing, she hears a voice.

"Hannah," Logan moans from somewhere in the distance. "Hannah."

She sees him out on the lake, barely visible in the gloom, sitting on an island, leaning against a dried-up old tree.

"Are you hurt?" she shouts.

"Yes," he says, his voice choked with sandpaper hoarseness. "I've been shot."

"Oh, shit," Hannah whispers.

She's unsure what to do. The feeling of helplessness she had when Logan was saving the girl begins to wrap itself around her in a paralyzing squeeze.

No, she thinks. I have to do something.

She thinks of Logan's quick, unhesitating action when the girl was drowning, and this breaks her paralysis.

She kicks off her shoes and strips off her clothes. She stands in her bra and underwear on the cold rock and steels herself for the swim.

"I'm coming," she shouts to Logan, and then she runs into the lake.

The water burns like liquid fire.

She gasps, unable to catch her breath. It feels as if her lungs are being compressed by the cold. She flaps her arms and kicks her legs, and still she feels like she's getting nowhere. In the moonlight, the water looks black, like she's swimming through oil. She has the urge to turn around, swim back to shore, and climb up on the rock out of the water's icy grip. She wills herself to fight forward.

I'm not going to die here, she thinks. And neither is Logan.

She pulls herself onto the shore of the island and crawls to Logan. His skin is ghost white.

"Hey," he says to her, his voice a whisper.

"Hey," she says, not knowing what else to say.

His eyes drop for a moment to her body. "This is a good look for you," he says, and his mouth curves just slightly into the hint of a smile.

"What happened?" Hannah says.

"Claire and I broke up," he says. Then he points to a hole in his stomach trickling blood and says, "This was her good-bye present."

"What about those two?" Hannah says, pointing toward the bank where the two dead bodies lay.

"My old partner," Logan says. "She played them just like she played me."

"Come on," Hannah says. "We need to get you to shore."

"There's no point," Logan says.

"Don't give me that shit," Hannah says. "I need you to hang on. I need you to fight."

Logan shakes his head. "Even if you get me to shore, and we

somehow make it down to the telephone, we can't call an ambulance."

Hannah stares at him in disbelief. In the moonlight, his face looks like a skull.

"The hospital will have to report a bullet wound," Logan says. "They'll connect me to Marco's and Jasper's deaths. And maybe you too. How are you going to keep your job at the newspaper when you're being investigated?"

Hannah feels that sense of panic again. Then the solution presents itself.

"I have an idea," she says. She grabs him by the face and looks hard into his eyes. "I need you to come with me, Logan. I need you to swim across this lake and hike down the mountain with me."

"What's your idea?"

"Just trust me," she says. "You trusted me with your story earlier today. I need you to trust me again. Get down the mountain with me, and I'll take care of the rest."

She helps him to the bank, and they slip together into the black burning water.

CHAPTER 23

I'M FLOATING IN DARKNESS so pure it feels like death.

Then I wake with a start, my heart thumping like a kick drum, my skin clammy and hot.

I'm lying in a strange room. The walls are wood-paneled, decorated with wildlife paintings. A soft light comes in through the window, telling me it's evening.

How long have I been asleep?

I try to sit up and feel a throbbing pain in my stomach. I look and see white bandages stretched across my abdomen. I notice for the first time that there's an IV hooked to the bed frame with a wire hanger. It's feeding fluid into my arm.

I swing my feet off the bed and onto the floor. I'm wearing boxer shorts but nothing else.

My mouth is dry, and I snatch a plastic water cup from the nightstand and drink it down. I yank the IV needle out of my arm. I grab the blanket from the bed and wrap it around my shoulders, stepping out of the room.

My legs are weak.

I round the corner of the hallway and step into a kitchen, and then I recognize where I am. I'm in the cabin of the girl who was drowning. There is the phone by the refrigerator that I used to dial 911.

I walk into a spacious living room with a floor-to-ceiling picture window looking out over the lake. There is a fire crackling in the fireplace. Sitting in a plush leather chair, Hannah is looking out the window, watching snow falling down in fat flakes.

She sees me and gives me a smile so beautiful and so genuine that I can't believe I ever fell for Claire.

"So *this* was your idea?" I say, looking around the house.

"I told you to trust me."

"How long have I been out?"

"Almost twenty-four hours," she says. "Do you remember anything?"

I take a chair next to her and pull the blanket around me. Out the window, the sun is setting. There is already a layer of snow on the lawn and deck, and it doesn't look like the storm will let up anytime soon.

"The last thing I remember," I say, "was going into the water and knowing I was going to die. I remember thinking, *I hope Hannah doesn't blame herself that she wasn't able to save me.*"

Hannah fills me in on the rest. We made it to the shore and then stumbled down the mountain, with her supporting most of my weight and me practically unconscious on my feet. She knocked on the door of the house and asked the father of the girl I'd saved for help. I'd forgotten she'd told me he was a doctor.

He was nervous, afraid he was getting involved in something illegal, but he figured he owed me, she explained. He shot me full of sedative, pulled the bullet out, and sewed me back up. Then he gave Hannah a big bottle of antibiotics and another of painkillers, and he packed up his girls and took off.

"They drove back to the Bay Area this morning," she says. "The house is paid up for four more days. I can watch over you until you're ready to go back to your house and take care of yourself. I'm sure the storm will let up by then."

"You saved my life," I say.

She shrugs. "I learned from the best."

"Is there anything I can do for you?" I say. "To repay you?"

She looks at me sincerely. The firelight twinkles in her brown eyes.

"You can be the person I know you are," she says.

We're quiet for a few minutes, enjoying the serenity, then she asks what I'm going to do about Claire.

"Let her go," I say. "She can have the diamonds. I want out of that life. For good."

"She shot you," Hannah says. "She shouldn't get away with that."

"A wise man once told me there's no honor among thieves," I say. "Everyone who lives that life ends up dead sooner or later."

"I'm not sure that's good enough for me," Hannah says. "She shouldn't get away scot-free."

"Have they found the bodies yet?" I ask.

She shakes her head no. "I called my editor and told her I was sick and wasn't coming in this week. She would have mentioned a double homicide if anyone knew about it. I doubt anyone's gone hiking up there because of the snow."

Outside, the snow is really coming down. This early in the season, it will probably melt off within a few days.

I picture spending those days curled up in front of the fire with Hannah, talking, getting to know her.

"So, what are you going to do now?" Hannah says. "Your trust fund is gone."

"I guess I'll get a job," I say.

"This might help tide you over," she says, reaching into her pocket.

She pulls out a diamond the size of a small marble and holds it between her thumb and forefinger, its surface sparkling in the firelight.

"Where did you get that?"

She explains that when we got to shore, she was trying to put my hiking shoes onto my feet when something glinting in the moonlight caught her eye. The diamond was wedged into a crack in the rocks.

"I bet there are more up there," she says.

I shrug. "I already got what I wanted," I say.

"What's that?"

"To be here with you."

She tries to hide her smile, and I can't tell if it's the glow of the firelight or her skin, but it looks like she's blushing.

EPILOGUE

THE WOMAN LOGAN KNEW as Claire and Marco knew as Jill—and whom other people have known by other names—walks through Union Station in Los Angeles. Orange light from the setting sun pours in through the big windows. She walks in tight jeans and tall heels, with a black leather jacket cinched around her body and a Louis Vuitton handbag slung over her shoulder. Her luxuriant golden hair bounces around her shoulders as she struts over the marble floors.

A group of college-aged boys turn their heads and watch her. A tired-looking woman with two kids in a double-stroller eyes her. A middle-aged man in a Lakers sweatshirt does a double-take as she walks by.

The woman settles into a seat to wait for her train. She can feel the eyes on her—jealous eyes, lustful eyes—and she loves the feeling. She is on top of the world. She's rich. She's confident. And, after a week, she's still feeling quite elated about how things went down at Lake Aloha. It couldn't have worked out better.

She'd fooled Logan from the start. He'd never suspected a thing until she'd put a bullet into him. And Marco, the thug who'd brought her in? She didn't even have to double-cross him. Logan took him out for her.

The only inconvenience was that she had to pick the diamonds up off the ground. She's certain she left some behind, but it couldn't be helped. She didn't have a lot of time. She needed to get back to Logan's house and wipe down anything that might have her fingerprints or DNA on it.

She knows she did a half-assed job, but that bitch from the newspaper showing up had made her antsy to get out of town.

It didn't matter. The police would search Logan's house once they found his body on that island, but they wouldn't look too hard. The evidence at Lake Aloha would tell a pretty clear story: three crooks had a dispute and killed each other.

Yes, the whole thing couldn't have worked out much better.

There's a television mounted on a nearby wall that she's been ignoring. It's tuned to one of those all-day news channels, and when she hears the words "Lake Tahoe," the broadcast suddenly catches her attention.

The anchor is explaining how cross-country skiers found two dead bodies in a hiking area near Lake Tahoe. The words "double homicide" are stamped along the bottom, as the screen shows footage of police cars at the snow-filled parking lot by Echo Lake.

They must not have found Logan's body yet, she thinks. She'd been checking the *Lake Tahoe Gazette* website for the past few days and had seen that it had begun snowing the day after everything went down.

If they don't find Logan's body until spring, or even next summer, then that's even better for her.

She is starting to smile, but then her face freezes as the broadcast continues.

There is a police sketch placed prominently on the screen—

an excellent rendering of her own face. The artist couldn't have done a better job if she'd been posing in person.

"Police are looking for this woman for questioning," the reporter states. "A witness saw her leaving the hiking area the day of the homicide."

The reporter continues, "The *Lake Tahoe Gazette* is reporting that the woman has used the aliases Claire and Jill, and she was last seen driving a Toyota Tacoma pickup. Authorities believe she has ties to the Los Angeles area."

She grits her teeth, thinking of that bitch from the newspaper. But how would she know about the name Jill? And how did the reporter know what she drove?

The TV anchor moves on to other news, a warehouse fire in New York, but the woman stares at the TV in a daze, trying to make sense of what she just saw.

There's only one explanation: Logan is still alive.

That bitch from the paper went to Lake Aloha and saved him. Then, when the bodies were discovered, she told police she'd been hiking there and saw a woman come out alone.

She can't quite figure out all the details. It is hard to believe Logan could make it back down the hill, but even if he had, he'd need medical attention. And a hospital would certainly report a gunshot wound to the police. Maybe the police know more than the TV is reporting.

Whatever. It doesn't matter. Logan could go ahead and enjoy his retirement in Lake Tahoe without his diamonds. She'd gotten away with it.

But as she glances around the terminal, she feels again like all eyes are on her. Not jealous eyes this time. Not lustful eyes.

Suspicious eyes.

She reaches into her handbag, her fingers brushing against the bag of diamonds, and pulls out her sunglasses. She puts them on and looks around, trying to act casual. There are people everywhere stealing glances her way. A man who'd been watching the news is gawking openly at her. Two security guards standing by the bathroom keep glancing at her as they talk.

She stands up and starts walking toward the exit, trying to exude the confidence she'd had just five minutes earlier, pretending the stares don't bother her, pretending everything is all right. She is good at pretending, after all. She fooled Marco. She fooled Logan. She can fool anyone she wants.

But, she realizes, it's harder to pretend when the person you're trying to fool is yourself.

ABOUT THE AUTHORS

James Patterson has written more bestsellers and created more enduring fictional characters than any other novelist writing today. He lives in Florida with his family.

Max DiLallo is a novelist, playwright, and screenwriter. He lives in Los Angeles.

Andrew Bourelle has published numerous short stories in literary magazines and fiction anthologies, including *The Best American Mystery Stories*. He teaches writing at the University of New Mexico.

"I'M NOT ON TRIAL. SAN FRANCISCO IS."

Drug cartel boss the Kingfisher has a reputation for being violent and merciless. And after he's finally caught, he's set to stand trial for his vicious crimes—until he begins unleashing chaos and terror upon the lawyers, jurors, and police associated with the case. The city is paralyzed, and Detective Lindsay Boxer is caught in the eye of the storm.

Will the Women's Murder Club make it out alive—or will a courtroom shocker ensure their last breaths?

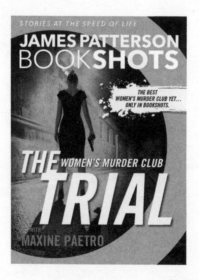

Read on for a sneak peek at the shocking new Women's Murder Club story. Available only from

BOOK**SHOTS**

IT WAS THAT CRAZY period between Thanksgiving and Christmas when work overflowed, time raced, and there wasn't enough light between dawn and dusk to get everything done.

Still, our gang of four, what we call the Women's Murder Club, always had a spouse-free holiday get-together dinner of drinks and bar food.

Yuki had picked the place.

It was called Uncle Maxie's Top Hat and was a bar and grill that had been a fixture in the Financial District for 150 years. It was decked out with art deco prints and mirrors on the walls, and a large, neon-lit clock behind the bar dominated the room. Maxie's catered to men in smart suits and women in tight skirts and spike heels who wore good jewelry.

I liked the place and felt at home there in a Mickey Spillane kind of way. Case in point: I was wearing straight-legged pants, a blue gabardine blazer, a Glock in my shoulder holster, and flat lace-up shoes. I stood in the bar area, slowly turning my head as I looked around for my BFFs.

"Lindsay. Yo."

Cindy waved her hand from the table tucked under the spiral staircase. I waved back, moved toward the nook inside the cranny. Claire was wearing a trench coat over her scrubs, with a button on the lapel that read SUPPORT OUR TROOPS. She peeled off her coat and gave me a hug and a half.

Cindy was also in her work clothes: cords and a bulky sweater, with a peacoat slung over the back of her chair. If I'd ducked under the table, I'm sure I would have seen steel-toed boots. Cindy is a crime reporter of note, and she was wearing her on-the-job hound dog clothes.

She blew me a couple of kisses, and Yuki stood up to give me her seat and a jasmine-scented smack on the cheek. She had clearly come from court, where she worked as a pro bono defense attorney for the poor and hopeless. Still, she was dressed impeccably, in pinstripes and pearls.

I took the chair across from Claire. She sat between Cindy and Yuki with her back to the room, and we all scooched up to the smallish glass-and-chrome table.

If it hasn't been said, we four are a mutual heart, soul, and work society in which we share our cases and views of the legal system, as well as our personal lives. Right now the girls were worried about me.

Three of us were married: me, Claire, and Yuki—and Cindy had a standing offer of a ring and vows to be exchanged in Grace Cathedral. Until very recently you couldn't have found four more happily hooked-up women. Then the bottom fell out of my marriage to Joe Molinari, the father of my child and a man I shared everything with, including my secrets.

We had had it so good, we kissed and made up before our fights were over. It was the typical: "You are right." "No, you are!"

Then Joe went missing during possibly the worst weeks of my life.

I'm a homicide cop, and I know when someone is telling me the truth and when things do not add up.

Joe missing in action had not added up. Because of that I had worried almost to panic. Where was he? Why hadn't he checked in? Why were my calls bouncing off his full mailbox? Was he still alive?

As the crisscrossed threads of espionage, destruction, and mass murder were untangled, Joe finally made his curtain call with stories of his past and present lives that I'd never heard before. I found plenty of reasons not to trust him anymore.

Even he would agree. I think anyone would.

It's not news that once trust is broken, it's damned hard to superglue it back together. And for me it might take more time and belief in Joe's confession than I actually had.

I still loved him. We'd shared a meal when he came to see our baby, Julie. We didn't make any moves toward getting divorced that night, but we didn't make love, either. Our relationship was now like the Cold War in the eighties between Russia and the USA, a strained but practical peace called détente.

Now, as I sat with my friends, I tried to put Joe out of my mind, safe in the knowledge that my nanny was looking after Julie and that the home front was safe. I ordered a favorite holiday drink, a hot buttered rum, and a rare steak sandwich with Uncle Maxie's hot chili sauce.

My girlfriends were deep in criminal cross talk about Claire's holiday overload of corpses, Cindy's new cold case she'd exhumed from the *San Francisco Chronicle*'s dead letter files, and Yuki's hoped-for favorable verdict for her client, an underage drug dealer. I was almost caught up when Yuki said, "Linds, I gotta ask. Any Christmas plans with Joe?"

And that's when I was saved by the bell. My phone rang.

My friends said in unison, "NO PHONES."

It was the rule, but I'd forgotten—again.

I reached into my bag for my phone, saying, "Look, I'm turning it off."

But I saw that the call was from Rich Conklin, my partner and Cindy's fiancé. She recognized his ring tone on my phone.

"There goes our party," she said, tossing her napkin into the air.

"Linds?" said Conklin.

"Rich, can this wait? I'm in the middle—"

"It's Kingfisher. He's in a shoot-out with cops at the Vault. There've been casualties."

"But—Kingfisher is *dead*."

"Apparently, he's returned from the grave."

MY PARTNER WAS DOUBLE-PARKED and waiting for me outside Uncle Maxie's, with the engine running and the flashers on. I got into the passenger seat of the unmarked car, and Richie handed me my vest. He's that way, like a younger version of a big brother. He thinks of me, watches out for me, and I try to do the same for him.

He watched me buckle up, then he hit the sirens and stepped on the gas.

We were about five minutes from the Vault, a class A nightclub on the second floor of a former Bank of America building.

"Fill me in," I said to my partner.

"Call came in to 911 about ten minutes ago," Conklin said as we tore up California Street. "A kitchen worker said he recognized Kingfisher out in the bar. He was still trying to convince 911 that it was an emergency when shots were fired inside the club."

"Watch out on our right."

Richie yanked the wheel hard left to avoid an indecisive panel truck, then jerked it hard right and took a turn onto Sansome.

"You okay?" he asked.

I had been known to get carsick in jerky high-speed chases when I wasn't behind the wheel.

"I'm fine. Keep talking."

My partner told me that a second witness reported to first officers that three men were talking to two women at the bar. One of the men yelled, "No one screws with the King." Shots were fired. The women were killed.

"Caller didn't leave his name."

I was gripping both the dash and the door, and had both feet on imaginary brakes, but my mind was occupied with Kingfisher. He was a Mexican drug cartel boss, a psycho with a history of brutality and revenge, and a penchant for settling his scores personally.

Richie was saying, "Patrol units arrived as the shooters were attempting to flee through the front entrance. Someone saw the tattoo on the back of the hand of one of the shooters. I talked to Brady," Conklin said, referring to our lieutenant. "If that shooter is Kingfisher and survives, he's ours."

I WANTED THE KING on death row for the normal reasons. He was to the drug and murder trade as al-Baghdadi was to terrorism. But I also had personal reasons.

Earlier that year a cadre of dirty San Francisco cops from our division had taken down a number of drug houses for their own financial gain. One drug house in particular yielded a payoff of five to seven million in cash and drugs. Whether those cops knew it beforehand or not, the stolen loot belonged to Kingfisher—and he wanted it back.

The King took his revenge but was still short a big pile of dope and dollars.

So he turned his sights on me.

I was the primary homicide inspector on the dirty-cop case.

Using his own twisted logic, the King demanded that I personally recover and return his property. Or else.

It was a threat and a promise, and of course I couldn't deliver.

From that moment on I had protection all day and night, every day and night, but protection isn't enough when your tormentor is like a ghost. We had grainy photos and shoddy footage from cheap surveillance cameras on file. We had a blurry picture of a tattoo on the back of his left hand.

That was all.

After his threat I couldn't cross the street from my apartment to my car without fear that Kingfisher would drop me dead in the street.

A week after the first of many threatening phone calls, the calls stopped. A report came in from the Mexican federal police saying that they had turned up the King's body in a shallow grave in Baja. That's what they said.

I had wondered then if the King was really dead. If the freaking nightmare was truly over.

I had just about convinced myself that my family and I were safe. Now the breaking news confirmed that my gut reaction had been right. Either the Mexican police had lied, or the King had tricked them with a dead doppelganger buried in the sand.

A few minutes ago the King had been identified by a kitchen worker at the Vault. If true, why had he surfaced again in San Francisco? Why had he chosen to show his face in a nightclub filled with people? Why shoot two women inside that club? And my number one question: Could we bring him in alive and take him to trial?

Please, God. Please.

OUR CAR RADIO WAS barking, crackling, and squealing at a high pitch as cars were directed to the Vault, in the middle of the block on Walnut Street. Cruisers and ambulances screamed past us as Conklin and I closed in on the scene. I badged the cop at the perimeter, and immediately after, Rich backed our car into a gap in the pack of law enforcement vehicles, parking it across the street from the Vault.

The Vault was built of stone block. It had two centered large glass doors, now shattered, with a half-circular window across the doorframe. Flanking the doors were two tall windows, capped with demilune windows, glass also shot out.

Shooters inside the Vault were using the granite doorframe as a barricade as they leaned out and fired on the uniformed officers positioned behind their car doors.

Conklin and I got out of our car with our guns drawn and crouched beside our wheel wells. Adrenaline whipped my heart into a gallop. I watched everything with clear eyes, and yet my mind flooded with memories of past shoot-outs. I had been shot and almost died. All three of my partners had been shot, one of them fatally.

And now I had a baby at home.

A cop at the car to my left shouted, *"Christ!"*

Her gun spun out of her hand and she grabbed her shoulder as she dropped to the asphalt. Her partner ran to her, dragged her toward the rear of the car, and called in, "Officer down." Just then SWAT arrived in force with a small caravan of SUVs and a ballistic armored transport vehicle as big as a bus. The SWAT commander used his megaphone, calling to the shooters, who had slipped back behind the fortresslike walls of the Vault.

"All exits are blocked. There's nowhere to run, nowhere to hide. Toss out the guns, now."

The answer to the SWAT commander was a fusillade of gunfire that pinged against steel chassis. SWAT hit back with automatic weapons, and two men fell out of the doorway onto the pavement.

The shooting stopped, leaving an echoing silence.

The commander used his megaphone and called out, "You. Put your gun down and we won't shoot. Fair warning. We're coming in."

"WAIT. I give up," said an accented voice. "Hands up, see?"

"Come all the way out. Come to me," said the SWAT commander.

I could see him from where I stood.

The last of the shooters was a short man with a café au lait complexion, a prominent nose, dark hair that was brushed back. He was wearing a well-cut suit that had blood splattered on the white shirt as he came out through the doorway with his hands up.

Two guys in tactical gear grabbed him and slammed him over the hood of an SUV, then cuffed and arrested him.

The SWAT commander dismounted from the armored vehicle. I recognized him as Reg Covington. We'd worked together before. Conklin and I walked over to where Reg was standing beside the last of the shooters.

Covington said, "Boxer. Conklin. You know this guy?"

He stood the shooter up so I could get a good look at his face. I'd never met Kingfisher. I compared the real-life suspect with my memory of the fuzzy videos I'd seen of Jorge Sierra, a.k.a. the King.

"Let me see his hands," I said.

It was a miracle that my voice sounded steady, even to my own ears. I was sweating and my breathing was shallow. My gut told me that this was the man.

Covington twisted the prisoner's hands so that I could see the backs of them. On the suspect's left hand was the tattoo of a kingfisher, the same as the one in the photo in Kingfisher's slim file.

I said to our prisoner, "Mr. Sierra. I'm Sergeant Boxer. Do you need medical attention?"

"Mouth-to-mouth resuscitation, maybe."

Covington jerked him to his feet and said, "We'll take good care of him. Don't worry."

He marched the King to the waiting police wagon, and I watched as he was shackled and chained to the bar before the door was closed.

Covington slapped the side of the van, and it took off as CSI and the medical examiner's van moved in and SWAT thundered into the Vault to clear the scene.

BOOK**SHOTS**

AVAILABLE NOW!

CROSS KILL

Along Came a Spider killer Gary Soneji died years ago. But Alex Cross swears he sees Soneji gun down his partner. Is his greatest enemy back from the grave?

ZOO II

Humans are evolving into a savage new species that could save civilization—or end it. James Patterson's *Zoo* was just the beginning.

THE TRIAL

An accused killer will do anything to disrupt his own trial, including a courtroom shocker that Lindsay Boxer and the Women's Murder Club will never see coming.

LITTLE BLACK DRESS

Can a little black dress change everything? What begins as one woman's fantasy is about to go too far.

LET'S PLAY MAKE-BELIEVE

Christy and Marty just met, and it's love at first sight. Or is it? One of them is playing a dangerous game—and only one will survive.

CHASE

A man falls to his death in an apparent accident....But why does he have the fingerprints of another man, who is already dead? Detective Michael Bennett is on the case.

James Patterson's
BOOKSH🔥TS
Flames

LEARNING TO RIDE

City girl Madeline Harper never wanted to love a cowboy. But rodeo king Tanner Callen might change her mind…and win her heart.

THE McCULLAGH INN IN MAINE

Chelsea O'Kane escapes to Maine to build a new life—until she runs into Jeremy Holland, an old flame….

"DON'T MAKE A SOUND. NOT A SINGLE SOUND."

Someone is luring men from the streets to play a mysterious, high-stakes game in the English countryside. Former Special Forces officer David Shelley will go undercover to shut it down. But this might be a game he can't win.

The hunt is on.

Read the shocking new thriller *Hunted*, available only from

BOOKSHOTS

LOOKING TO FALL IN LOVE IN JUST ONE NIGHT?

INTRODUCING BOOKSHOTS FLAMES:

original romances presented by James Patterson that fit into your busy life.

FEATURING LOVE STORIES BY:

New York Times bestselling author Jen McLaughlin

New York Times bestselling author Samantha Towle

USA Today bestselling author Erin Knightley

Elizabeth Hayley

Jessica Linden

Codi Gary

Laurie Horowitz

…and many others!

COMING SOON FROM

HER SECOND CHANCE AT LOVE MIGHT BE TOO GOOD TO BE TRUE....

When Chelsea O'Kane escapes to her family's inn in Maine, all she's got are fresh bruises, a gun in her lap, and a desire to start anew. That's when she runs into her old flame, Jeremy Holland. As he helps her fix up the inn, they rediscover what they once loved about each other.

Until it seems too good to last...

Read the stirring story of hope and redemption
The McCullagh Inn in Maine, available only from